## Also by Ray Hobbs and Published by Wingspan Press

## Published Elsewhere

I0645893

# AN EYE TO THE FUTURE

## RAY HOBBS

Wingspan Press

Published in the United States and the United Kingdom
by WingSpan Press, Livermore, CA

The WingSpan name, logo and colophon are the trademarks
of WingSpan Publishing.

ISBN 978-1-63683-055-1 (pbk.)
ISBN 978-1-63683-956-1 (ebook)

Printed in the United States of America

www.wingspanpress.com

This book is dedicated to the affectionate memory our late companions Puster, Heathcliff, Perdie, Bert, Polly, and Jack, who was with us for only a short time, but who nevertheless left a deep and lasting impression on our lives.

RH

As ever, I wish to acknowledge the invaluable support and assistance of my brother Chris in the preparation of this book.

RH

# AN EYE TO THE FUTURE

# A South-East Coastal Town

## 1976

## 1

# Jack

Nobody likes a scene. There are those who say, usually with some vehemence, depending on the situation, that they're not afraid to create one, but some people say all kinds of things in the heat of a given moment. Being an essentially even-tempered soul, Barry wasn't one of them, which meant he had no say in the current proceedings. The scene was entirely of Christine's making.

'Don't think I'm coming here again while you've got that *fiend* in your flat!' She was incensed, and Barry knew her well enough not even to consider reasoning with her. Instead, he held the door open for her to leave. She swept past him, catching him carelessly with her huge shoulder bag as she stepped over the threshold and on to the pavement. Wrenching her car door open, she delivered her final salvo. 'You deserve each other!'

Barry looked self-consciously along the street and winced. Lucy Hart from the bookshop was putting out the milk bottles and she was looking his way. She couldn't have failed to hear the disturbance at the door. In fact, with Christine revving her engine and spinning her tyres as she took off, the noise was sufficient to alert the entire neighbourhood. If embarrassment had been measurable, the kind he felt on that occasion would have been well inside the red sector.

His relationship with Christine had been heading for the hills, anyway. It couldn't have limped on much longer, but he'd intended finishing it in a civilised way, rather than with the doorstep drama that had just taken place. That it had happened in that way was largely Jack's doing.

There was a kind of flatmate no sensible person would willingly consider, let alone accept. All the loneliness in the world could never give rise to such a voluntary alliance. Only someone as soft-hearted as Barry could have taken him in.

Jack could be dismissive, solitary and, it was no exaggeration to say, completely selfish. He would accept everything that came his way and even demand it. He would turn up for supper, when he would display a rare hint of friendship and disappear soon afterwards from the flat, returning late, silent and insular at first. Then at some stage he would assume occupation of Barry's room, where he would purr loudly, creeping further and further up the bed until sleep claimed both him and, eventually, his reluctant host.

When he first arrived at the studio, he was scrawny, bedraggled, infested, and bleeding from various wounds. Patches of grey and white fur were missing and one eye was completely closed, its lids sealed by a foul crust of congealed blood. Heaven alone knew what horrors existed behind them, and no one could have criticised Barry, had he taken him immediately to the RSPCA to be put to sleep. He was patently homeless and helpless, and what appeared to be his ninth life had nothing to recommend it, so it seemed the only course to take. Even so, he hesitated. The poor creature was pathetic and forlorn, and life had been particularly cruel to him. Almost before he realised what he was doing, Barry was scanning the Yellow Pages for the nearest vet.

Several days and a significant extension of his overdraft later, Barry collected him from the vet's surgery, disinfected, deflea-ed and minus his left eye. And it didn't end there. He had to go back for a tapeworm injection and vaccination because for some reason they couldn't do it all at once, so Barry quickly became acquainted with the true nature of sacrifice.

Having given him a home with a brand new cat flap, Barry bought him a bed, which he scorned in favour of his host's, and fed him on the best Sainsbury's could supply, only to find that he was sloping off to the teashop for breakfast every morning.

In spite of all that, though, Barry had become used to ordering his life to accommodate his feline companion's vagaries and, in a masochistic sort of way, had come to accept him.

Christine had returned that Sunday from visiting her parents, and they'd spent the evening at the pub. It wasn't a good idea, mainly because the bar was full of people Barry knew, and that provided her with the perfect audience. It appealed to her heavy sense of humour to relate anecdotes that illustrated his various shortcomings, real or imagined. It possibly had something to do with her being a PE teacher; she spent her working hours assessing and criticising the children's efforts, and it spilled over into her private life. Added to that, she seemed to have come back, for some reason out of sorts, and Barry was bearing the brunt of her dissatisfaction. Her preoccupation that evening was with his driving.

'He peers over the steering wheel like Mr Magoo,' she told Gavin Peckett, Barry's regular drinking partner, 'and he's too vain to wear his glasses, so he can't possibly see where he's going.' Gavin had the decency to keep quiet. It was just possible that he found her observations amusing, but he wasn't at all keen on her. She went on relentlessly. 'With an old wreck like his, you'd think he'd be a bit more careful.'

Barry found it difficult to recognise either himself or his car from that description, and it had never seemed to him that his driving was at all dangerous. Also, his glasses were only for close work; he didn't need them for driving, but that was a mere detail, insignificant beside her catalogue of criticism. Barry watched her telling a story about him with malicious satisfaction, and decided she would have to go. He really couldn't remember why he'd taken up with her in the first place, except that she was quite attractive in a healthy, robust sort of way, and he was going through a phase in which athletic women with bright, copper-coloured hair held a special kind of appeal for him.

3

In his alcohol-mellowed state, he wasn't sure why they found themselves at his flat that night, because they usually went to her place. Maybe he was being uncharacteristically assertive. It was just possible, but there they were. He'd fully intended finishing with her, but he was side-tracked. He'd had quite a lot to drink and was therefore more susceptible than usual. At all events, he went along with the one pastime for which she'd never criticised him, and peace and harmony existed, at least for a while, at number thirty-three, Woodley High Street.

It couldn't last, and the end came completely without warning. He never heard the cat flap swing shut, and the padding of small furry paws on the stair carpet was beyond the range of human hearing. The first intimation he had of Jack's return was the frantic scrabbling of his claws against the overhanging duvet as he lunged for the bed and didn't quite make it. The problem stemmed from his having only one eye. Without binocular vision, he couldn't judge distances, an impediment that made him incredibly clumsy. Barry had lost count of the number of times he'd tried to jump into a chair and fallen short of it. Optical physics, however, was the last consideration on Christine's mind at that moment. She screamed and tried to jump across the bed, an impossible manoeuvre with Barry's weight pinning her down. She yelled, 'What is it?'

'It's Jack,' he sighed, reaching for the bedside lamp.

'It's horrible!' He must certainly have seemed so, crouched in the glow of the lamp, fixing his one green eye on her and growling. It was a low growl, not very loud, but it was no less menacing, and Jack was clearly determined to make his resentment known.

'Get off me!' She shouted. 'Get off, quick!'

Barry hesitated, unsure for the moment which of them she was shouting at, and then she lunged upwards, pushing him off the bed. He fell backwards between the bed and the wardrobe, whacking his head against the tall mirror, so that he was stunned and helpless for a minute. However, had he been naïve enough to expect sympathy from Christine, disillusionment would have been swift and telling.

'You should have that bloody thing put down! It's dangerous! It's vicious! Hell's bells, it attacked me!' All the time she was shouting, naked and enraged, she pointed at Jack, then at Barry, so that he wasn't sure who was supposed to be the greater villain. From his position on the bed, Jack continued to growl, his back arched in defiance and the light of battle gleaming in his eye. Meanwhile, Barry, who had never been able to maintain any sense of dignity in a crisis with his lower half exposed, was searching urgently for his underpants, which had disappeared in the hurling of the duvet and everything else that got in its way. Having found them, he girded himself and faced her tirade.

'He didn't attack you,' he said as calmly as he could. 'He found you in his place, and if you hadn't reacted so violently he wouldn't have behaved the way he did.' It seemed perverse in the light of Jack's undeniable failings, but someone else criticising him was another matter altogether, and in spite of those shortcomings, Barry felt quite defensive of him at that moment.

The recriminations continued, however, until they were both dressed and downstairs, with Jack shut safely in the bedroom, and that was when she made her explosive exit.

Christine was only the latest in a succession of unusual women who came into Barry's life at around that time. Certainly, there was no shortage of straightforward, uncomplicated ones, but he still found himself becoming involved, one way or another, with the oddest characters, and spending a great deal of time pondering the reason for it without arriving at even a hint of an answer.

It wasn't as if there were anything particularly remarkable about him. His appearance was quite commonplace; he had medium-brown hair worn on the collar in the fashion of the time, and blue eyes that tended to be slightly bloodshot on occasions. He had just a tendency to gain weight, which he usually controlled by diet, and occasionally by the more drastic expedient of exercise. He dressed in a fairly restrained way too, formally when he was at work, and tidily at other times. Service life had kept him well away from the Swinging Scene, about which he knew little, anyway, and he was working hard now, largely oblivious to outside influences, to become established with his own studio, recently acquired at considerable expense. All in all, he was the kind of character who could be lost in a small crowd, and who would attract no more attention than the next anonymous being. At least, that was what, in his apparent naivete, he believed. It was around that time that he met Claret.

# 2

# Claret and Lucy

He'd seen Claret several times on the check-out at the Sainsbury's outside Ashford. She would have been difficult to miss, because she really was lovely, with dark, shining hair and, by contrast, a pale complexion that accentuated her deep, brown eyes. Her face was a photographer's dream, and it was a pleasant surprise when she recognised him. It happened a little over a week before the incident with Christine.

'You're Barry Craven, aren't you?'

'That's right.'

She began checking out his purchases: an oven-ready meal, a tube of shaving cream and a bottle of wine. 'I live in Woodley,' she explained. 'I've seen you around.'

'Oh yes?' There wasn't much else he could say.

'Yes, that's two pounds forty-seven.' She pushed a button on the till and said, 'I need to have some photos done, as it happens.'

He took a five pound note from his wallet and handed it to her with a business card. 'Give me a ring when you're ready, and we'll make an appointment.' Then, as an afterthought, he asked, 'What are they for?'

She gave him the change with an ingenuous smile. 'Modelling.'

'Oh, you want a portfolio. Won't your agency arrange that?'

'I'm not with an agency. I want some photos I can take round the agencies to see if I can get any of them interested.'

'I see.' He was running his eye discretely over what he could see of her slender figure when he became aware that a woman in the queue behind him was glaring at both of them and looking at her watch. 'Give me a ring,' he said, 'and we'll arrange a session.' He picked up his carrier and left.

In his experience, not everyone who said they'd make an appointment actually got around to it, but he was rather hoping she'd phone him. She had a kind of naïve charm that he found appealing, and he decided that working with a subject like her, however inexperienced she might be, would be a welcome change from the bread-and-butter work he'd been doing, especially the weddings. He had to prepare for one the next day, and he was viewing the prospect with some apprehension. It was a shame, because, as a guest, he could enjoy all that a wedding had to offer. The friendly atmosphere, the vicarious excitement and the extravagant clothing appealed to him as strongly as they might to anyone. Unfortunately, however, as a photographer, he hardly ever got a straightforward one. All too often, something would go wrong. Sometimes, the bride would be late, and often tearful during the ceremony, so that repair work had to be carried out, and everything would have to be done at the rush. Then he'd get the group together for a shot, and some interfering relation would rearrange them. There was almost invariably a member of the party, often an extrovert uncle, who thought he knew better than the photographer. Some even criticised his choice of equipment, an area to which amateurs were unfailingly drawn. It was surprising how many self-styled experts attended the average wedding. Then there were the children, highly excited after sitting through the ceremony, and bursting with suppressed mischief. It was fair to say that some of them were fine. All too often, however, there was a spoilt little bugger who went all out to make the job impossible. No, wedding photography wasn't the scene for Barry, and he was right not to look forward to this one.

As it happened, the wedding itself went unusually well, almost to the end, in fact, which was when Wesley dropped the camera, and then, in his haste to retrieve it, flipped it under a rear wheel of the departing limousine, which left it crushed beyond repair.

'Wesley, you clumsy—' Barry stopped himself. There were still guests within earshot, and it was, after all, a genuine accident.

Wesley was Barry's weekend assistant, which meant that on Saturdays he accompanied him to weddings. When they had no wedding, he made himself useful in the studio. He was a willing soul but, at sixteen, he was still struggling with the trials of late adolescence, which made him prone to a number of unfortunate conditions, including chronic clumsiness.

'Oh hell,' he said almost tearfully. 'I'm sorry, Barry.'

Barry wasn't too happy, either. It wasn't as if the camera were particularly valuable; with things as they were, a Hasselblad or a Rolleiflex was beyond his pocket. It was an inexpensive Japanese alternative, and it was insured, but the fact remained that he would be without a medium format camera until the insurance company paid out. He took a very deep breath and said, 'It's not the end of the world, it's insured, and the main thing is that you got the film out before you started your juggling act.'

Wesley continued to berate himself until Barry told him to get into the car and stop moaning.

He sat in miserable silence on the way back to the studio, so that when they'd unloaded the gear, Barry took him two doors down the street to the teashop to cheer him up. He wasn't being saintly, he just felt sorry for him. He hadn't suffered from that kind of problem when he was Wesley's age, but he'd known a few kids who had.

The teashop was part of a bookshop that had been closed

9

for several months, but then it had re-opened and Barry had taken to calling in regularly. The interior was low-beamed, like most of the shops in the street, with chintz curtains and cushions and white-emulsioned walls, which gave it an atmosphere of sedate calm and coolness. In that blistering summer the coolness was most welcoming.

Only one table was taken, by an elderly couple, and he led Wesley to one several feet away, where he had enough space to spread himself without being a nuisance or a hazard to them. He gave him the menu. 'What's it to be, Wesley? Tea and cakes?'

'Please,' he nodded. Like so many in his age group, Wesley didn't waste words, even on the deserving.

'It'll do your acne no good at all,' Barry warned him, watching his jaw drop. 'I'm only kidding,' he relented. 'Have whatever you like.'

Wesley grunted his relief and lapsed into silence again. He really wasn't terribly good company, but where there was a flicker of life and enthusiasm, improvement was always possible.

Presently, Lucy, the proprietress came to take their order. Slim and with fair, shoulder-length hair, she was attractive in a completely natural way, with a flawless complexion.

She greeted them. 'Hello, you two. You're looking very serious.' With a hint of mischief, she said, 'Don't tell me – you've just done a wedding.' She knew how Barry felt about them.

Wesley coloured and looked down at the table. Barry said, 'We had an accident with the equipment this afternoon.'

She raised her eyebrows, but made no comment, evidently aware of Wesley's discomfiture. 'Are you ready to order?' She had a lovely smile, and a gloriously smooth complexion that would look magnificent on slow film.

'Yes, Wesley would like tea, a scone and probably a cake as well, if I know him, and I'll settle for a pot of English Breakfast, please.' His waistband was feeling just a trifle taut.

She wrote the order on her pad and turned to Wesley. 'And which kind of tea would you like, Wesley?'

'Mm?'

'Have the same as me,' Barry advised him. He nodded mutely, and Lucy made a note on her pad before leaving them. Wesley's social skills needed a lot of attention before he could be turned loose on clients.

When their order arrived, Barry watched his protégé heap four cubes of sugar into his cup, like a brickie's labourer mixing cement, and decided to postpone his education until another day, when he might feel more equal to the task. Wesley went on to put away a scone and a wedge of chocolate cake, finally mumbling about having to go.

'All right, Wesley.' Barry took out his wallet and handed him three one-pound notes. 'Here's your money.'

He looked embarrassed, and Barry thought he was going to apologise for the camera incident again. It would have been interesting to see if he could manage a whole sentence this time, but he simply said, 'Thanks for the tea. See you next week,' and he was away. He was probably still feeling awkward and, as he wasn't a great communicator, Barry was obliged, more often than not, to read between somewhat cryptic lines.

The elderly couple were leaving as well. Barry watched as Lucy brought their change and receipt. It was difficult not to watch her, but there was no point in exciting himself. He'd always found her extremely attractive as well as delightful, but she was already involved with someone, a junior partner in a firm of solicitors in the town. Barry had met him once, and that occasion had been enough. He was smooth, self-assured, tall, dark and totally sickening. Once over the initial disappointment, however, he reconciled himself to the fact that Lucy was a friendly neighbour, and a helpful one, too, as she was happy to feed Jack on the odd occasions when he had to be away.

She saw the couple off, picked up an ashtray and a cup and saucer, and came over to his table. He'd been trying not to smoke as heavily of late, but he was more than ready for a cigarette at that moment, and he lit one while she sat down in the place Wesley had recently vacated.

'Tell me about this afternoon,' she said.

He described Wesley's performance with the camera, and her amused smile became a sympathetic grimace.

'Was it insured?'

'Of course.'

'But what will you do while you're waiting for a replacement? Have you got something else you can use?'

'Oh yes, I'll manage.' Her fleeting concern pleased him. It wasn't the sort of reaction he usually got from women, but that wasn't surprising, as it wasn't the kind he was used to seeking. He found the platonic thing new and different, something that had never featured in his single-minded progression from one carnal crisis to the next.

They continued to chat about the problems of building up a small business. In the short time he'd known her, he'd learned that Lucy had inherited the bookshop and teashop from her mother, and that she'd tried unsuccessfully to sell it, finally opting to run the business herself, but that was all he knew.

'What did you do before this?'

'I was a museum assistant.'

'Really?' It was a world about which he knew nothing. 'How did you get into that?'

'It seemed quite natural. I did modern history at university, and I didn't fancy teaching, so I opted for the museums service. I enjoyed it, but it's appallingly badly paid, so I wasn't too unhappy about taking on the business.'

'It seems popular,' he said. 'It should do well.'

'I hope so. For now, I'll be happy if I can find a new waitress. As you can see, the temp from the agency let me down today.' She shrugged. 'I'm interviewing one on Monday, but I know very little about her.'

'I hope you find the right one soon,' he said. 'It must be frustrating, having to close the bookshop to do this.'

'Believe me, it is.' She looked at him enquiringly, possibly feeling that the conversation had been all about her. 'Didn't you once tell me you'd learned the photography business in the forces?'

'Yes, in the Fleet Air Arm.' It seemed odd to a lot of people, but that wasn't surprising.

She poured the last of the tea into their two cups. 'Now that I've emptied the pot, I'll get you some fresh tea,' she told him, signalling Esme in the kitchen. 'What kind of thing did you get up to?'

'We did more cine than still photography, really. We had to film deck landings and take-offs, as well as anything that was needed for posterity. They managed to keep us pretty busy.'

'I suppose that makes sense. What made you join in the first place?'

Barry waited until Esme had placed a pot of fresh tea on the table. They thanked her and, in answer to Lucy's question, he said, 'I ran away to sea.'

'No.' Her smile was one of disbelief.

'Don't tell me I'm the first fortune seeker you've ever met.'

'I think you must be.' She was still smiling.

'I worked in an office for two years after I left school, and I was bored mindless with it. Worse than that, though, I wasn't happy at home. I had an overbearing elder brother, and parents who could see no wrong in that, and I couldn't see things improving, so I joined up.'

'It was a good move, obviously.' She was serious again.

'It gave me everything I needed,' he agreed, 'including a secure home and a profession.'

'That all makes sense, but I don't understand why you left all that behind, if it was so good for you.'

'Ah well, there was some very ugly writing on the wall. The two general elections came shortly before my nine years were up, and we knew then that the politicians were looking to save money by scrapping the last of the aircraft carriers, so I left before I was pushed. I was very lucky to find a job as a studio assistant.'

'And then you came here.' She smiled as she said it. 'How's it going? It's portrait work you do, mainly, isn't it?'

'That's right. Business is trickling in. What I really need is to win a professional competition or do particularly well in one. For now, I have to take on all kinds of work, just to keep things together.'

Mischievously, she said, 'Including weddings.'

'I'm afraid so. I'm also on the scene-of-crime rota, which helps.'

'Oh?' The information evidently surprised her. 'I imagined the police would have their own photographers.'

'A lot of forces have started employing their own people, but the work's contracted out here for the time being, and I'm happy to do it.'

'What does it involve?'

'I'm on call seven days each month, twenty-four hours a day, and I have to photograph evidence. Sometimes it's malicious damage or burglary, sometimes injuries and even an occasional body. I also have to attend road traffic accidents.'

She shuddered. 'I don't know how you can cope with seeing all those things.'

'It's different when you're not involved. You get used to it. The worst part is being called out in the middle of the night, or working all night and then having to carry on through the day.'

'I can imagine.' Suddenly, she remembered something. 'You had a client this afternoon.'

'Did I?'

'Yes, a girl came in to ask if I knew whether you were going to be closed all day. I said I imagined you would be, and she seemed disappointed.'

'I suppose if she's keen enough, she'll call again.' The memory of the girl at Sainsbury's prompted him to ask, 'Can you remember what she looked like?'

'I can.' There was no hesitation. 'She was tall and very slim, with long, dark hair. Very pretty. I've seen her in the town and at Sainsbury's, where she works, but I can't say I know her, particularly. Were you expecting someone?'

'Sort of, but I thought she might phone first.'

In fact, he'd only been back at the studio a few minutes when the phone rang.

'Hello, is that the photographer?'

'Barry Craven, yes.'

'It's Claret from Sainsbury's. I'm ringing up about having some photos done. I came round this afternoon but you was closed.'

'Yes, I was doing a wedding.'

'Lovely.'

He let that pass. 'Would you like to make an appointment?'

'Yeah, how much is it, by the way?'

'I could do you a portfolio for thirty pounds.'

There was an awkward silence, and then in a subdued voice she said, 'I didn't think it would be as much as that.'

'Honestly,' he told her, 'that's not expensive. A lot of studios would charge you more. Is it a problem?' It was a silly question, given her reaction, but he was possibly as disappointed as she was.

'Yes, I can't manage that much.'

Maybe he could shave a bit off the profit margin. 'What can you afford?'

'I've got seventeen quid.' She hesitated and said, 'Maybe if you didn't take as many pictures....'

'Have you done any modelling?'

'Yes, I got some work through Belles Images. It wasn't a lot though.'

'I see.' He knew the firm. It was a cowboy concern and he was surprised they were still in business. 'What sort of thing did you do?'

'Just local things, shows in a couple of local stores. The problem is they've gone bust and I've got to find somewhere else.'

'I'm sorry.'

'Oh well, I'll just have to go on saving up. Thanks anyway.' Before Barry could say anything else, she'd rung off, and it was then that he realised how much the thing meant to her. She'd sounded choked. It was ridiculous. He was in business to earn a profit, but he was disappointed because he couldn't help her.

⁓⬦⁓

Gavin Peckett leaned his considerable bulk against the bar at The Three Tuns, and eyed him pityingly. 'You can't go through life feeling sorry for people, you know,' he said. 'It's bound to take its toll on you eventually.' Gavin was a plumber, and he reckoned that being called out to emergencies and having to deal with people under stress had made him an expert on human behaviour. 'You'll be taken for a soft touch again and again,' he said.

'It's a bit difficult to change now,' Barry told him. 'I've been doing it for as long as I remember.'

'Well in that case there's no hope for you, my son.' He signalled to the barmaid with his empty glass and called for two more pints. 'Mind you,' he said, his eyes suddenly twinkling, 'if this girl's as fit as you say she is, you could always do her a favour. She might return the compliment. You never know your luck.'

'No,' Barry protested, 'I don't work like that, and anyway, she's only a kid.'

'How old is she?'

'I don't know. Not very old. All I know is she's over eighteen because she serves me with booze at the check-out and she doesn't have to wave it at a supervisor the way the younger ones do.'

'That makes her old enough,' he said, 'so I really don't see what your problem is.' It was as Barry had long suspected, Gavin had no scruples at all. For the moment, however, his attention had wandered, and he pointed towards the door. 'Maybe that's more in your line.' Barry followed his gaze. The bar was filling up, but he could see that Gavin was pointing to Lucy. She and her solicitor chap were making their way into the restaurant. She caught Barry's eye and waved.

16

'No way,' he told Gavin. 'You can see she's catered for.'

'Barry, my son,' he said patiently, 'you just need to play your cards right, that's all.'

Gavin made things sound so simple, but as far as Barry was concerned just then, life was a huge complication. There was a wrecked camera, a portfolio session that didn't happen, an attractive and agreeable woman who was beyond his reach, and a business that wasn't expanding quickly enough. He leaned against the bar and suddenly his elbow felt cold and wet. The sleeve of his suede jacket was trailing in beer and the day was complete.

# 3

# Two Problems Solved

Two weeks later, he went to a local stud, where he'd been asked to photograph a stallion, and he decided on the way back to call in at the teashop for a late lunch. Enough time had passed since the embarrassment of Christine's hysterical departure that he felt sufficiently recovered to show his face again.

He'd sometimes wondered how the High Street came to get its name. With the exception of a few very minor side turnings it was the only street in Woodley that qualified it as a town rather than a village, by virtue of its having a few shops, a pub and restaurant, and a tiny but handy branch of Lloyds Bank.

Actually, the shops, though few, were very good. They had to be, to survive the way they did in so small a town. There was an excellent post office and general store that kept the kind of food items usually only found in larger places. Also, a little way up the street from the studio, there was an expensive but exceptionally good hairdressing salon.

The rest of the High Street consisted of dwelling houses of various ages and designs, most of them with a small patch of garden to the front, and an array of colourful window boxes and hanging baskets. It was a charming place, and Barry considered himself lucky to have found the studio there.

On that day, with its white-painted buildings, the street

was like a great shimmering reflector in the mad August heat, so it was a relief to go into the coolness of the teashop and sit in a corner away from the window. A waitress he hadn't seen before came to take his order. She was very young; he imagined she might be a school-leaver and he wondered if she was the one Lucy had mentioned. Her long hair was swept back and pinned, and some of it had worked loose, because here and there, wisps of blonde hair lay on her shoulders in a way that seemed out of place in a restaurant, but which would look most appealing through a lens under diffused lighting.

'You ready to order yet?'

'Yes, I'd like a prawn salad, please.' His waistband was feeling the merest fraction restrictive again, and drastic measures were appropriate.

'We ain't got no prawns left. Sorry.'

'All right.' He looked at the menu again. 'Chicken salad?'

'No, we ain't got no chicken left neiver. Sorry.'

He changed his mind about the soft lighting. She only had one expression: downright vacant. 'Have you got any Cheddar cheese?'

'Yeah, we got that.'

'In that case, will you do me a ploughman's lunch?'

'What's that, then?' Her vacant expression dithered for a moment.

'A cheese salad with pickles.'

'I don't know. I'll go and ask.' She disappeared into the kitchen and re-emerged a moment later. 'Yeah, we can do you that farmers' fing.'

'Oh good, and I'd like a pot of coffee while I'm waiting, please.'

'Right.'

He was thankful they weren't out of coffee. He needed it after all that. He sat back and lit a cigarette, ashamedly his fifth that day. It was all Christine's fault, but he'd settle down in a few days.

Just then, Lucy came in and spotted him. 'May I join you?'

'Please do. Are you taking a late lunch too?'

19

'Yes, lunchtimes can be quite busy in the bookshop. People go shopping during their break, so it pays to take mine later.'

'There's not much left. I'm having a "farmers' fing" because you ain't got no chicken and you ain't got no prawns, neiver.'

She sighed. 'I gather you've met Michelle. She's the nearest I can get to raw talent. She's very raw, and maybe the talent will come later if I'm lucky.'

'A bit like Wesley when he joined me,' he suggested.

'Well, in that case, there's hope for her.' Addressing the menu, she asked, 'What's the "farmers' fing" you mentioned?'

'A cheese salad.'

Michelle arrived with the coffee and deposited it in front of him, a little taken aback to see Lucy.

'Michelle, will you get me the same as Mr Craven's having and a pot of coffee, please?'

Michelle hesitated for a second, perhaps wondering who Mr Craven was, and then reacted. 'Right, Miss.' She hesitated again. 'Miss, that grey-and-white cat's here again. Have I to feed him?'

'Yes, please. Jack usually calls for lunch at about this time.'

It was news to Barry, who thought he only went there for breakfast. He thought about the depleted menu. 'I don't think he'll be terribly excited about cheese and pickles,' he said.

'That's all right,' Michelle assured him, 'he can have the bits of ham and chicken that we can't give the customers. You know, all the rind and fat and stringy bits—'

'Thank you, Michelle,' said Lucy. 'Will you go and feed Jack, please?' Seeing Michelle hesitate, she prompted, 'The cat.'

Michelle departed, and Lucy turned to Barry. 'And what have you been up to?'

'I've been photographing a horse.'

'I didn't know you did animals.'

'I do occasionally.'

'I suppose people are as keen to have their animals photographed as their children.'

'They are, but this one's special. He's a stallion at stud, and I must say he'll make an excellent picture. His owner was going

20

into raptures about the size of his neck, but somehow I didn't see that as his most prominent feature.'

'You're jealous.'

'Of course I am, and he hasn't got a cat like Jack to cramp his style.'

A little coyly, she said, 'Look, I don't want to pry, but what did Jack do, exactly?'

He hesitated, because he still found it embarrassing. 'He came home unexpectedly and caught me in a compromising situation with my girl... my *ex*-girlfriend.'

Lucy smiled. 'What did he do?'

'He frightened the life out of her.'

'Jack? But he's not at all aggressive.'

'Not much. She's only the second he's seen off the same way. He's a thug.'

'Oh, poor you.' She was laughing immoderately.

'Feel free to make light of my misfortunes, Lucy. I'll try to wear my embarrassment bravely.'

'I'm sorry, but it's so unusual.'

'Well, this time it was possibly fortuitous,' he admitted. 'The thing was coming to an end, anyway. He just spared me having to do the deed in cold blood.'

She stopped laughing and wiped her eyes with a paper napkin. 'Were you being squeamish?'

'I'm afraid so. I can't help it.'

'But Jack's not, apparently.'

'Not in the slightest.'

Lucy shook her head in wonder, and then said, 'You know, I'm not keen on names like "Tiddles" and "Fluffy", but Jack's an unusual name for a cat, isn't it?'

'Yes, I named him after a character I knew years ago when I first went to school.'

'Oh, tell me about him.'

He hesitated. It wasn't the most appropriate subject for a mealtime, but the food hadn't yet arrived, so he set about answering her question. 'It was because of his attitude, you see.'

Michelle came with a tray bearing two 'farmers' fings' and a pot of coffee, and he waited until she was gone. Then, having started, he had to continue. 'I met Jack Rushworth on my first day at school when we were five years old. He was dirty. I mean long-term dirty. Even at five, the poor kid wore very strong glasses because he was so short-sighted, although I don't know what he could see through them because they were always filthy, too, like coal cellar windows. He wore hob-nailed boots as well. I kept asking my parents for boots because so many of the kids wore them, and I felt left out of things, but they wouldn't let me have them, because they were only for poor kids.'

'You wouldn't have found them at all comfortable, I'm sure.'

'I don't suppose I would.' Out of politeness, he allowed her the interruption whilst wondering, as he often did, why women felt obliged to do it. 'Anyway, naturally enough, Jack became a convenient victim for bullying, until I took his side.'

'Oh, that was noble of you, Barry.'

'Not noble, really, so much as…. I suppose I just felt sorry for him.' He stopped and asked, 'Where was I?' Her interruption had broken his train of thought.

'You took his side.'

'Yes, and then a teacher came out and broke up the fight. I wasn't too unhappy, though, because I reckoned I'd done the right thing.'

'There's no doubt about that.'

'Anyway, you'd think he owed me a favour for that, but he evidently didn't think so.'

'What did he do?'

'When we were having our turn in the sand pit—' He broke off when Lucy laughed. 'Didn't you have sand pits at your school?'

'I'm sure we did. It's the mental picture that's creasing me.'

'All right, I'm thick-skinned enough to take it.'

'I'm sorry.'

'Anyway, one of the girls who were with us told the teacher that Jackie Rushworth was throwing sand. Now, we hadn't been there very long, and there were forty-five of us, so I suppose Miss Watkins hadn't got to know everyone, and somehow she thought I was Jack Rushworth. At all events, I got a beating-up from her and Jack never said a word. He just let me take the punishment that should have been his.'

'That's awful.'

'So you see, it seemed an excellent name for an ungrateful little sod.'

Lucy's smile gave way to a thoughtful look. 'Maybe Jack, I mean *our* Jack, isn't as ungrateful as you think. He got you out of a difficult relationship, after all.'

'That's true, and the one before it wasn't brilliant.'

'Did he break that one up for you as well?'

'Yes.'

Touching his arm sympathetically, she said, 'You don't have much luck with women, do you?'

'It must seem so sometimes,' he admitted soberly.

'So maybe Jack's trying to tell you something.'

'You mean that he knows best?' It sounded ridiculous as he said it.

'It's possible. Animals judge purely by instinct.'

'In that case, I wish he'd give me a few pointers, because I'm certainly open to advice.'

Thoughts of Jack set him in the direction of Sainsbury's. There were some things he needed, and he knew he was out of cat food. Jack wasn't exactly starving, as Barry had discovered earlier, but he'd still expect supper to be on the floor at six o-clock, as usual, if not earlier.

He drew up in the car park and the heat hit him again. He hurried into the supermarket and made a bee-line for the fruit and vegetable section, not because he wanted either, but simply to enjoy the blissfully cold air that surrounded them. When he felt sufficiently cooled, he headed inevitably for the oven-ready meals, changing his mind half-way and settling for a prepared pizza. It was shameful really, but he'd never taken to proper cooking. He kept telling himself that it was only like developing and printing, that it was just a matter of dunking something in liquid at a certain temperature for a given time, but laziness always took the upper hand. He made a resolution to start cooking. In a month's time, or maybe when the weather cooled down a bit might be a good time to start. If he were honest with himself, though, he knew it was unlikely to be more than a good intention, but it made him feel slightly more virtuous, and he continued to the pet food aisle and picked up two tins of meat and a box of the usual cat biscuits. There was a picture of a cross-looking cat on the front of the box. He was sure it wasn't meant to look fierce, but that was nevertheless the effect it had – being Persian put it at an immediate disadvantage – and he wondered how many buyers had been put off by it. He could have taken a far better picture than that. Cats weren't the easiest subjects to photograph, but he'd taken some pretty good ones. If Jack had one redeeming quality, it was that he made a very good photographer's model. He was unfazed by spot lamps and even studio flash, and he was usually happy enough to let Barry shoot off an occasional roll of film. He put the box back and took one with a better picture on it. Jack wouldn't notice the difference.

Realising he'd forgotten to get coffee, he went back for it, and in doing so, happened to glance towards the check-out where Claret was taking her place behind one of the tills. A supervisor was doing something with it, so he assumed she'd just come on shift. The memory of his conversation with her returned. Poor kid. She was keen to have those pictures, but she hadn't a clue about what was involved, especially the cost. She was innocent. Just sitting there, she looked innocent, with that same naïve charm that had appealed to him in the first place. As he stood in the aisle watching her, an idea came to him. She could help him make his competition entry.

He hurried over to her till. No one else had noticed it was open. She saw him coming and smiled.

'Hi.'

'Hi, I'm sorry you were disappointed about the photographs.'

She shrugged and began checking his things out. 'It's all right. I should have realised.'

'No, you weren't to know, but listen, I've had an idea. I need a portrait model for an important project, and I think you're just right for it.'

Her expression was a mixture of surprise and doubt. That alone would have made a superb picture. 'I haven't done any photographic work,' she said.

'You've got to start some time.'

'Do you think I could do it?'

'I'm sure you can.' He looked behind him to see a woman pushing a loaded trolley towards him. She had two restless toddlers in tow and was unlikely to take kindly to waiting, so he said hurriedly, 'If you'd like to do it in exchange for your portfolio, give me a ring.'

He watched disbelief morph into bliss. She stared at him without saying a word, but he knew how she felt. Her mouth was still open when he paid for his stuff and left. He'd solved two problems at one stroke, which made him feel pretty good, too.

# 4

# Deborah

It was Saturday morning, the sun was shining, and the day was full of promise. Barry had a couple of 'people' sittings booked, and that was always good. The only missing element was Wesley, and he couldn't find him anywhere. He'd heard his arrival as he was making a studio shopping list. He remembered the squeal of brakes and the muffled crash as Wesley parked his bike against the wall. He'd heard the bell ring and the door slam as he came into the office, but after that, nothing. It was most odd, because it wasn't like Wesley to be quiet about anything. He couldn't usually walk through a doorway without kicking the architrave. He checked the downstairs loo. The door was wide open and there was no sign of him so there was only one other place he could be. Barry opened the door of the studio changing room and there he was. At least, he thought it was Wesley. His hair was slicked back with goodness-knew-what kind of preparation and he reeked of cheap after-shave. The effect was unnerving, but the most striking feature of his transformation was the total absence of spots. Instead, there was a pale blotchiness about his face. Barry stared at him, and Wesley lowered his eyes guiltily. It wasn't necessary to search far to find the reason for his discomfiture. The make-up cupboard was open and a stick of concealer lay on the dressing table in front of him. It was the kind of thing that was used to cover blemishes. Some of the more self-conscious clients were sufficiently clued up to use it before a photo session, and it seemed that Wesley had been doing his homework too.

As the hapless youth gazed downward, it occurred to Barry that, at twenty-nine, he was ill-equipped to play the Dutch uncle, but someone had to. 'It isn't a good idea,' he said gently.

Wesley's tone was expressionless, as usual. 'What isn't?'

'Putting that stuff on your spots. In fact, the more muck you put on them the worse they'll be.' There was no reaction, but he went on. 'The best thing you can do is to rinse your face with lots of clear water every time you wash, to get all the soap off.'

He frowned miserably. 'I do, but it doesn't do any good.'

'It will, given time. It happens to everyone, you know.'

There was a flicker of new interest. 'Did you have 'em?'

'Of course I did.'

'I don't suppose it mattered as much in them days.' Clearly, Wesley regarded teenage problems, like teenage itself, as a product of the nineteen-seventies.

'Of course it mattered. I was as conscious of it as you are, and bear in mind, in those days I had a whole ship's company to poke fun at me, close on two thousand men. How do you think I felt about that?'

'Hm.' Like all Wesley's grunts, it was open to interpretation, and Barry took it that he was conceding a point. Still, the lad's meagre confidence had taken a jarring and Barry felt he had to help him restore some of it. 'We have a family group at ten o'clock,' he reminded him, 'and I want you to receive these people in the office. Introduce yourself by name and tell them that you're my assistant, and that I'll be with them shortly. You can show them the dressing room in case they need to make any final adjustments, and generally welcome them. You can do that, can't you?'

'I think so.'

'I'm sure you can, and you know, your professional image is part of the firm's image. It's very important.'

'Right.' He didn't sound terribly certain.

'Remember that clients don't give a bugger about acne. They just want to be treated as if they're special, and I know you can do that.'

'Right.' He was sounding more positive, and it seemed that it was finally making sense to him.

'So wash the concealer off, and then you can check the lights in the studio.'

Barry returned to his order. It seemed to him that the kind of image Wesley needed most was an improved one of himself. It wasn't going to develop overnight, but a bit of responsibility might set things in motion.

He was quite pleased with the way Wesley welcomed the family into the office. His delivery could have been smoother, but he was downright suave by his own standards. From his vantage point in the passage-way, Barry heard him take them through to the studio and point out the changing room, and it was at that point that he decided it was time to introduce himself.

They had with them a boy of about eleven or twelve and a girl who must have been a couple of years or so younger. She was shy and she clung to her mother, unsure of what was expected of her, but the boy couldn't have been more different. For one thing, he couldn't leave his hair alone. He kept patting his elaborate quiff into place and checking it in the studio mirror, like a playboy about to make a conquest. He had a long nose, a superior expression and protuberant lips. All in all, he set Barry in mind of a pre-pubertal version of the stallion he'd photographed the previous day. He took an immediate dislike to him, but business was business, and he had to take whatever came along. He arranged them together on the chaise longue; the parents in the middle, the girl with her mother and racehorse-features with his father, who, now Barry thought of it, must have passed the race-horse gene on to his son.

Barry stood behind the camera and hesitated. From that angle, he was conscious of the boy's nostrils. He motioned to him. 'Just lower your chin a little and look straight at me,' he said in what he hoped was a coaxing manner. It wasn't easy when the subject was so unappealing.

The boy's mother glanced across at him and said, 'Do as Mr Craven says, Jonathan.'

Jonathan threw her a bored look before returning his condescending gaze to Barry. Then, nodding at the camera, he asked, 'Is that all you've got?'

'This is a specialist portrait camera,' Barry told him.

He wasn't impressed. 'My uncle has a Nikon,' he informed him, smirking as he spoke, 'with a motor drive.'

Barry smiled blandly and said, 'Motor drive, you say?' It was very difficult, taking deep breaths without showing it, and the little sod was really winding him up. 'Well, they say this is the age of labour-saving devices, don't they?'

'What else have you got?'

'I have various cameras, but I use this for studio portraits because it's the best kind for the job'.

'If you say so.' He remained unimpressed, which didn't surprise Barry.

'Are you keen on photography?'

'I do some,' he said, sounding like a dilettante who dabbled a little when his busy calendar allowed, 'with my uncle.'

'Well then,' he said, 'you and I appreciate how lucky your uncle is to have a Nikon *with a motor winder*. That's really something, isn't it?' The boy was still smirking when Barry took the first shot. His father looked less confident, while his mother shifted uncomfortably before favouring Barry with a camera smile. The girl started to relax a little as well, so he concentrated most of his efforts on her for the time being.

After a few frames, Mr Racehorse asked him to take some pictures of Jonathan. It wasn't the most inviting task, but business was business. He called Wesley and asked him to bring some more cut film. 'Okay,' he agreed, 'but shouldn't I take some of your daughter too?'

'Naomi's very shy,' her mother explained.

Barry had a pretty good idea why. 'Don't worry,' he assured her, 'she'll be fine.'

So it was agreed, and for the next several frames, Jonathan gave him the benefit of his distinguished bearing. It was less like a series of celebrity stills, which may have been his intention, than a set of mug-shots of a spoiled brat, but the customer was always right, so Barry took them and then called again for Wesley. 'Wesley, will you take Mr and Mrs Thomas and give them coffee or tea, whichever they prefer, while I take some pictures of Naomi?'

'Yes, Mr Craven.'

He was working well. Barry waited for them to leave the studio and then turned his attention to Naomi. 'There's nothing to worry about,' he told her, taking the Pentax from the safe and fitting a portrait lens. 'We're going to take some super pictures that you're going to be proud of.' She didn't seem convinced, and he couldn't blame her. He dragged the chaise longue away from the backdrop and motioned to her to sit down. 'There now. This is going to be easy.' He talked to her while he adjusted the lights. 'Have you got a boyfriend?' He saw her shyness increase. 'Because when he sees these pictures he's sure to want one.' He winked slowly and was rewarded with a tentative smile. 'Tell me about him,' he teased.

'I haven't got one,' she whispered.

'Go on, a lovely girl like you? You're pulling my leg.'

'I haven't.' The smile broadened and he caught it.

'You're kidding. You've got to be kidding. I bet you've got lots of boyfriends all fighting over you. I know these things.'

'No I haven't.' She was getting into the game now and her face was becoming much more animated.

'I can't believe that, Naomi.'

'I haven't!' He caught her with her mouth wide open. It was a superb shot, perfectly natural and right for a girl of her age.

'Well you jolly well should, and you will very soon, believe me.' There was a hint of her earlier shyness, but the smile was genuine and he caught that too.

He managed a few more before they were interrupted by a scratching sound. He opened the studio door and scooped Jack up.

Wesley loomed in the doorway. 'I'm sorry,' he said, 'I tried to stop him.'

'It's okay. Don't worry.' Barry held Jack for a minute. He was looking at Naomi, and he was purring in a reassuring way, so he put him down. He usually behaved well in the studio, and Naomi evidently held some fascination for him. He made a leap for the chaise longue and, for once in his life, he made it in one. She held out her hands and Jack climbed over her, sniffing her tentatively at first. After that, it was true love, as he slipped his forepaws over her shoulders in one of his arms-round cuddles. They didn't happen often; Jack was very selective and a bit reserved but every now and again he allowed his feelings to surface. The look of pleasure and surprise on Naomi's face was indescribable, and Barry caught it.

After all that, he had mixed feelings when the family were about to leave. The session with Naomi had been quite magical, especially after Jack's entrance, and that made up for a great deal. Wesley had done well too, right up to the end, when Barry had given him the unused film to put back in the fridge. He couldn't have asked more of him, which was as well, because that was where the transformation suffered a hitch. It was Jack's fault really. When he saw a refrigerator, he envisaged food. He'd never seen anything edible come out of the studio fridge but he still followed Wesley there on the off-chance that his luck might change, and that was when, in his eagerness, he crept a little too close, and Wesley stood on his paw. As Barry opened the office door to let Mr Racehorse and his family out, there was the kind of ear-splitting yowl that only an agonised cat could produce, followed by the clatter of the contents of the fridge landing on the floor, and Wesley's startled yell. 'Fucking cat!'

He took Wesley to lunch at the teashop, partly because of his efforts that morning – he considered that he could be allowed an expletive in the circumstances – but chiefly because he was in a happy frame of mind. The little session with Naomi had been rewarding in itself, and he had another appointment to look forward to in the afternoon. Added to that was the prospect of a session with Claret the following Monday.

It wasn't long before Michelle came to serve them, and this time there was no difficulty over the menu. Everything was available, including Wesley's shepherds' pie, although Barry couldn't imagine how he could face it on such a hot day. Even though it was cool in the teashop, the sight of Wesley's steaming plate made him uncomfortable. Still, he couldn't have everything. Wesley had shaped up remarkably well that morning, and he even looked the part in a light-weight, flared suit and paisley tie. Being tall and slim, he looked fine in flares. He'd caught Michelle's attention too. She'd been back twice to enquire if the food were satisfactory, and it would have been difficult not to notice her surreptitious glances in his direction. If it came to that, Wesley wasn't exactly unaware of her presence, and Barry wondered if the day might present a turning point in his fortunes. He said, 'She's nice, isn't she?'

'Who?'

'Michelle, the waitress.'

Wesley mumbled something incoherently and attacked his shepherds' pie with renewed concentration, but Barry wasn't about to let things slide. 'I reckon she fancies you. Why don't you ask her out?'

He raised his face from the cloud of steam and hissed, 'Give up, Barry, you're embarrassing me.'

'You'd like to, though, wouldn't you?'

'Barry!' He was squirming.

'Back in a minute,' Barry told him. Wesley looked relieved until he saw him making for the kitchen.

Esme, the cook, was picking up Jack's bowl. 'Hello, Barry,' she called. 'Jack was in earlier than usual. He must have things to do this afternoon.'

'We'll never know, Esme. Actually I'm looking for Michelle.'

Esme gave him a strange look as Michelle emerged from the pantry, carrying a tray of coffee things. She looked surprised to see him, too.

'Michelle, my mate Wesley in there,' he said, pausing until she nodded, 'would really like you to go out with him.' Her look of surprise waned as if she'd known it all along. 'He's ever such a nice lad,' he went on, 'but he's very shy. Why don't you go and ask him out?' He knew that girls did that sort of thing, although it was unheard of when he was their age, but he was still taken aback by the promptness of her response.

'Okay.' That was all she said. She pushed open the door to the dining room and went through.

Esme shook her head in bewilderment. Barry decided to have a word with Lucy in the bookshop.

He found her checking invoices. She seemed relieved by the interruption.

'Hi, Barry,' she said. 'What's new?'

'I think I've got Wesley fixed up with Michelle,' he told her.

The idea seemed to amuse her. 'They'll make the perfect couple.'

'We'll see. Wesley's shaping up now, you know.' He told her about the morning session and Wesley's part in it, leaving out the accident with Jack, and she was impressed. Then she remembered something. 'Of course, you had Guy's brother and his family in, didn't you?'

'Guy's brother?' He was completely thrown. Guy was the smooth solicitor, but Barry hadn't been aware of any connection. Now he thought about it, though, there was a physical similarity, especially about the nose.

'Yes, that was Guy's brother Matthew and his family.

Guy said they had an appointment with you. Actually, he wasn't very pleased, because he'd offered to take the pictures himself, but June, his sister-in-law, insisted on having it done professionally. They don't get on terribly well.'

'Really?' Things were falling into place. 'So Guy must be the uncle who has a Nikon with a motor drive.'

She frowned. 'A what with a motor what?'

'A Japanese camera with a device that works the shutter like a machine gun.'

'That's right. Presumably, Jonathan told you about it.'

'Yes,' he said guardedly, 'he wasn't impressed with what I was using.'

'He wouldn't be. Don't worry. I'm not keen on him either. Naomi's different though. How did you find her?'

'She was lovely, and I got some excellent pictures of her.'

'I'm amazed you were allowed to. Matthew usually keeps her firmly in the background. He can't let anyone steal the limelight from Jonathan.'

That tallied perfectly with Barry's impression of him. 'Ah well,' he said, 'he wanted some pictures of Jonathan, so I suggested I took some of her, just to be fair, and in any case I'm not going to charge them for hers.'

'Why ever not?'

'I got them to sign a model release form, instead, so that I can use them.'

'I see. Well, good for you. It was high time she had a bit of attention.' She smiled mischievously. 'How did that go down with Matthew?'

'It took him completely by surprise.'

'Good. He's a pompous twit. It runs in the family, you know. Guy can be a bit like that sometimes.' She looked at her watch. 'Look, if you're here for a while I'll come and have coffee with you.'

'Fine.'

She put the 'Closed' sign on the shop door and locked it, and he followed her through to the dining room. It was good to know that Guy was less than perfect.

They joined Wesley, who was still looking embarrassed, although not altogether displeased with himself.

Barry asked him, 'Have you broken the ice?'

'Stop it, Barry.'

'Yes,' Lucy agreed, 'don't be cruel.'

Wesley's embarrassment increased, however, with the reappearance of Michelle who was trying hard to avoid looking at him.

'Coffee all round, please, Michelle,' Lucy asked her. 'You'd like coffee, wouldn't you, Wesley?'

'Um, please.' He was squirming, and Barry decided to stop teasing him. It was time to talk about something else.

As it happened, it was Lucy who changed the subject by asking, 'What will you do with those pictures of Naomi?'

'I don't know yet. A friend of mine's writing a book on portrait photography, and he might be interested in them. I'll find a use for them eventually. I've got lots of pictures that I've just filed away, well, shoved into a drawer actually. You never know when they might be useful.'

'I must say I'm very surprised about Naomi. She's always been so shy.'

Suddenly Wesley spoke up. 'It's part of a photographer's job, putting people at ease.'

Barry was startled. Wesley didn't usually contribute much to a conversation, and he wondered how much was due to his new image and how much was down to the fact that Michelle had appeared with the coffee. He seemed desperate to keep the conversation going, possibly to avoid further embarrassment.

'It's very important, and Barry's really good at it,' he told her.

'Yes,' she said, 'I imagine he is.' She turned to Michelle. 'Thank you, Michelle. Now everyone else has gone, would you like to get yourself a cup and saucer and join us?'

'Thanks, Miss.' Her suggestion obviously appealed to Michelle.

'"Lucy" will do,' she told her. '"Miss" makes me feel like an elderly spinster.'

'Right, Miss... Lucy.'

'So,' said Lucy, returning her attention to Wesley, 'there's obviously a lot more to being a photographer than taking pictures.'

'Oh yes, there's the processing side as well.' He glanced at Barry, who motioned to him to go on. He was doing well. 'You can change the whole character of a picture after you've taken it, just by the way you print it.'

Michelle joined them in time to hear what Barry thought was a surprisingly articulate description of creative printing. It really had been Wesley's morning.

Deborah Williams arrived promptly at two o'clock and Wesley brought her into the studio. Barry wasn't sure what he'd been expecting, but he was quite stunned by what he saw, although it was unlikely that she would have the same effect on everyone as she had on him, because her appeal was of a particular and peculiar kind. She was young, and attractive in the usual way, with fair hair and light blue eyes, highlighted by thin-rimmed glasses, and even in that hot summer, a very pale complexion. She wore no make-up, and her dress was one of the large-patterned halter-neck creations that were so popular, but those were simply details. It was her natural expression that appealed to Barry. It was one of detachment, an almost childlike simplicity that had no place in the real world, so that, from the moment she entered the studio, she fascinated him.

'I understand you want something that can be reproduced in the media,' he said.

'That's right. I've written a piece for a journal and they want a recent photograph to go with it.'

'They'll want it in black and white, then?'

'Yes, black and white's fine.'

In the absence of a medium-format camera, he loaded a

cassette into the SLR and fitted an eighty-five millimetre portrait lens. 'Which journal is it?'

'Cybernetics Monthly,' she told him. It didn't mean a thing to him, and he thought she got that impression, because she explained, 'It's a journal for the computer industry. I'm a systems analyst.'

'What's that?'

'A sort of translator,' she explained patiently. 'I talk to customers in everyday language about what they want, and then I give the information to the programmers, who speak anything but everyday language, in a way that they can understand.'

'I see.' He peered through the viewfinder. 'I'm just going to move the lights. I'm getting a reflection from your glasses.'

'I'd rather keep them on. I wear them all the time.' She motioned vaguely in their direction and he was encouraged to see that her ring finger was unadorned.

'It's no problem.' He shifted the spot lamp so that it was shining down on her. 'There, that should do the trick.' He returned to the camera, and confirmed that all was well.

He took eight frames and despite all his efforts there was very little change in her expression. Each image, however, contained an element of the same fascinating quality that had impressed him from the beginning.

He took out the film, asking, 'How soon do you want to see the proofs?'

'As soon as possible, really. The quicker I can get one off, the sooner my article will be published. When can you have them ready?'

'You could have them on Monday.'

'Really?'

'Oh yes. Do you live locally?'

'Sort of. I live in Elmston.'

'I thought I hadn't seen you about.'

'No, I'm usually fairly busy. Actually, Monday's a bit difficult. I'm in the office all day and I've got a meeting after work.'

'I suppose you'll have to dash off and eat after that.'

She gave him look of mild surprise. 'No, 'I'll have eaten at work, but you'll be closed, surely.'

'The studio will be, but if you'd like to meet me for a drink, I can bring the pictures then.'

She considered that for a moment, and then said, 'All right. Do you know the Wig and Gavel?'

'Yes.'

'I'll be there shortly after seven.'

'Fine. I'll see you there.'

And that was that. Wesley and he were both fixed up. It had been a useful day. He saw her to the door and returned to find Jack regarding him pensively from the office chair, almost as if he were sizing up the situation, but Barry didn't care. What could a cat really know?

Gavin had already formed his opinion. 'The quiet, thoughtful types, Barry,' he said, 'they're the ones.' He lifted his glass and gave him a meaningful look. 'You won't miss Christine now.'

Barry nodded in agreement. It was early days. He'd only made a tentative date with Deborah, but he was hopeful. 'Yes, someone who'll think before speaking, instead of mouthing off all the time.'

'Not just that.' He put his glass down impatiently. 'I mean she'll go like a bloody ferret. The quiet ones always do.'

He'd misread Christine completely. Despite her failings, of which Barry was only too aware, she had a healthy physical appetite. In fact, that was probably one of the reasons he'd held on to her for so long. However, only a week had elapsed since her departure. It was too soon for withdrawal symptoms, and his mind was on higher things, at least for the time being. 'No, no, I wasn't thinking of that particularly.'

Gavin nodded confidently. 'You will.'

'I've no doubt.' He was distracted by Lucy and Guy going into the restaurant.It was odd that they used the same place so often, rather like an old married couple. Not that Lucy fitted that description. She looked sublimely young and fresh, unlike Guy. He was very staid, somehow, like someone who had found success too early, so that life had no new experience to offer, only acceptance of the same old things. Barry wondered quite what she saw in him and, for once, there was not even a hint of envy in the thought, because his interest lay elsewhere.

# 5

# The Session

It must have seemed a very different direction to Lucy that Monday morning. She was belatedly drawing out the awning over the bookshop window when Claret arrived at the studio, suitcase in hand. Barry picked up the case and waved to Lucy before following Claret into the office.

'I see you took me at my word,' he said. 'You must have got half your wardrobe in this thing. It feels like it, anyway.'

'Not really, but it's all fairly new, like you said. There's nothing old or worn.'

'That's right.' He took her into the studio and put her case in the changing room. She was dressed for the moment in jeans and a plain white tee-shirt and, oddly enough, it was the first time he'd seen her standing. She was easily five feet nine. The beautician had done a superb job on her make-up, and her hair had been trimmed but left loose, so that it provided all kinds of framing possibilities.

He asked her, 'What would you like? Coffee or tea?'

'Tea would be lovely, if that's all right. I didn't have time for one this morning. I had to get me dad off to work, an' then me brothers come down wantin' their breakfast, so it was a bit of a rush.'

'Fine. I'll leave you to adjust your hair and make-up and I'll be with you in a minute.' He went off to put the kettle on, wondering a little about what she'd just told him, although,

40

for the moment, he was more interested in starting the session.

When he returned, he found her flicking through one of the back numbers of *Vogue*.

'Is this the sort of thing we're going to do?' She indicated the open page featuring an advertisement for Gucci shoes.

'One of them. We'll certainly do body parts.'

She looked alarmed. 'What's that?'

'Relax. I'm talking about hands, feet and legs.' He pointed to the Gucci advertisement for an example.

'Oh, that's all right.'

'What we have to do is highlight all your potential qualities so that we're not tying you down to one line. That way you'll stand a better chance of finding work.' He turned a few pages to show her various poses associated with clothes, perfume and jewellery. Inevitably there was a picture of a naked model. 'How do you feel about doing some semi-nude poses?'

'What do you mean by *semi*-nude?'

'Well, minus your clothes, but with the essential parts covered up.' It was going to be necessary. He'd already decided to give her the best possible chance by putting together a comprehensive portfolio. Most professional models didn't seem to give a damn about nudity, but he was mindful of the fact that she was very young and, seemingly, innocent.

She shrugged her shoulders. 'I'm going to have to take me clothes off sooner or later.'

'Quite right.' He poured tea into her cup. 'Help yourself to milk and sugar.' He watched her tip milk and a heaped spoonful of sugar into it in a way that reminded him of Wesley. It was amazing that she managed to maintain the kind of figure she had. 'There's something that's been puzzling me,' he told her.

'What's that?'

'What made your parents call you Claret?'

'Yeah, it's different, isn't it? I like it 'cause it's me favourite colour, but me mum decided on it at the last minute. She was nine months gone at the time and she was doing a bit of shopping. Well, she hadn't thought of a name, and then suddenly she saw it in a shop window and she liked it, so that was it.'

'A wine merchant's window?'

'Yeah. How did you know?'

'I have a nose for these things. Never mind, it's a lovely name.'

'I like it,' she agreed. 'One of me brothers has an unusual name an' all. He's called Bailey.'

He couldn't resist asking, 'Did your mum get that out of a wine merchant's window as well?'

'No.' She stared at him as if wondering why he should draw such a conclusion. 'It was me dad. He was keen on rock and roll when it first come out, and there was this singer called Bill Haley.'

'I can just about remember him.'

'Yes, well he thought Bill was a bit ordinary, and Haley sounds a bit iffy. Know what I mean? So he called him Bailey 'cause it has a bit of both names in it.'

'Of course.' It made a kind of sense. 'What's your other brother called?'

'Cliff.' She became curious again. 'What are we going to do first?'

'An ordinary portrait, just to get you relaxed. Then we'll do the hands.'

'The hands?'

'Yes, you've got lovely hands. You might find yourself modelling nail polish or hand cream, or maybe jewellery. You never know. Hand models are always in demand. Of course, you could find yourself holding up toilet tissue or washing up liquid on a TV commercial, and that's also quite lucrative.'

'What's that mean?'

'Lucrative? It means it pays well.'

'Oh, right. What do you want me to wear?' She was taking the job seriously.

'Have you got a plain shirt?'

'Yes, I brought everything you said.'

'Okay, slip that on and come in when you're ready.' He went into the studio and switched on the lights.

After a minute, Claret came in and he could tell she was nervous. She looked at the camera, then at the lights and reflectors, and the camera again, like a patient contemplating the contents of a dentist's consulting room.

'There's nothing to worry about,' he told her. 'Just sit here,' he said, pointing to the cushioned end of the chaise longue, 'rest your head lightly on your hand and look straight at me. There's no need to smile. Just look at me as if I've dumped a load of shopping on your belt.'

He knew he'd probably throw the first few exposures away, but they would help to relax her, and then he'd get much better shots.

He took several more, moving her slightly each time to change the lighting effect, and she began to unwind until it was clear that she was actually enjoying the process, so he reloaded the Pentax and took some close-ups of her face and hands.

'That's fine,' he said. 'Now I'd like you to wear your favourite dress, something that makes you feel really good. Oh, and don't wear a bra with it.'

'Why not?'

'Straps,' he explained. 'They can ruin the whole effect.'

'Right.' She leapt up and disappeared into the changing room, the nerves forgotten. It was like a party game. He moved the lights back to the area in front of the backdrop and pushed the chaise longue out of the way to clear a large space. He hadn't done that kind of thing for ages and he could barely wait to get started.

When Claret returned she was wearing a cocktail-type dress, appropriately in wine red. She had said it was her favourite colour, and it went beautifully with her dark hair and her skin tone. The only problem was the lipstick, which was far too light. However, after a few minutes in the changing room, she was perfect.

'Right, I'm going to take a Polaroid first, so that you can

see how fantastic you look.' He checked the Polaroid. 'Okay, sideways on. That's it, and looking over my shoulder dreamily. Go on. Dreamily. Terrific!' He took the shot and waited for the print. It was a beauty. He showed it to her, enjoying her pleasure at seeing herself in the kind of pose she must only have imagined.

'We're going to go through various poses now. I'll tell you what to do, and then all you have to do is enjoy it.' He fixed the motor drive on to the camera. It had to be the most over-used gadget in the history of photography. Certainly, he'd no idea what Guy used his for, but Barry knew when his was invaluable, and that was in the kind of sequence they were going to shoot next. In his brief experience of working with models, he'd found that the sound of the repeating shutter often excited and electrified them, sometimes with surprising results.

He put her through a series of conventional poses and a few of his own and, as the camera whirred and clicked, she responded better than he'd imagined. She was putting everything into the session, her camera-shyness lost in the sheer enjoyment of what she was doing, and Barry was enjoying it possibly as much as she was.

After that, the lingerie poses were relatively easy once they'd got over the problem of some of the stuff she'd brought with her, which wasn't terribly exciting. It was asking a lot of a girl of her age to produce really stylish underwear, apart from the ever-popular g-strings, but the basic stuff she had wasn't going to do her any favours. At his suggestion, she found a translucent slip and blouse to wear over it, and that softened the effect without detracting from her lovely curves, so they got some excellent shots.

'Okay,' he said, 'you can relax now. I'll switch the studio lights off and make some more tea.'

'Great, I'm sweltering under this lot.'

'You will. Make no mistake, it's hard work. Successful models make a good living, but they earn every penny of it.'

'That's all right. I don't mind.' She was looking at him

anxiously. 'Have we finished?' She was like a child enjoying a treat, fearful that it was time to go home.

'No, there's more. I just thought you needed a rest.'

'That's all right then, only....'

'What?'

'Can I have coffee instead of tea?'

'Of course. That's what I'm going to have. I can't really drink tea after breakfast. It doesn't taste right.'

'Me neither. I just needed tea this morning when I came, 'cause I hadn't had a bloody fing since I got up. There wasn't time.'

It was the second time she'd mentioned the morning's rush. He was curious. 'Does your mother live with you?'

She shook her head matter-of-factly. 'No, she left us a few years ago. Why do you ask?'

'Only that you mentioned having to see to your father and your brothers. It made me wonder, that's all.'

'Yeah, me dad needs looking after, and me brothers are on leave just now. They're in the forces.'

'Both of them?'

'Mm, they're twins. They're not identical at all, but they do everything together. They always have.'

'I see. I'd have thought they'd be quite self-reliant.'

'They like to think they are, but they're idle sods. Me dad's the same. They all expect to be waited on when they're at home.'

'They'll have to look after themselves when you get modelling work and you have to be away.' It was as well to warn her.

'That's true.' She looked thoughtful, as if the idea had only just occurred to her.

He took the tray from the changing room and went out to make coffee. He found Jack in the passage, so he poured some milk into a saucer and watched him ignore it. It was probably too cold for his taste. He could be very picky. Jack watched Barry make the coffee and followed him into the studio, where he made for the chaise longue where Claret was sitting. This time his aim was erratic, and he collided with the wooden frame before hauling himself on board.

'He's a bit clumsy,' Barry explained. 'It's because he only has one eye.'

'Yes, poor little thing.' Claret's sympathy had been immediately aroused by his bungled and painful assault on the furniture. 'What happened to the other eye?'

'I think he lost it in a fight. He was in a hell of a state when he came here.'

'That's awful.' She was stroking him and he was purring loudly. It gave Barry an idea.

'Before we finish, I think it would be a good idea if we did some more hand shots, this time with you holding him. It would show them in an interesting way, and you can do it in your ordinary clothes at the end.'

'Okay, but what are we going to do next?' Again, she was like a child on a treat.

'I thought we'd do some full-figure stuff. There's a plain white towel in the changing room. You can use it as a prop.'

She frowned. 'What do I want that for?'

'Something to do with your hands,' he said, 'and you can use it to keep things decent.'

'Oh, you mean with me clothes off?'

'That's right. If you're still happy about it, that is.'

'Well, it's part of the job, isn't it?'

He wasn't convinced that she was totally sold on the idea. 'It can be,' he said. 'As I told you before, you need to present as many options as you can, so that you don't miss any opportunities, but in the end it's up to you. I'm not going to persist with it if you're not keen.'

She looked at him pensively. 'I don't mind if it's like the photos in *Vogue*. I mean, like I said, it's part of the job. I just don't want to do anyfing... you know....'

'I know, and you won't. Not with me. It'll be in the best taste, and you won't have to show your naughty bits. I'll make sure of that.'

She brightened immediately. 'Oh, that's all right then,' she said, laughing self-consciously.

'What have you seen that made you so worried?'

'Calendars an' books an' fings.'

'Dirty books?'

'Yes. I found one in me brothers' room when I was hoovering once. It was horrible. I didn't fink they went in for that sort of fing at all.'

He shook his head to reassure her. 'You don't need to worry, Claret. I don't do porn, and you needn't either.'

'I didn't fink you would, really.'

It was a tricky area. Things that had been seen as indecent a decade or two earlier were being increasingly accepted. The popular Pirelli calendars were pushing away some of the old taboos, and the law was becoming far more accommodating, but there was still a dividing line over which Barry was not prepared to go. He wasn't at all prudish; he simply drew the line between an acceptably artistic image and a picture for men in dirty raincoats.

Claret finished her coffee in a happier frame of mind. 'I know you wouldn't want me to do anyfing like that,' she said,

'That's right, you can trust me, but don't for goodness' sake run away with the idea that you can trust just anyone.'

# 6

# A Hitch in Time

The Wig and Gavel was one of Elmston's landmarks. No-one seemed to know exactly how long it had been there, but the half-timbered, leaning structure, despite additions and alterations made before the building became listed, placed its origin firmly in the sixteenth century. It stood as a stubborn reminder of Elmston's history, like an elder citizen who watches the machinations of progress with a disapproving, yet dignified eye. There was an upstairs room, where countless judges had sat, but the law courts were now situated across the road in new, business-like premises, more in keeping with the concrete and glass character of the modernised town centre.

Barry went into the lounge bar and ordered a drink. He usually drank beer, but he'd decided that vodka and tonic seemed more appropriate on such an occasion. He gazed around the bar, conscious of his suede jacket, now returned from the cleaners minus beer stains, but somehow temporarily bereft of its friendly familiarity. He was quite pleased, however, with the effect of the panel-front trousers and square-patterned shirt.

People were sauntering into the bar, ordering drinks, and he was deciding which table to take when Deborah arrived. He saw her, backlit by the brilliant sunshine in the doorway and was conscious of her tight, light-blue cotton top and her long, loose skirt, which was almost translucent. Her feet were tucked into thong-type sandals that made the toes seem twice as long as normal, and it struck him as an odd way to dress for the office. In fact, the overall effect was much the same as he remembered from the studio, somehow unworldly and fascinating.

She peered into the bar, recognising him with a half-smile, and he stepped out to meet her.

'Hello. What would you like to drink?'

'Lager, please.' There was no hesitation. She was obviously an habitual lager drinker. He was still glad he'd opted for the vodka, though. It was civilised and it didn't hang on the breath. He caught the barman's eye and ordered the lager. Turning to Deborah again, he noticed that she was still wearing no make-up. It had been a minor problem when he set the lights to photograph her. His home was in the north of England, where it wasn't unusual for women to be seen without make-up, but it seemed out of place in the south. There was no suggestion of perfume either, and he wondered if maybe she were allergic to certain cosmetics. He had no doubt he would find out before long.

The lager came, and they found a table near the window.

'Tell me about this thing you do,' he said. 'I really don't know the first thing about computers.'

'That's the whole point of my job. I organise software for people who don't understand it, but who know what they want it to do. At least, they usually know what they want. I work for a time-sharing company.'

'What's that?'

'Time-sharing? It's a way of paying for the use of a computer without having to buy one. Firms that can't afford or justify an in-house computer have a choice. They can manage without, but that can be time-consuming and inefficient, or they can have their work done, especially accounts, by a batch bureau, in which case they have to work to the bureau's collection and delivery times, and that's not always convenient. On the other hand, they can buy computer time from someone like us. We install a terminal in their office. It's like a teleprinter, and it's linked to our computer by telephone through a thing called a modem, a device that sends a signal along a telephone line, that can be read by a computer. They can put in the data whenever they choose, and call up the information they want, as and when they need it.'

'Fascinating.' It all sounded very space-age to Barry, and not at all the kind of thing that interested him, but it was the beginnings of a conversation. 'You mentioned something earlier called software. What is it, exactly?'

'Software is the programmes that enable the computer to perform its tasks. That's all.'

He could tell she was bored with the subject, and that was fair enough if she'd been doing it all day.

She asked, 'Have you brought the photographs?'

'Of course.' He took the packet from his inside pocket and handed it to her. Her enquiry and the way she made it seemed a little abrupt, but he reminded himself that she was unusual.

She slit open the packet and took out the presentation folder containing the photographs in transparent sleeves, glancing at it oddly before opening it.

'These are good,' she observed. 'They should be satisfied now.'

'I'm sure they will be. I've never had a complaint.'

'I sent them a picture from a photo booth,' she explained, 'and they said it wasn't good enough to be reproduced.' She said dismissively, 'It seems to matter to them.'

'I imagine presentation's very important to editors. It's quite understandable. Anyway, they won't have a problem with them,' he assured her.

'I hope not. How much do I owe you?'

'Seven pounds fifty.'

She fumbled in her shoulder bag and took out a cheque book and pen, hesitating before writing the name.

'Just "Barry Craven",' he prompted her.

'Right.' She wrote the cheque and gave it to him. 'It's a

lot more than the photo booth, but I need to get this thing published.'

'As important as that?' He was beginning to feel nettled. She'd admitted that she'd tried to get by with a cheap snapshot from a booth, and then hinted that his service was expensive.

She nodded. 'It's something that needs to be said.'

'Ah.' There wasn't much more he could say.

She eyed the plastic folder again and asked, 'Is this what you do all the time? Photographing people like this?' It sounded like an accusation.

'People and animals.'

'Animals? Pets?' Her scorn was undisguised. It *was* an accusation.

'Not just pets,' he told her. 'I photographed a stallion at stud last week. He wasn't actually working at the time, but I'm sure you know what I mean.'

Whether she did or not was unclear, because there was no change in her expression, so he went on. 'And I shot a portfolio this morning, for a girl who's trying to get into modelling.' Immediately, he realised his mistake. The pursed lips told him that he might as well have said 'prostitution', and he experienced the familiar draining sensation of disillusionment. 'I take it you don't approve of that.'

She didn't answer immediately. Instead, she took a drink from her glass and said, 'I suppose that sort of thing appeals to a mindless few.'

The disenchantment was complete. 'On the contrary,' he told her. 'I've met models who are highly intelligent, educated people. Students sometimes do it to eke out their finances but, for those who become successful, it can be a very lucrative career, and who can blame anyone for taking advantage of that?'

'Taking advantage is just what it is, nothing more than an opportunity to make money.'

'It pays many a mortgage.'

'And it could do an awful lot more,' she said, tapping the table with her fingers. 'Do you realise that what one selfish

51

parasite pays for a designer dress could feed a third-world family for months?' She made a gesture of disgust. 'Those models are starving themselves into skeletons to wear over-priced creations on the catwalk while honest victims of third-world famine are going without food simply because they have none.' Just when he thought she was finished, she went on. 'And what about all those people killed by the earthquake and tidal waves in the Philippines?' She obviously read the papers. 'All because their economy is incapable of protecting them against those things, even though their president lives in extravagant luxury.'

Barry was beginning to lose the thread of her argument but she was well and truly into her stride, like a war horse with a union card. She wasn't exactly glaring, so much as gazing steadily at him in accusation, as if he were responsible for it all. It made him angry but, instead of retaliating, he said, 'I gather you're into politics.'

'I am, as it happens. Aren't you?'

'No, I'm not.' Memories of the miners' strike and the three-day week had left him completely intolerant of politicians, right, left or centre and, more recently, the economic crisis the country was still enduring had only served to harden his attitude. He took out a packet of cigarettes and offered her one, which she refused with a shake of her head, so he lit one. Normally, he would have asked her if she minded, but judging by the way things were going, he reckoned she was likely to object to anything. 'I've had my fill of politics,' he said. 'In any case, all my energy goes into keeping my business alive, and that's a full-time preoccupation these days.'

'Yes,' she said, transferring her gaze to the window, 'there's a lot of complacency about, but I'm pleased to say that I'm far from complacent. I want to change the way society works, and there's nothing wrong with that. It's called Having a Social Conscience.'

That did it. If anything was going to alienate him and make him thoroughly bloody-minded, it was a condescending, superior smart-arse sticking labels on concepts. When anyone said, 'It's called', he felt his patience close down. 'Look,' he said, controlling himself with difficulty, 'it seems that we've found a topic on which we'll never agree, so maybe we should talk about something else.' As potential relationships went, this one had already hit the bottom of the bin with a loud clang, but he couldn't see any point in arguing for the rest of the evening.

Returning her gaze to him, she said, 'Don't worry about it. I need to go soon, anyway.' She underlined her remark by looking pointedly at her watch.

'Fine.' It was too. The whole thing had been a mistake. He made a half-hearted attempt at conversation for the next ten minutes or so, and then he walked with her to her car. It was a very smart Vauxhall Firenza that was new enough to be expensive, but just too old to be a company car. It was difficult to see how it conformed to her vision of an egalitarian utopia.

He drove home in a sour mood, berating himself not only for blundering into quite the wrong assumption, but for building up on the thing as well, imagining that it might become more than a casual affair. He felt an utter fool. By that time, he should have learned his lesson. Things just weren't going his way, and there was only one cure for it. He would embark on a period of celibacy. If something turned up in the next few months, fair enough, but for the time being, at least, he was retiring from the arena.

He let himself into the flat, finding Jack on the bed as usual. Instead of ignoring Barry, as he so often did, he roused himself to greet him. They sat together, and Barry stroked him. 'It's just as well it all fell on its arse, Jack,' he confided, 'you wouldn't have liked her either.'

⸺⸺◈⸺⸺

By the end of Tuesday morning, he was thoroughly morose, and it wasn't simply because of the previous evening's fiasco, although he was still kicking himself about that. The fact was that he'd been staring at the bookings, or rather the absence of them, for the next two weeks, and it was enough to dishearten the most ardent optimist. Business just wasn't coming in. It wasn't particularly surprising. Most people were feeling the effects of inflation, and luxuries were the first casualties of stringency. If he were honest, though, the cupboard wasn't entirely bare. He still had the forensic work, thank goodness. Even so, he saw his future as a portrait photographer, and he had to find some way of getting to the people with money to spend and, more importantly, to those who had the inclination to spend it, but try as he would, he couldn't think of a way. In the meantime, the bank manager was pestering him about his overdraft and, with the bank rate at around twelve percent, Barry wasn't too happy about it either. He had the radio on that morning while he was working, but he wasn't really listening. It was only providing background noise, which had been mildly soothing until ABBA began to sing 'Money, Money, Money'. It was the last thing he needed to hear. He decided to adjourn to the teashop. He would have lunch and then spend the afternoon printing the films he'd shot of Claret.

When he arrived, he found the shop fairly empty, which surprised him until he looked at his watch. He must have spent longer than he'd realised, agonising over the bookings. He took a seat at what he'd come to think of as his table, in the corner away from the window and lit a cigarette. It wasn't long before Michelle came to him, notepad in hand.

'The only thing we're out of is the steak and kidney pie,' she informed him. 'That's all gone.'

'Good, I couldn't have faced it anyway. Will you get me a prawn salad, please, and a pot of coffee?' His trouser waistband was still feeling ever-so-slightly snug, although he was sure beer had nothing to do with it and that his lunchtime diet held the key.

'Prawn salad and a pot of coffee.' She wrote the order laboriously on her pad. 'Right.'

'Did you enjoy yourself with Wesley at the weekend?' He had to know.

She smiled shyly. 'Yeah, it was all right.'

'I'm glad.' He was genuinely glad one of them had moved off the hard shoulder. She returned to the kitchen, and he wondered idly if Jack might be in there, because he hadn't seen him for a while. It was common knowledge that cats typically had two homes, and their owners sometimes found out about it years later, if they ever did. However, Jack was downright blatant about his alternative haunt, and Barry knew he was as likely to find him there as in his flat. His thoughts were interrupted when Lucy joined him at the table, her eyes twinkling with good-natured curiosity.

She asked, 'How was the heavy date?'

'How did you know about that?'

'Michelle told me.'

'Ah.' Wesley must have mentioned it to her, and now it was popular gossip. It certainly didn't make him feel any better. 'The only thing about it that was heavy,' he said, 'was that it never got off the ground.'

'Oh hard luck. What happened?'

'Very little. I just found that I'd formed a completely wrong impression of her.' He told her about the afternoon in his studio, when Deborah had appealed to him in such an unusual way.

'You're a hopeless romantic, Barry. What made you change your mind?'

'I discovered very quickly that she had no personality worth mentioning and a massive chip on her shoulder about the evils of capitalist exploitation.'

'Dear, oh dear. No wonder you were looking so unhappy when I came in.'

'It's not that,' he explained. 'I'd just been looking at my empty work diary.'

'As bad as that?'

'Well, there's nothing until the middle of next week, and it's thin after that. Actually, I wonder if you'd mind feeding Jack for a few days while I nip up home. I may as well do a duty trip now that things are so quiet.'

'Of course I will.' After a moment's thought, she said, 'I've still got your key from last time. Jack will be fine.'

'Thanks very much.'

'When are you going?'

'Tomorrow morning. I imagine I'll be back on Sunday night.'

Michelle brought his order, and Lucy was giving her hers when Guy came in. He was all Barry needed, the sort of character who could never have experienced his kind of problem, financial or romantic. In fact, there was no doubt at all about the latter, because he'd already pulled Lucy.

'I thought I'd find you in here,' he announced. Everything he said was an announcement or a sharp interrogation. He also had a way of twitching one side of his mouth downwards with certain vowels, that might have been fascinating, had he been simply a passing acquaintance. In his current mood, Barry just resented him.

Lucy looked up, pleasantly surprised. 'Guy, I thought you were with a client.'

'I was, but he had to be back at his office, so I decided to call in here.' He drew a chair from a vacant table and sat down.

'I'm cat-minding this weekend,' she told him. 'Barry's off to Yorkshire.'

His habitual sardonic smile broadened. 'The satanic mills? My dear chap, how awful for you.'

Barry ignored his remark, and his silence was conveniently camouflaged by Michelle's appearance with a quiche for Lucy. Guy waved his hand to her. 'Be a good girl and bring another cup and saucer, will you? I'll join my friends for coffee.'

That didn't impress Barry either, especially as it was his coffee he was taking for granted, and by no stretch of the imagination could they be called friends.

'So what's been happening?' He addressed his question to Lucy.

'We were discussing the state of business,' she told him. 'Actually, I've been finding it rather slow, recently, as well.

I keep thinking that I should try some kind of side-line that would bring in customers from a wider area. I read an article in a magazine recently, about the growing market in historic photographs, and I've been wondering about that, about local scenes particularly.' She looked expectantly at Barry, but before he could say anything Guy stepped in with one of his characteristically authoritative pronouncements.

'Forget it. You've got to be in the right place at the right time to pick those up, I'm afraid, and the dealers are already snapping them up.'

Barry wasn't aware that dealers were doing anything of the kind, but he was prepared to learn. However, Guy never bothered to elaborate, so he was left in ignorance.

'What about reproductions, then?' Lucy was obviously hooked on the idea of period prints, and Barry thought it was a good idea. There was a lot of interest in local history. There must be pictures to be had, and the idea of sepia prints appealed to him as well.

'It can't be done,' Guy insisted. 'It just isn't possible to get the same effects. For one thing, the materials are no longer available. You have to realise that a great deal of progress has been made in the science of photography over the last thirty years or so. I'm sorry, you'll just have to think of something else.' He favoured Barry with a smirk, as if checking that his superior knowledge of the subject had registered.

It was an example of what Barry's old petty officer used to call, 'the ultimate genetic mutation', meaning, 'talking bollocks', but he kept quiet for Lucy's benefit. He knew she would have found an argument embarrassing.

'Yes, I suppose I will,' she agreed.

Barry put his glasses on and looked at the prints that were drying in the darkroom. He was delighted with them, and he knew Claret would be. It made him eager to get started on the competition pictures, but that would have to wait until he returned from Yorkshire, or 'the satanic mills', as that insufferable creep had called it. Burley-in-Wharfedale was just a spit away from the National Park, one of the most beautiful areas in Britain. There were doubtless lots of people who assumed that the county consisted entirely of soot and racing pigeons, but that didn't excuse Guy for voicing his ignorance in that patronising way.

He looked again at one of the black and white prints. It was a three-quarter back view of Claret, and she was holding a dress up, as if she were considering wearing it. She was completely nude, but at that angle, and with her left arm half-extended and masking her breast, there was only an impression of the innocence that he always associated with her. In fact, he found it charming. He was very pleased as well, with the lighting, which had cast strong shadows to accentuate her long curves. Because of the way she was holding the dress, very little of its detail was visible, so there was no distraction from the shape of her body and the atmosphere she had created. The picture had a timeless quality.

He opened the darkroom cupboard and searched towards the back, where he was pretty sure he still had some sepia toner.

⁖⁖⁖

It was only five minutes or so before closing time when he got to the bookshop, and Lucy was serving a customer, so he hung around until she was free.

When she could speak to him, she said, 'Hello Barry, are you packed and ready to go?'

'No, but it won't take long.'

'I don't suppose so. I imagine you won't be packing your cameras this time.'

'Why do you say that?'

'I just thought you were taking a break from work.'

'I am really, but I always carry one, and it's not really work all the time. He put the picture on the counter. 'Take a look at that, but don't handle it. It's not properly dry yet.'

Lucy examined the photograph and expressed surprise. 'What a super picture! It's the model girl, isn't it?'

'Claret, yes, but what do you think of the effect?'

'It's brilliant. I mean, you can see in a way that it's contemporary, but it's got a period feel about it. Maybe Edwardian, I don't know, because there's nothing to pin it down to any particular time. It's not just the sepia, there's something else as well.'

'That's what I thought when I saw it in black and white. After what you said at lunch-time, I decided to do a tint just as a try-out.'

'Well, it worked incredibly well.' She looked again at the picture. 'She's a beautiful girl, isn't she?'

'She certainly is, but think about this, Lucy. I can do period-style portraits to order, in costume. If you put any business my way, I'll pay you commission, and I can also get Claret to pose for some prints you can sell in the shop. She'll be fully-clothed, of course, living locally, as she does. What do you think?'

'Absolutely. I think it's a wonderful idea.'

'And the local prints you're interested in shouldn't be too hard to find, if we advertise in the papers.'

'I agree. Guy was completely wrong about them. We never had much difficulty getting them for the museum. The only problem was the condition they were in after so many years.'

'Retouching's not usually a problem, and as long as the copyright's paid for fair and square, I can copy and enlarge them.'

'Really?'

'Oh yes.'

She gave him a strange look. 'You kept very quiet about this at lunch-time.'

'Yes, well, there are times when it's better not to argue.'

'Guy annoyed you, didn't he?'

He wasn't going to make an issue out of it. There was no point in that, so he said, 'Just a bit.'

'I know.' She looked half-apologetic. 'He can be like that, but he can be very sweet sometimes.'

Barry nodded doubtfully. 'I'll take your word for it.'

# 7

# Hard Sense

Barry sat outside the Listers' Arms in Malham watching a crowd of hikers, who were feeding the ducks on the pond. The pub was about to close for the afternoon, and he'd already decided to stay there. He wasn't alone, because an elderly couple with a similarly elderly and amiable mongrel sat nearby, apparently content to watch the slow stream of visitors go by.

Barry lit a cigarette and continued to enjoy the scene. Malham hadn't changed much since his last visit to the Dales, and he, too, was content just to sit there.

His parents had been apologetic. They'd had to go to Ilkley to keep an appointment, but he'd been quite happy to wander about on his own. He'd been busy, too, shooting a cassette of colour film purely for his own satisfaction. It might have been triggered by Guy's sneering unpleasantness, but Barry wasn't about to waste his time trying to change his mind about anything. All the same, he reflected, it was odd that a thing like that could have stung him to that extent. He might have brushed it off without much thought at one time, but he seemed to be bridling at the pettiest annoyances. Maybe he did need the break, just to restore some kind of perspective to his reasoning.

Certainly, business was slow, and that was a source of genuine concern. Far and away, the most lucrative side was the weddings. It wasn't a particularly pleasant thought, but he had to work on the damned things, and he had to tackle them with more confidence as well. He'd been far too ready to talk about the things that had gone wrong, so that even Lucy, good-natured though she was, seemed amused by his catalogue of misfortune.

So much for the business, then. What about the rest? There'd been that interlude with Christine, and the ludicrous business with Deborah. He was still smarting about that, because the answer was staring him in the face. The only thing that had been at fault was his own attitude. Lucy was right to call him an inveterate romantic. He saw things as he wanted them to be, rather than as they were. It was true and he had to face it. He pondered that for a while, becoming increasingly gloomy.

On the positive side, however, there was Claret. His interest in her was solely professional, and he'd enjoyed that session with her more than anything he'd done for a long time. It was all because of her, as well. It was her attitude to the job, which was so fresh and guileless that the session had been sheer pleasure. He genuinely wanted her to be successful.

He became conscious, after a while, that he was under scrutiny, and he realised that the couple next to him were looking in his direction.

The woman spoke to him. 'Are you all right, love? You look as if you've lost a quid and found a tanner.' It wasn't a local accent. It was more Lancashire: Burnley or maybe Rochdale.

'Yes, I'm fine, thanks. I was miles away, thinking about work or, at least, the kind I want to do. Unfortunately, I'm not making much progress.'

'You haven't come to a gradely place like this to think about work, have you?' The accent was definitely Rochdale.

'No, I haven't,' he agreed. 'I just caught myself doing it.'

The man asked, 'What is it that you do?'

'I'm a photographer. I have a studio in Kent.'

'Kent? You don't sound like a southerner.'

'No, I'm from Yorkshire. I'm visiting my folks in Burley-in-Wharfedale.'

He nodded approvingly. 'That's a grand place to live. We're from Milnrow. D'you know it?'

'Yes.' He knew it vaguely, having driven through it on his way to Rochdale. It confirmed his suspicion about their accent.

'We spent our honeymoon here, in nineteen thirty-two. That's why we're here today. It's our forty-fourth wedding anniversary. We come back every year, on or about the day. Of course, it's easier now I'm retired. We can come whenever we like, really.'

'That's nice. Congratulations.' Barry gestured towards the pub door. 'I'd buy you a drink, but they've stopped serving.'

'Eh, don't worry about that, lad.'

He found himself warming to them. 'What did you do,' he asked, 'before you retired?'

'I were a weaving overlooker, and Hilda worked in the mill as well until we started a family, didn't you? That's where we met, and we've been together ever since, apart from during the war, of course. I had to retire early when the mill closed down, but we've been all right since then.'

They looked completely right together, yet there was a suggestion of sadness about them as well. Whether it was to do with his enforced retirement, or something that had happened to the family he'd mentioned, Barry had no idea, and he wasn't going to pry. He had a better idea than that. 'As it's your wedding anniversary,' he said, 'will you let me photograph you both? Then, if you give me your address, I'll send you some prints as a sort of anniversary present.'

The man looked at him in surprise. 'That's very nice of you, lad. Much appreciated.' He watched him take the camera from his pocket. 'That looks like a gradely camera you've got there.'

'It's very good,' he agreed, 'and it goes everywhere with me.'

The woman squinted at it warily. 'What sort is it? It's not Japanese, is it? You know how Lancashire folk feel about them buggers.'

He saw her husband squeeze her hand, and he said, 'No, it's a Leica. It's German.' Then, conscious that she might find that equally offensive, he added, 'I'm afraid no one makes cameras in Britain nowadays.'

'That's all right,' she assured him, 'just as long as it's not Japanese.'

He stood back and framed them, the two of them holding hands and the dog at their feet, and took the picture. Then, as an afterthought, he looked at the dog. It was black, and grizzled about its face, and it lay with its body against the man's feet and with its head across hers. Barry was conscious of two clasped hands, four human legs and a supine dog, now looking lazily and vaguely in his direction. It was a superb picture, and he couldn't resist taking it.

The man watched him and said, 'She's old, you know. She must be fifteen by now. Her eyesight's failing, but she's happy enough.' Sensing that he was talking about her, the dog wagged her tail languidly and raised her head before resuming her comfortable position.

Barry took some more pictures of the couple, and they chatted for a while before deciding that it was time to go. He walked with them to their car, and after the dog had climbed stiffly into the back, he was surprised to see the woman open the driver's door and lean across to unlock the passenger side for her husband. It seemed a little odd until he realised that the man was quite breathless after his short walk. He settled into his seat and held out his hand to shake Barry's. 'It's been very nice to meet you, lad, and thank you for your kindness.'

'Don't mention it, it's nothing at all.'

'Well,' he said, 'just you remember, business will buck up if you work at it. Take it from me, it's the only way. Big ideas are no substitute for hard work. You'll have disappointments and disasters, but you'll get over them if you keep your feet on the ground, so don't go sticking your head in t' gas oven just yet. Life's for living, not for moping about.'

'I'll remember,' he promised. 'Goodbye.'

He spent Saturday with his mother and father, mainly in the garden. It started well, in the brilliant sunshine to which everyone had grown accustomed, but as the day went on, the atmosphere became increasingly sticky and oppressive and as the clouds thickened they went indoors, mainly to escape the ubiquitous thunder bugs that invaded the food, drink and, most annoyingly, themselves. His mother was philosophical. 'Well, at least, the weather held off until we'd finished lunch.' Barry was also thankful. The Yorkshire puddings alone had been worth coming home for. As usual, his mother had done her best to feed him up, as she put it, before he returned to the exotic south, where food was presumably a rare commodity. With his brother Daniel and his wife now living in the Midlands, and therefore not currently a distraction, she worried about Barry's eating habits to the extent that she often sent him food parcels consisting of cakes, gingerbread, tarts, and all the most unhealthy things imaginable. Secretly, he found it all far too tempting, and he was over-burdened with the stuff. That was where Wesley came in handy. Whilst he had never met Barry's mother, he regarded her as one to be worshipped from afar, the Goddess of Plenty. Barry sometimes wondered, when he saw Wesley tucking into the latest offering, if his own mother ever fed him.

He picked up the newspaper and scanned it briefly. The main stories were familiar ones. There was the poor state of the pound, industry in recession and furious exchanges in the Commons between James Callaghan and Margaret Thatcher. The sport section offered no relief, only news of the county's latest cricketing embarrassment. He put the paper down when he heard the music on television signal the end of Professional Wrestling, and he hoped he might be able to get some sense out of his father. He was the most peaceful person imaginable but, on Saturday afternoons and Wednesday evenings, he was transformed. He would watch two men in trunks or leotards throw each other around a ring, and he would be totally involved, living each clinch and foul, shouting raucous, bloodthirsty advice, berating the referee for dereliction of duty, and finally, if things went according to his wishes, banging with his fist on the arm of his chair as he counted a pin-fall or knockout.

His excitement finally subsided and Barry attracted his attention. 'Dad,' he said, 'Would you say that the recession in the textiles industry's as bad in Lancashire as it is here?'

He looked thoughtful for a moment, and Barry was thankful he'd calmed down. 'I'd say it's worse, if anything,' he said. 'They were hit by cheap imports before we were, and there are places in Lancashire where cotton's the only industry. What made you think of that?'

Barry told him about the couple he'd met in Malham, and about the woman's insistence on knowing that the camera wasn't Japanese.

'A lot of people feel like that about Far Eastern goods nowadays, and it's not surprising. We seem to be besieged with things from over there. I'm glad you did that, though, Barry. It'll be nice for them to have that photograph. I imagine it'll mean a lot to them.'

'I'm just glad I met them.'

His parents looked at him strangely, but he didn't really want to explain himself. The idea was only half-formed, but somehow the old man had been right. Success really was a question of hard work. They'd lived their lives by common sense, so they knew all about that and, in an imperfect world, if that meant taking work that didn't necessarily appeal to him, then that was what he had to do, at least for the time being. The rest he had to play by ear.

Fortunately or unfortunately, their attention was diverted by Cedric, the dog, who was cowering under the table and shaking uncontrollably.

'It's the weather,' his mother explained. 'He knows it's going to thunder. I just wish it would get on with it and clear the air. Does it bother your cat when it's like this?'

'Jack? No, he takes it in his stride.'

'What on earth possessed you to give him that name?'

'I named him after Jack Rushworth at school.'

'That dirty lad with the runny nose?' She was nonplussed.

'Well, they have things in common.'

His mother sniffed disapprovingly. 'I hope he's not a dirty cat. They're very clean animals, as a rule.'

It was amazing how quickly a homecoming became an occasion for small-talk, although it wasn't such a bad thing really, and maybe he did expect a little too much out of life.

After a few large but desultory raindrops, the long-awaited storm came, and it persisted well into the night, with thunder rolling around the valley, as if, in its anger, it had lost its way, and lightning turned the sky into brilliant daylight. Eventually it subsided and Barry drifted into sleep, lulled by the gentler patter of raindrops against the window.

In the morning, the sky was still grey, promising yet more rain, but the air smelt fresh and clear. It seemed the perfect morning for a new start. He was going to take up his life in Kent, not just as he'd left it, but with a kind of resolve that left no room for half-baked ideals and ambitions. From that moment, he was going to keep his feet squarely on the ground, taking whatever work came his way, and leaving nothing to chance, so that the disasters and embarrassments of the past would never be repeated.

He said goodbye to his parents and got into his car. All at once, he was conscious that he was sitting in a pool of cold water, and it rushed through the material of his trousers like ink through blotting paper. A glance at the side window told him everything. He'd left it partially open when he parked the car, and he'd forgotten to close it before the storm. It was several hours before his new-found resolve returned to its former strength.

꒰ᓀ˙ᓂ˙ᓀ꒱

A combination of a delayed start, several road works, and an accident on the A1 meant that he arrived at the Dartford Tunnel towards the end of the rush hour, so it was early evening by the time he arrived home. He decided against calling on Lucy, partly because of the time, but mainly because Guy's white BMW was parked outside the shop. Instead, he unloaded the car and went up to his flat. There was no sign of Jack, although that wasn't unusual. Instead, his food bowl stood, washed and dried on the kitchen counter with a note beside it in Lucy's girlish handwriting.

> *Jack fed and watered. Fresh milk in the fridge.*
> *Parcel for you in the shop.*
> *Hope it all went well,*
> *Lucy X*

The milk was a nice thought. It had slipped his mind to buy some on the way back. He put the kettle on to make tea before checking the answering machine. There were two of the usual abortive calls and one old message that he'd forgotten to erase, but he was still determined not to be depressed by the lack of business. He was going to take the advice of the old boy in Malham and make the most of any opportunity. He poured the tea and took a bottle of milk from the refrigerator. How thoughtful it was of Lucy to do that. And that was another thing. There was nothing to stop him asking her round for an occasional drink if he felt like it. It wasn't as if Guy had an exclusive claim on her. It was a pleasing thought, and one which he took to bed.

# 8

# Making a Splash

After the storm of the previous night and the long journey, Barry slept very soundly, apart from when Jack came in and woke him up to welcome him home. It was typical of him that he would ignore his benefactor for days on end, and then, as if on impulse, he would climb all over him, usually at the least convenient moment, purring and stroking the side of his mouth against any part of him he could reach. It was one of the funny ways that might have seemed normal for a cat, but Barry preferred to think it made him an individual.

Elmston Police phoned to ask if Barry was available for the following week, and he confirmed that he was. With that settled, he spent the rest of the morning developing the slides he'd taken in Yorkshire. He was quite pleased with them, especially those he'd taken of the old couple. Encouraged by the thought, he took out the gold-leaf lettering set and began laboriously to make some presentation mounts. He completed the first one and held it up to inspect it.

*Mr and Mrs A. Fielden*
*On the Occasion of their 44th Wedding Anniversary*
*Malham, 27th August, 1976.*

They would be pleased with that. He looked at his watch and realised it was lunchtime.

For some reason, the teashop was almost full, and he found Lucy helping to take orders. His usual table was occupied, so he had to take the remaining one, next to the kitchen, which meant that he saw Lucy several times, both coming and going, before he had a chance to speak to her. Eventually, she paused in mid-errand, to ask, 'Has Michelle taken your order?'

'Yes.'

'Oh good. Things are hectic, as you can see, but I'm not complaining.'

'I should think not.'

She looked over her shoulder. 'Most of these people will be leaving soon. If you're still here I'll come and join you.'

'I'm in no hurry. How was Jack? Did he behave himself?'

She appeared to consider the question. 'By his own standards, or generally?'

He was wondering how to answer this when there was a call from the kitchen and Lucy turned to go. 'I'll have to tell you later,' she said, 'but I will say that he didn't exactly ingratiate himself with Guy.'

Barry wasn't at all unhappy about that, but he was intrigued all the same. Michelle brought his order, and he poured a cup of coffee and watched as one by one, the tables slowly emptied. Soon, he would know the nature and extent of Jack's misdemeanour.

Lucy put her plate down opposite him and sat down. 'So, how was your trip?'

'Well worth the journey. Thanks for the milk, by the way.'

'It was no trouble.'

'I brought you some Wensleydale cheese, the genuine stuff. It's on the shop counter.'

'Thank you. I'll look forward to that. Actually, there's a parcel for you in there. Someone tried to deliver it on Friday, so I took it in.'

'Thanks for doing that.' He was still dying to know what had happened. 'What did Jack do?'

She sighed deeply. 'Well, once he'd got the idea that you weren't there and I was feeding him, he moved in with me.'

'What a friendly soul.'

'Yes, well, for most of the time anyway, and Guy came over on Saturday evening.'

'Quite a house-full, then.'

'Oh yes, three was most certainly a crowd. Guy doesn't like having animals around – he's terribly fastidious – and he made much of sweeping invisible cat hairs off the furniture and complaining about animals being unhygienic.'

'How unreasonable.' Secretly, he wasn't at all surprised.

'It's one of his little foibles,' she said in a defensive tone that Barry hadn't previously noticed. 'We all have them. Anyway, he made no secret of the fact that he resented Jack's presence, and I think animals know when someone dislikes them, don't they?'

'Most animals, I suppose, but I always thought Jack was particularly thick-skinned.'

'Thick-skinned or not, he let Guy know how he felt about him by tipping a glass of red wine over him. He was wearing a very light suit. It was cream-coloured. Unbleached calico, I think.'

Barry could imagine the poser wearing something like that, but he kept that thought to himself, also containing the glee that the mental picture gave him.

'Yes, we were having a drink when Jack leapt on to the chair arm beside him. Then, quite deliberately, he reached over with one paw and flipped the wine so that it flew all over Guy's suit.'

'How remarkable.' Good old Jack. Barry was quite proud of him, although perhaps he shouldn't have looked quite so pleased, because it was evident that Lucy was nettled by his attitude.

'That's not how Guy saw it. I've never seen him as angry. He was shouting and swearing like nobody's business.'

Barry said nothing, but sighed and shook his head.

She eyed him impatiently. 'Come on, Barry. I know you've taken against Guy for some reason, but you must see how annoying it must have been for him.'

'I suppose so,' he said. 'What about your furniture? Did any of the wine land on that?'

'A little bit. I got the stain out in the same way as I got it out of Guy's suit, with white wine.'

'Really?'

'Yes, it's very effective, but Guy's still furious about his suit. He says if he could legally hold you responsible for Jack's behaviour, he'd give you the cleaning bill.'

It was the first time he'd known Lucy be anything less than her usual warm self towards him. Granted, he hadn't taken the thing particularly seriously, but he still felt that Guy had made much of an unfortunate accident. 'He needn't worry himself about the legality of it,' he told her quietly. 'I'll pay his cleaning bill, and I'm sorry about your furniture. If you give me the details, I'll replace the wasted wine, obviously.'

'Oh, Barry, there's no need for that.' She raised her hand in an impatient gesture, and it was then that he saw the thin gold ring set with three diamonds. No wonder she was so tight-lipped about his attitude.

'When did this happen?' He pointed to the ring.

'Yesterday. He was working up to it on Saturday when we had the accident with the wine. That just delayed things a bit.'

'Congratulations.' It was all he could say. He couldn't imagine how she could possibly commit herself to a pompous clown like that, and he was completely floored. The day had begun with so much promise, only to fall flat on its backside.

He put the parcel on his office desk and opened it. As he'd expected, it was the replacement for the wrecked camera and lens. It was a lovely job, too, a more recent model than the one he'd lost. At any other time, he'd have been delighted with it, but he wasn't in the mood to appreciate anything. He put it away in the safe and then checked the answering machine. There was a message from David King asking Barry to call him back. He was rather surprised. David was a successful photographer with a studio in Elmston. Barry had met him a couple of times at various functions, but he couldn't imagine why an experienced photographer would want to speak to him. He dialled the number and David answered. After the usual pleasantries, he came to the point.

'Have you anything booked for Saturday week, Barry?'

'Not so far.'

'Oh good. I wondered if you'd do a wedding for me. I'm in a bit of a fix as it happens.'

Barry heard himself say, 'Of course I will.' If it was one of David's weddings there wouldn't have to be a problem. His usual clientele expected the best, and paid handsomely for it. He was nervous already.

'That's good of you, and a huge relief, Barry. The thing is, my father's funeral's that Friday, and I have to go to Cornwall.'

'Oh hell, I'm sorry to hear that.'

'Thanks, but it wasn't unexpected. Anyway, I'll have to stay over, so if you'll do the wedding, that relieves me of a huge problem.' He went on to give Barry the details and describe what was required. It was pretty straightforward, but he was staggered by the price David had quoted. He could have done two weddings pretty lavishly for the same sum.

'It's all yours, Barry,' he said. 'I'll get back to the bride's parents and tell them about the arrangement. Then, if they need to get in touch with you about anything, they can. Thanks ever so much.'

Having put the phone down, Barry sat back and considered the implications. He had to be absolutely sure of everything this time, leaving nothing to chance. And what then? If everything came together, which it must, it might very well lead to more business. He had absolutely no intention of specialising in weddings, but there could be other spin-offs. It was quite an opportunity.

He returned to making the mounts for the Fielden pictures. He'd learned that they had a daughter and a son. For all he knew, they might have grandchildren too, but he decided to send them just three prints. They might be embarrassed if he sent them more, but he thought they'd be happy with those, and he felt he owed it to them.

Otherwise, he was still feeling floored about Lucy's engagement. Actually, it had surprised him at lunch-time that he'd felt that way. He'd consciously given up on her when he first learned about Guy, but something must have been lurking deep down, to make him react the way he had. It was just too bad, and anyway, he was supposed to be taking time out from that sort of thing. He decided it was better not to dwell on it, and maybe it would be a good idea, in view of the current climate, to give the teashop a miss for a while. It was a shame, but probably the best thing to do. He finished the last of the mounts and put them aside. He had to go shopping, and he had on his list a carton of single cream, which was to be Jack's reward for the wine-throwing stunt.

# 9

# Belinda

The wedding was at St Mark's in Denford, a village that was about three miles south of Elmston but, to all appearances, deep in the countryside. The church was charming as well, with a lych-gate as old as the building, and rose beds all the way to the church door. It was a beautiful setting, especially as the weather, which had been unsettled since the storm, had improved for the weekend, and the morning sunshine completed the scene.

They'd made a detour to the police station that morning, to pick up the pager. He would be on call from six o-clock that evening and he didn't want to do everything at the last minute. Even so, they were well ahead of time, so they sauntered off in search of the vicar. They found him in the chancel, laying out the marriage certificate and register on a table, presumably placed there for the purpose.

The vicar eyed the new camera. 'Ah, the photographer,' he observed. 'Now, the rules are very simple. There must be no flash photography during the hymns, the prayers and the blessing, but I shall pause after the pronouncement that the couple are man and wife, so that you can take one then.' He stopped and scratched his head, as if he had lost the thread of what he was saying. 'Oh yes, and you mustn't include the organist in any of your photographs. He gets very nervous and it puts him off his playing.'

'Fine, Reverend.' That suited Barry. He peered round the vestry door and saw the organist leafing fussily through his music. He didn't want to photograph him anyway. He was an ugly sod. They returned to the lych-gate to wait for the wedding party.

Guests were arriving, some making their way down the path to the church, others clustering around the lych-gate and chattering with one another. The groom and best man had gone to take their places, and eventually the assembled guests too, disappeared into the church. The bride's mother came to introduce herself to Barry before following them. He and Wesley then stood for a while with the bridesmaids, who were very young, self-conscious and excited. Then, a few minutes after the due time, the car drew up with the bride and her father. Barry went forward and took the first picture as the car door was opened.

The rest was easy. There were no hysterics, no interfering relations, and no difficult children; in fact, it was the most perfect wedding he'd ever attended, and there was a bonus. He'd seen her among the guests who'd gathered at the lych-gate before the wedding. She had dark brown hair, and she was very slim, with a tiny waist that curved down to the cutest legs, the shape of which was clearly visible, in the slight breeze, through the skirt of her thin red dress. All at once, his pretensions to the monastic way of life were as naught. It was inevitable that he should look out for her after the service, and she wasn't difficult to find. She appeared to be with the family party, although she hung around, talking to various other guests after the bride and groom had left for the reception. He was packing the equipment into his car when she came to talk to him. She had a particularly open smile that impressed him immediately.

'Hi! Are you coming to the reception?' It was like being greeted by an old friend.

'Oh yes, they want me to see it through to the end. Well, the Going Away anyway.'

'Good, I'll see you there.' She watched him lock the case in the back of the car and said, 'I gather you're really a portrait photographer.'

That was what David King had told the bride's parents. It made him sound rather grand, but the difference was only a matter of detail, and he was happy to go along with David's description. 'Yes,' he said, 'but I'm happy to help out.'

He was conscious of Wesley looming over the car, always an inhibiting factor, but the girl continued to chatter freely, so that Barry had to say very little. He learned, among other things, that her name was Belinda and that she was a cousin of Janice, the bride. Finally, she made her way to the reception, and Wesley and he followed on.

Eventually, they arrived at the Parklands Hotel in Elmston, where they were quickly back in business. There were photographs in the hotel's picturesque grounds, and they spent some time in gathering scattered relations, but eventually the party moved on into the banqueting suite. Barry handed the Leica to Wesley and sent him off to get whatever pictures he could, having warned him on pain of death to return it in one functioning piece. He had no intention of including any informal pictures in the final presentation, but it would be practice for him, and it would also keep him out of the way while Barry renewed contact with Belinda, something he intended to do as soon as he could.

There were some very boring speeches by the best man and the groom, and it seemed an age before the cake was cut and the couple finally went to change for the honeymoon. Barry made his way to where Belinda was sitting between two elderly, bored guests. She seemed pleased to see him.

He asked her, 'Are you staying in the hotel?'

'Hell, no, I wouldn't be found dead here. Hotels are supposed to be fun places, and there's no chance of that here.' The people on either side of her shifted uncomfortably, but she didn't seem to notice. Even if she did, she gave no sign of caring. 'I live not far from here anyway, in Kingsford. Do you know it?' Kingsford was only a few miles from Woodley. It had been a village for centuries, but a proliferation of new housing estates had turned it into a suburb of Elmston.

'Yes, I live in Woodley.'

'Good. Come over for a drink later on if you're not doing anything. Make it about eight. That'll give me time to sober up after this thing. Have you got something to write with?'

He handed her his pen, and she wrote her address on the back of her place card.

'Right,' he said, 'I'll be there, about eight.'

In fact, it was nearer twenty-past when he arrived, having driven most of the way in third gear. The problem had begun shortly after he left home, and he found it impossible to get into top gear. He tried double-declutching, but there was something hard and nasty clogging up the works, so in the end, he had to settle for a slow journey.

He pulled up outside the address Belinda had given him. It was a modern detached house on an estate that had been built only in the past few years. The houses were almost identical, and the gardens were pretty much the same too. It wasn't quite what he'd expected.

He rang the doorbell and waited, and was about to ring again when Belinda came to the door with a towel round her shoulders. Her hair looked damp.

'Hi, come in. I won't be a minute.' She showed him into an untidy but comfortable sitting room, where he waited for her. It was furnished with the basic things, but there were few of the trappings of domesticity, no photographs, pictures, or any suggestion of family life. He was quite intrigued.

After about fifteen minutes, she reappeared looking splendid. Her dark hair, now dry, was shining and she was wearing a short skirt and blouse that did everything for her slender figure. He'd only seen her dressed for the wedding, and for most of that time, her features had been masked to some extent by a large, floppy hat. The sunny expression that had impressed him earlier was still there, only more so, and it was accentuated by a sparkle of latent fun in her eyes, which were further enhanced by long lashes.

'Right, I'm ready,' she announced. 'Sorry to keep you waiting. Now, shall we go to the pub? It's just round the corner. We can walk there.'

'Fine,' he agreed. 'We couldn't go far in my car anyway. It's not well.'

'That's too bad. They can be a pain, can't they?'

They left the house and walked up the road. He asked, 'Do you live here alone?'

'No, I share the rent with another girl, but she's away in Cambridgeshire, visiting her family. The people who own the house are in Saudi. It's been very convenient, but they're coming home soon, so we'll have to find somewhere else.'

'I see.' That explained a lot. They turned the corner and walked a hundred yards or so to the pub.

Not surprisingly on a Saturday evening, it was quite full, but Belinda ran a practised eye round the bar and spotted a corner table. 'I'll grab that table,' she told him. 'Mine's a Campari and soda.'

He managed to get served, and threaded his way through the crowd to where she was sitting. The stools were all taken and he had to perch on the banquette beside her, delightfully conscious of her perfume and her physical proximity. For her part, she seemed not to notice, but chattered away about the wedding, regaling him with bits of family gossip punctuated with mischievous laughter.

'I nearly died when Janice's father described Edward as "a fine young man of excellent character." He's the most boring sod imaginable, but just right for Janice.' Clearly, she had a low opinion of them both. 'She wanted me to be a bridesmaid,' she said, 'but I persuaded her that an entourage of little girls would look far better and much more bridesmaidenly.' She stopped and asked, 'Is there such a word?'

'If there wasn't, there is now,' he assured her.

'Good, but honestly, could you see me in one of those pink dresses they were wearing?'

'Perhaps not.' They were a little on the short side, but the bridesmaids were only about twelve years old. Actually, the skirt she was wearing was rather short and, seemingly oblivious to the effect it had on him, she crossed her legs carelessly and continued with her irreverent commentary on the day's proceedings. He didn't need to say much. She was remarkably easy to be with, and it came as a surprise when the landlord called Last Orders.

He asked, 'Would you like another drink?'

'Not really. Let's go back and have one at my place. It's too hot in here.'

As they walked back to the house Belinda clung to his arm, occasionally stroking the sleeve, so that he felt an exciting sense of inevitability. Everything was coming right all at once, quite suddenly, in fact, and he made a mental note never to part with his suede jacket, his lucky charm.

Once inside the house, Belinda stopped as if she had just remembered something. 'I hope you like brandy,' she said. 'It's all I've got.'

'I do, but perhaps I shouldn't. I've got to drive home. Coffee would be fine, really.'

'Don't drive. It's not worth the risk, and the coffee's not up to much. It's a new one I tried, and it's like cats' pee. Stay here instead.' She didn't wait for his reply, but disappeared for a moment and returned with a bottle and two glasses. He sat on the sofa, and she joined him to pour the brandy, somewhat generously, he thought. He picked up his glass and inhaled the vapour, something he always enjoyed doing.

'Don't bother with that,' she told him, 'it's only cooking. Just a minute.' She leapt up and picked up an ashtray which she set down on the coffee table. 'There, make yourself at home, as you're stopping.' She sprawled comfortably beside him again, all legs and temptation.

He lit a cigarette, and was about to speak when she looked

at her watch and said, 'Eleven o' clock. Janice should have broken her duck by now.'

He almost choked on the brandy.

'Seriously, she was saving herself for him. She made a big thing of it, the silly cow. I mean, life's too short, isn't it?'

Thus encouraged, he slipped an arm round her shoulders and she moved closer, still smiling as he kissed her. For the first time in ages, fortune also seemed to be smiling on him, right until the moment his pager bleeped.

He made his way laboriously in third gear to the location he'd been given on the Canterbury road. Needless to say, he was annoyed and unbelievably frustrated. Belinda hadn't been terribly impressed either; in fact, there'd been quite an atmosphere when he left, especially when he told her he'd no idea how long he might be. It was a road traffic accident, and they could be quite complex. It wasn't all bad news, though, because they'd arranged to meet again, at his flat.

It was beginning to rain, but he saw the flashing lights some distance away, and he was thankful he hadn't taken more than a sip of the brandy.

There was a line of stationary cars, and he deduced, as there was nothing coming in the other direction, that the road was completely closed, so he pulled out and approached the posse of police cars, waving his identity badge at a number of busy officers. An inspector he'd never met approached him.

'You the duty photographer?'

He nodded.

'Inspector Charnley, Traffic Division.' He introduced himself as if he expected a fanfare. 'You took your time getting here.'

'I left immediately. My gearbox has developed a fault.'

'Well you'd better get your stuff unpacked. We haven't got all night.'

Barry wasn't impressed with Inspector Charnley's manner, or his manners, if it came to that. The senior officers he'd dealt with before had been altogether more civilised, but he bit his lip and took the equipment from the police van, loading a roll of film into the camera and taking it to the scene of the accident. Charnley was waiting for him.

'It would appear,' he intoned, 'that the motor cyclist skidded and fell in front of this motor vehicle. We're going to need photographs of the points of impact and the tyre marks of both vehicles.'

Mercifully, the injured biker had been taken away, but Barry could see the driver of the car, obviously very shaken, sitting in one of the police cars, and he felt sorry for him. Charnley watched Barry photograph the front of the car, head-on and from each side, and asked, 'Are they all you need?'

'As far as the car's concerned, yes, they are.' He didn't think it was one of his duties to remind him that it was the senior officer's responsibility to identify the features to be photographed. Instead, he indicated the damaged motorbike, and Charnley pointed out what was required. Barry did what was needed before going on to photograph the tyre marks.

After what seemed an age, he was allowed to leave, and he ground his way home in very low spirits. He was wet, tired, disappointed, and generally displeased, especially with Inspector bloody Charnley. As far as Barry was concerned, the less he had to do with him, the happier his life would be, but he had a feeling he'd be seeing more of him.

As the garage was filled with the junk he couldn't fit into the flat, Barry parked the Triumph on the tiny apron of ground beside the studio and, with the front wheels up on ramps, he crawled underneath to remove the gearbox. Its replacement was still in the boot. He'd spent ages that Sunday morning, trawling the Yellow Pages before finding what seemed to be the only reasonably local scrapyard that had a gearbox for a Triumph Herald 13/60, only to find that they wanted forty-five pounds for it. It was supposed to have done a very low mileage, but he would have expected it to be gold-plated at that price. However, he needed one quickly, so he had to settle for it.

He eased the old one to the ground and shifted it towards the side of the car so that he could lift it out of the way. As he did so, he heard the rasping of an exhaust and he crawled out to see Guy parking his BMW outside the bookshop. He got out and glanced in Barry's direction with the look of amused scorn he doubtless reserved for blokes in overalls who were reduced to mending their own cars. Barry contented himself with the knowledge that if the synchromesh ever went on his gearbox it would cost him the equivalent of the national debt.

He was opening the boot when the pager bleeped from inside the car, so he hurriedly wiped his hands and switched it off. Past experience told him that it usually happened at the most awkward times, so he wasn't entirely surprised.

He spoke to a girl at the police station who told him he was needed at another road traffic accident. It wasn't far away, as it happened, but he still had a transport problem. 'I've just taken the gearbox off my car,' he explained, 'so I'm going to need transport.'

'Oh, can't you drive it, then?'

He swallowed his impatience, realising that he must have asked a few silly questions in his time about things he didn't understand. 'No,' he said, 'it won't go without a gearbox.'

'Oh, I see.'

'Can you send a car for me?'

She paused. 'I don't know. I'll ask.' He imagined she must be very new to the job. She returned to the phone after a few seconds. 'Yes,' she confirmed, 'they're sending a car for you.'

A police car wasn't the kind of thing he particularly wanted outside the studio. It could easily create the wrong impression, so he could only hope it would pass unnoticed.

It was a traffic car that came, one of the white ones with a red stripe, that the irreverent masses called a 'jam sandwich', so it couldn't have been more conspicuous. He locked up the studio quickly and climbed into the back. The two officers in the front didn't appear to be in much of a hurry when they greeted him. The driver indicated the Triumph, still on the ramps and pointing uselessly at the sky. 'What's the matter with your car, then?'

'The synchromesh has gone on fourth gear,' said Barry, wishing they would just drive off before one of the neighbours got the idea he'd been arrested.

The officer shook his head sympathetically. 'Fourth is always the first to go.'

'It's unusual with them, though,' his mate said. 'Triumph gearboxes are pretty good.' Someone Barry vaguely knew was driving up the road and, worse still, Guy's BMW was pulling out. Perhaps they wouldn't notice him, although it was a futile hope in the circumstances. The police driver engaged first gear and pulled out behind them. His mate was more impatient. 'What's the hold up, Dave?'

'It's that slowcoach in front of the "Beamer",' the driver told him. 'Let's get round 'em.' It was the worst possible time for them to develop a sense of urgency. On went the siren and flashing lights and, before Barry could duck down, he caught sight of Guy and Lucy staring at him as they passed them.

Dave asked, 'You all right, mate?'

'Just about.' Half the neighbourhood would be expecting to see him on the six o-clock news, but other than that, he was fine. He wondered what else might happen to make life complete, and he asked, 'Is Inspector Charnley at the incident?'

'Hitler? No, he's not on duty until tonight, thank God.' Suddenly he and his mate exchanged anxious looks. 'He's not a mate of yours, is he?'

'No way.'

'That's all right then. Funny bloke, Charnley.'

'I know.'

'No, I mean weird. He's a shit with people, but did you know he breeds Siamese cats?'

'You're joking.'

'He does, and he's daft about 'em. Funny, isn't it?' They relaxed again, and so did Barry to some extent. Cats or no, it was a small blessing that he was off-duty, and one for which, in his over-stressed condition, he was thankful.

Having been delivered safely home by the friendly officers, Barry lost no time in getting back into his overalls and fitting the new gearbox. He was determined not to be caught in that situation again. Thankfully, it all went smoothly. When he took the car out to test it, he found that the gears worked perfectly.

He went inside to develop the wedding pictures. The couple would be away for a fortnight on their honeymoon, but he didn't want to leave it too late. For one thing, he'd no idea what surprises the constabulary might have in store for him.

Apart from nipping outside for an occasional cigarette, he spent the rest of the afternoon in the darkroom. He was pleased with the proofs of the wedding pictures, and he left them drying while he enlarged some of Claret's. He would phone her later and ask her to come and see them.

She looked at the label on the wine bottle and smiled. 'Did you get this 'cause I was coming?'

'Yes.' It wasn't true, of course. He often bought claret, but the idea seemed to please her.

'I've seen people buy it at the supermarket, but I've never tried it.'

'Try some now.' He poured her a glass and handed it to her.

85

She took a sip, then closed her eyes and took another, finally putting her glass down and beaming like someone who's discovered the answer to the mystery of life. 'That's really nice,' she said. 'Mind you, it would be awful if I didn't like it, wouldn't it?'

'It would,' he agreed. 'You might have found something you liked much better, and then you'd have had to change your name to, maybe, Chateau Neuf du Pape, or Beaune Villages.'

She eyed him as she might look at a child who was talking nonsense. 'That would be silly.'

She was right, so he opened the folder of pictures on the kitchen table in front of her. 'There, I've enlarged the ones I think would be the most suitable. Have a look at those first.'

It was the nearest he could imagine to being a parent on Christmas Morning. He watched her sift through the enlargements in sheer delight. Eventually, she said, 'I can't believe this is really me. I look like a real model.'

'That's the idea.'

'These are fantastic, Barry.'

'I'm glad you think so, and let's hope they'll do the trick with the right agency.'

'They're bound to, though, aren't they? I mean, these pictures make me look like those girls in the magazines.'

He felt uneasy. Claret wouldn't be the first to expect instant stardom, and she wouldn't be the first to taste disappointment, either. 'Claret,' he said, 'you're a pretty girl, and these pictures are very effective, but the agencies look at hundreds of portfolios every week. It's anybody's guess what they're really looking for, so all you can do is to keep trying until you find one that's interested in your particular qualities.'

'But I don't know where to start.'

'That's all right. I'll lend you a book that has details of all the agencies worth considering, and it also tells you exactly how to go about introducing yourself to them. I'll put the pictures together in a presentation binder, and then you can make a start.'

# 10

# A Taste of Bliss

The week passed without major incident. Barry had one more encounter with Inspector Charnley, during which he matched the inspector's brusqueness with his own, with the outcome that Charnley became almost human. Other than that, he only had to photograph the evidence of two shop burglaries, both of which were reported at the start of work, so he didn't have to lose any sleep during the week.

On Saturday, Wesley arrived, although there wasn't an awful lot to be done. They spent most of the morning in the darkroom, finishing some prints and generally tidying up. It was a useful time for that, because, not being the most organised person, Barry found that things frequently stayed where they landed, at least until he found the time to have a massive clear-up.

Wesley was more than usually quiet, and Barry knew from experience that he was about to ask him for something. It surprised him, though, that it was taking so long. He'd never thought of himself as forbidding. Maybe it was just Wesley's age. In the end, he asked, 'What's on your mind, Wesley? Don't keep me in suspense.'

He fidgeted and looked around him, finally mumbling, 'Nothing really. It's just that, well... I wondered...' It was hard work for him, and Barry deliberately looked away. He tried again. 'I just wondered if you'd mind if I used the studio, I mean, when you're not using it.'

'Of course I don't mind. You need the practice. What do you want to do?'

He looked immensely relieved, and Barry thought, not for the first time, what a trial adolescence could be. Wesley stumbled on. 'I'd like to do some portraits.'

'So you should, but you'll need a model.'

'Michelle said she'd sit for me.'

'A good choice too. She'll photograph well.' Barry remembered his first impression of her when he saw her in the teashop. 'Yes,' he told him, 'there's no problem about the studio.' Actually, there was an element of chance in it. There were items in there that weren't exactly Wesley-proof, but he had to accept the risk some time.

'Thanks, Barry.'

'You're welcome.' He couldn't resist a leg-pull. 'You'll keep the session clean, won't you? I have the studio's reputation to maintain.'

'Yes, 'course I will.' The poor lad had turned as red as the darkroom safelight.

Barry patted him on the shoulder. 'Only kidding. I know your motives are pure. Pass me them over, will you?' He pointed to a pile of prints on the far corner of the dry bench. 'Most of them can be chucked, but there may be one or two that are worth keeping.'

Wesley picked up the pile and stared at the picture on top. He held it up for Barry to see, and asked, 'Are you going to use this one?'

It was one of Claret's out-takes, and Barry remembered it happening. It was at the beginning of the nude session, when he started the motor drive. The whirring had made her swing round in surprise to face the camera, the towel held carelessly to one side. It was a good picture, a natural nude pose, but much too blatant to be included in the portfolio. 'No, that one was an accident. They sometimes happen when you use the motor drive. Pictures can be more natural than you intend them to be.' He could see Wesley fighting back a grin.

'Did you print it by accident?'

He gave up and sighed. It was like that with Wesley. Every once in a while, he would produce a flash of sophistication. '*Touché*, Wesley, but don't run away with the idea that I spend all my time shooting tits and bums.'

He looked at the picture again and smiled. 'I never thought that,' he assured him. 'Do you want me to chuck this away?'

'No,' Barry told him, 'we'll keep it. It'll be a reminder that nobody's perfect, especially with a motor drive.'

Wesley became quite chatty after that, at least by his standards, and he told Barry about things that happened at college.

'The models we get,' he said, 'are quite old, so it's hard to make them look nice.'

'As old as me?'

'Yes, and some of them are older.'

'Eking out their pensions with a bit of modelling, I suppose.'

'Some older women are all right,' he conceded. 'Lucy at the teashop's really nice-looking.'

'But she's not very old.' He'd always imagined her to be about his own age.

'Twenty-eight,' he confirmed. 'Her birthday was last Sunday. That bloke she's going out with bought her one of them dangly things.'

'A pendant necklace?'

'Yes, he must be loaded.'

'He's certainly lashed out on jewellery lately.'

Wesley considered that. 'Yeah, but apart from that, I don't know what she sees in him. I think he's an arsehole.'

'I'd say that's a pretty accurate description of him, Wesley, but what's he done to upset you?'

He smiled nervously. 'I go in there quite a lot nowadays.'

He paused, and realising that Barry wasn't going to tease him about it, went on. 'He goes in a lot too and, every time he sees me, he says, "Ah, The Sorceror's Apprentice," all clever-like. He makes me sick.'

'Why does he call you that?'

'Because he reckons our equipment's old-fashioned. Mind you, I don't know what he knows about it.'

'I think his nephew must have told him about the Corfield.' He reminded Wesley of the Race-horse Family sitting. 'He may also have seen a sepia tint that I left with Lucy, and that wouldn't have pleased him after he'd told her with a great show of authority that the toner was impossible to get.'

'Pillock. He thinks he knows everything, just because he takes a few snaps.'

'That's right. When he starts again you should ask him to show you some pictures he's taken. That's the acid test.'

'That's a good idea, Barry. I will.'

Wesley seemed to be placated for the time being, and as his mind was seldom far from his stomach, announced that it felt like lunchtime. Barry decided to join him at the teashop. He'd stayed away long enough without being churlish.

⌒⌒⟡⌒⌒

He paid Wesley and put up the 'Closed' sign. It hadn't been a bad day. They'd cleared what outstanding work there was, and he'd spent some time with Wesley in the studio, experimenting with lighting so that he had some tangible ideas to work on.

Lunch at the teashop went well, too. Lucy and, inevitably, Guy had joined them, and whilst the atmosphere wasn't quite what Barry remembered, at least it had been fairly pleasant. Guy had avoided speaking to him as far as possible, of course. After all, what could he say to the irresponsible owner of a delinquent animal? At the same time, however, he'd left Wesley alone. Barry had been prepared to spring to his defence but it hadn't been necessary. The pleasantest thing of all had been seeing Wesley and Michelle very much at ease together. She was good for him.

He closed the downstairs doors and went up to the flat to shower and change. With his police commitment out of the way for the time being, Belinda was coming over, and he'd reserved a table at The Three Tuns, so it had the makings of a relaxed evening. He didn't have to drive, and with a bit of luck Belinda wouldn't either.

⚬⚬⚬

Not surprisingly, they saw Lucy and Guy as soon as they entered the restaurant. They seemed to go there most weekends, but Barry hadn't really thought about it when he made the reservation. It didn't matter anyway because, whilst Guy wasn't his favourite person, he didn't get worked up about him any more. He steered Belinda over to their table just to be sociable, and was surprised when she recognised Guy straight away. They seemed to know each other well, a realisation that Barry found disturbing. He'd expected better of her than that. He introduced her to Lucy and, after a few words, they went to their table, where the waitress was standing patiently with the menus under her arm.

Having made his choice, he observed Belinda as she ran her eye down the menu. Her dress was a very pale green, near enough eau-de-nil, and it was perfect for her skin tone. Spending much of his time looking at women through a lens made such things important to him. Her long eyelashes continued to fascinate him as well. He was sure they were her own, and he had to admit that, all in all, he was completely taken with her. He was also a little curious. He waited until the waitress had taken their order before asking her, 'How do you come to know Guy?'

For a moment, she seemed puzzled, and then with a look of realisation, glanced over her shoulder. 'Oh *him*. I went out with him very briefly. It was after he'd acted for me. I had

91

a bit of a shunt with my car about, oh, two years ago. Well, actually it was quite a big shunt, and the insurance company engaged his firm to represent me.'

'Bad luck, about the accident, I mean. Did he do a good job?'

She rolled her eyes upwards. 'No, he was bloody useless. I was done for driving without due care and attention, I got a walloping great fine and I lost my licence for three months. All he did was to tell the beaks how sorry I was. Oh, and he gave them details of my income and outgoings so that they could fine me a king's ransom. That's all.'

'I'm surprised you went out with him after that.'

'Yes, I am too, but he's quite good-looking, and I did rather fancy him. Still, we live and learn.'

The waitress appeared with their order, and she transferred her attention to that. Barry had a feeling he might find out more later, but that could wait.

They talked through the meal in a relaxed way about anything that came to mind, and it was thoroughly pleasant. He learned that Belinda worked in the general office at Rainham's, the department store in Elmston, which explained the elegant clothes she always wore and her immaculate sense of style. She was entertaining too, in an easy, frank sort of way, and he imagined she must have been indulged as a child. Things she told him led him to the conclusion that she expected, and usually got, most of what she wanted, and he might have felt misgivings about that with some women, but he was completely won over by her irreverent wit.

As they left the restaurant, Barry spotted Gavin Peckett waving to him and giving him knowing looks from the far end of the bar. He could be downright crude at times. Fortunately, however, Belinda hadn't seen him. Even so, Barry guided her out quickly, before Gavin could come over. He really couldn't have borne the embarrassment.

They crossed the road and passed Guy's BMW on the way to the flat.

'He's changed his car since I knew him,' Belinda observed, 'but he kept the number plate, the twerp.'

'Are those his initials?' He'd noticed the unfortunate combination before.

'Yes, Guy Ivan Thomas.'

It was very appropriate.

When they reached the studio, Barry unlocked the door and led Belinda up to the flat, where she perched on the sofa. 'You're not going to make coffee, are you, Barry?'

'Not if you don't want it.' For one awful moment, he thought she was going to tell him she had to go.

'Good.' She got up and came purposefully towards him to put her hands on his shoulders. 'That bleeper-thing of yours isn't going to go off again, is it?'

'No,' he assured her. 'I'm not on call for another three weeks.'

She rested her head on his shoulder in exaggerated relief. 'Oh good,' she repeated, 'I couldn't stand another postponement. Let's leave the coffee until morning.'

He closed the door behind them on that occasion, because the last thing they needed was another surprise visit from Jack.

Much later, there was a scratching at the door, which became insistent, and Barry was trying hard to ignore it when Belinda asked, 'Is that your cat?'

'Yes, it's Jack. He'll soon go away.'

'Oh, let him in. I like cats.'

'Better not.'

'Why not?'

'He's very prudish.'

She lay on her back and laughed. 'You're kidding.'

'No, really. He's not keen on anyone sharing my bed, and he gets horribly uptight about it. In fact, he can be very aggressive.'

She whispered teasingly, 'D'you think he's jealous? Maybe he wants you all to himself.'

'Something like that. He has some odd ways.'

She was silent for a moment, and then propped herself up on one elbow to ask, 'How well do you know that woman who was with Guy Thomas in the restaurant?'

'Fairly well. She has the bookshop and tearoom opposite the pub, where Guy's car was parked, and I go in there for lunch sometimes. I've done a bit of work for her as well, on some old prints that she sells.'

'I see.' She was quiet again, and he noticed with some relief that Jack had stopped scratching. He'd be sulking in the morning, but that couldn't be avoided.

Belinda stirred again to ask him, 'How long have they been engaged?'

'You noticed the ring, obviously. It happened a few weeks ago, but he's been showering her with jewellery lately.'

She made a noise that was somewhere between a snort and a laugh. 'I know one thing she won't be getting.'

'What's that?'

'This.' She snuggled up close again and delved with her hand beneath the sheet.

'Really?'

'Oh, he'll do it. After a fashion, that is, but it'll hardly be the experience of a lifetime. At least, if it is, it'll be the wrong kind of experience.'

'Tell me more.' He had to know.

'There's nothing more to tell, except that I don't know which was the most boring twenty seconds of my life: the first time with him, or the second. It certainly wasn't like this.' She launched another attack under the duvet.

'Careful, Belinda, please. You're not starting a lawnmower.'

'All right, I'll be gentle.' She eased herself up and knelt over him, leaning forward to kiss him, so that her hair fell around his face. Life could be blissful sometimes.

# 11

# Police Work to Paddock

He saw rather a lot of Belinda in the next two weeks. It would have been difficult to avoid her even if he'd wanted to, she was so ready to spend time with him, and he found it quite flattering. It seemed to him that she was the kind of person who threw herself into everything whole-heartedly. That had been his experience of her so far, and he found it entertaining and often surprising, albeit in an exhausting kind of way.

Unfortunately, however, her enthusiasm extended to finding out about everything he did, and that involved a close inspection of the studio and darkroom, so it was inevitable that she should find the frontal nude picture of Claret that had amused Wesley so much.

She looked at Barry suspiciously and asked, 'Do you do a lot of this?'

He told her about the portfolio and how the picture came to be taken. 'I only printed it because it's such a good, natural shot.'

Belinda continued to study the picture. 'You must be quite pleased with it,' she said, 'to have kept it.'

'Not at all. It's just a bit of fun. If I take a nude shot, it's for a good reason. In this case, it was to offer the model scope to try different kinds of work, and sometimes I've done it simply because it made a good picture. I don't do porn.'

'But you just called it "a bit of fun". There was a sharp edge to her voice that he'd not heard before. 'Who is this girl anyway?'

'I told you, she's doing some modelling for me, that's all. In case you're wondering, I don't mix business with pleasure and I don't go in for cradle-snatching, either.'

She eyed him uncertainly, but her tone had softened to some extent. 'How old is she?'

'Eighteen. That's old enough to do this off her own bat,' he said, pointing to the photograph, 'but too young to interest me in what you evidently have in mind.' He made an effort to lighten the conversation. 'You have no competition,' he told her.

It must have been what she wanted to hear because she was soon mollified, but the conversation left him uneasy, and he discarded the picture before it caused any more problems.

⚜

Within the next few days, Belinda seemed to have forgotten the incident. Instead, she was preoccupied with the impending return of the couple who owned the house she was renting, and her need to find new accommodation. As such things didn't happen immediately, and she was going to need somewhere very soon, it was no surprise when she suggested moving temporarily into the flat. Naturally, he had no objection to that and, as the awkward business over the picture of Claret seemed to have subsided, he was able to get on with his work in a fairly contented frame of mind.

The wedding pictures were very well received, and David King had called to congratulate him on them, which was quite a boost for him. It seemed that he was becoming known in other quarters as well. Elmston Camera Club had asked him to co-judge a competition. He would never grow rich on the kind of fee they were paying, but it would help to put his name abroad, and that was important.

Otherwise, the last week of September was hectic, in that he was called out on four nights by the police. Three of the calls were to road traffic accidents. Only one of them was attended by Inspector Charnley, and whilst he was his usual officious self, at least, he was no longer offensive. It seemed that Barry's earlier display of assertiveness had made a lasting impression on him. The fourth call, however, was to something completely different. A girl's body had been found in the bottom of a dyke on the marsh, and it was the most awful crime scene Barry had ever been called upon to attend. Having done scene-of-crime work regularly, he reckoned he was inured to most things, but he was sickened by what he saw, and he wasn't alone. DCI Jackson looked on, grim and silent as the pathologist made his initial examination at the scene, pointing out the features he wanted photographed. More-detailed photography would be required at the mortuary, but it was important to get whatever shots were called for at the scene. It seemed that she had been strangled and, beneath the floodlights, the marks were clearly visible on her throat. There were other bruise marks too, on her arms and legs. The latter were clearly visible because she was wearing neither tights nor underwear, and one of them coincided with a scar across one thigh. It was very prominent, possibly the legacy of a nasty childhood accident, but whatever had caused it was nothing compared with what had happened to her that night. Barry finished photographing the bruises as he was directed, folded the tripod and climbed out of the dyke. What remained of her clothing would be removed later, at the mortuary, and the body would be examined in detail, but everything seemed to indicate indecent assault followed by murder. It seemed that she had been dead only a few hours. Barry heard the pathologist estimate her age at between fifteen and eighteen.

Her body wasn't at all bloodied or mangled. As corpses went, hers was very clean. It was the hideousness of the situation that was so sickening, the taking of a young life, and quite possibly an innocent one. Those were Barry's thoughts as he leant against a police van, drawing on the chill night air and fighting the nausea that refused to subside. The sight of her still, white limbs as she lay in the bottom of the dyke left an impression on him that time was unlikely to erase.

⌇⌇⌇◈⌇⌇⌇

It was a relief to be called on again to do some animal photography. This time the subject was a mare that belonged to one of Lucy's friends. Relations with Lucy had never been quite the same since Jack's assault on Guy, but her business arrangement with Barry was still on, and happily, she had recommended him for this job.

Ram's Head Farm was just outside Denford, and he found it with little difficulty. He drove past several out-buildings of the soft red brick that, like the inevitable oast houses, was such a feature of the area, to park outside the farmhouse, and was immediately surrounded by an army of hissing geese. They seemed to arrive all at once, like hostile savages, and they scared the wits out of him. Nothing was going to make him leave the car, so he meekly sounded the horn, hoping to attract someone's attention.

Before long, deliverance arrived in the shape of a young woman clad in jeans, wellingtons and a waxed coat, who shooed the geese away before coming round to the car door with an apologetic grin. He opened the door tentatively and got out, having checked that the geese really were in retreat.

'Mr Craven? Fenella Billingham.' She extended a grimy hand, and he noticed that she was quite attractive in a hearty, open-air sort of way, with a pleasing, untidy mane of auburn curls. He imagined her to be around his own age, and that fitted with her being one of Lucy's friends.

'Hello, Mrs Billingham. That was quite a reception.'

'The geese? Yes, they can be intimidating all right.' She led him to the farmhouse door, chatting as she did so. 'Mind you, the one to look out for is Sam, the gander.'

'I'll watch him,' he promised.

'You do that, he's lethal.' She was smiling as she said it, so he could only assume she was joking, although he was prepared to give anything with a long neck and a beak an extremely wide berth. Mrs Billingham took him into the kitchen, where she indicated one of the chairs at a huge deal table. He put his bag on the floor and sat down.

She asked, 'Would you like coffee? I've just made some. May I call you Barry, by the way?'

'Please do, and yes, coffee would be welcome, thank you.'

'Good. I'm Fenella.' She took two mugs from a shelf on the dresser and filled them from a pot that was standing on the range. 'I gather you're a friend of Lucy.'

'I know her quite well,' he said, 'and we do a bit of business.' In truth, he felt that he hardly qualified as a friend any longer. It was something that had been troubling him. 'How do you come to know her?'

'We were at school together, so we go back a long way. Tell me, what do you make of this Guy character she's taken up with?' Her frankness was disarming, and he found it impossible to be anything other than equally candid.

'To be honest,' he said, 'I'm not impressed with him at all, but I find it safer not to criticise him in her hearing.'

'Me too.' She put milk and sugar on the table. 'Have you been in trouble as well?'

'Well, sort of, but it was my cat who really stirred things up.'

'Your cat?' She gave a laugh and waited in amusement and curiosity to hear the story.

He told her about the weekend he was away, when Jack had disgraced himself, and Fenella listened, wide-eyed, and finally seized with laughter. 'He sounds absolutely wonderful.'

'I suppose he is,' he agreed, feeling uncomfortably guilty at the thought. Jack had been very sulky and incommunicative for some time, making a point of avoiding Belinda and him when they were together, and Barry was sure it was because of his recent exile from the bedroom. Changing the subject, he asked, 'What sort of pictures are you looking for, Fenella?'

'Oh, my mare? Well, I'd like a head portrait and maybe one with all of her in it. Actually, she's in foal, but she's not showing it yet, and I wanted to get a photograph of her before that happens.'

'Fine. When's the foal due?'

'April.'

'It would be good to get some pictures of her with the foal, possibly when it's newly-born.'

She looked doubtful and said, 'When the foal's a few days old, perhaps.'

'That's a shame. I'm really keen to photograph a mare with a newly-born foal.'

Fenella shook her head. 'It's not a good time, Barry. She wouldn't be at all happy with too many people around, and the sound of a camera going off could easily unsettle her if she's foaling. In any case, you just can't legislate for these things. Quite often, they happen during the night when no one's about.'

'Okay, I'll be guided by you. In any case, I wouldn't use a camera with a noisy shutter, but you know best. Now tell me, what sizes of photograph are you looking for?'

'I don't know.' She frowned in concentration. 'About like this, I suppose.' She framed an imaginary picture with her hands. He was used to people doing that. In his experience, there was twenty by sixteen, ten by eight and 'about this size'.

'Ten by eight. That's fine, it doesn't really matter which camera I use.'

'Okay then, let's go out to the paddock.' She picked up a grooming brush and led the way.

The mare was at the far end of the paddock, but when Fenella called her, she came over readily. Fenella had described her over the phone as a dark-bay middle-weight hunter. Barry was learning all the time, but one thing he already knew from his own experience was that she would photograph well.

'This is Mandy,' Fenella told him, pulling out the mare's mane with the brush and tidying it.

He took out a packet of Polo mints and asked, 'Is it okay to give her one of these?' He knew how popular they were with horses.

'Oh yes, she'll love you for evermore. Keep your hand flat if you don't want her to take your fingers as well.'

He offered it to the mare on the palm of his hand, and she took it readily. 'She's not nervous, is she?' He remembered their conversation about mares and foals.

'Goodness, no, she's bomb-proof.'

He stroked and patted her with one hand while he took out his exposure meter, holding it over her to get an incident reading. For one awful moment, he thought she was going to take the meter from him, but he got the reading and transferred it to the Mamiya. He slipped inside the gate and framed the picture, clicking his tongue to her. She moved her head, and he took several shots. She wasn't at all fazed, so he thought he would try something different. He asked, 'Would you like to come in and take her attention?'

'Fine.' Fenella came in and, naturally enough, Mandy reacted to her, rubbing her mouth against Fenella's hand. Barry fixed a ninety millimetre lens to the Leica and moved around them, getting several promising shots of them together.

Finally, they left Mandy to graze, and returned to Barry's car. Happily, the geese's attention was diverted by something else and he was able to make a dignified exit. When he wound down the window to say goodbye, Fenella said, 'I've been thinking about that suggestion you made earlier, about photographing the foal. I still don't think it's a good idea for you to be here too soon after the foaling, but if I give you a ring, there's no reason why you shouldn't come soon afterwards, a couple of days or so. I don't think you'd be intrusive, and your cameras are very quiet, especially the little one.'

'Thank you, I'd really appreciate that.'

'Good, we'll do that then.' She paused for a moment as another thought occurred to her, and then asked him, 'Do you do a lot of animal photography?'

'Quite a lot, but not as much as I'd like.' In spite of

his determination to become established as a portrait photographer, he enjoyed working with animals and, after all, any kind of work was welcome.

'When you send me the proofs I'll have something to show my friends. I'm sure you could get quite a lot of business.'

He thanked her and drove off in a happy frame of mind. It was good to deal with someone as uncomplicated as Fenella, and Mandy had been an excellent subject too. Arthur Fielden's advice was paying off. Barry was taking all the work that came his way and, sooner or later, things had to improve.

Because of the prevailing circumstances, he'd taken to visiting the bookshop less frequently than before. He was sure Lucy had put the incident with Jack to the back of her mind, but he couldn't avoid the fact that she'd objected to his attitude towards Guy. It was fairly understandable, although it was a shame that their friendship should have deteriorated over something so trivial. It wasn't that she was being particularly unfriendly, but the easy familiarity they'd enjoyed seemed to have evaporated, and all that was left was the kind of politeness that existed between business associates.

He decided to call in on his way back to the studio because he wanted to speak to her about some photographs she'd found and which she wanted him to copy. It was lunchtime, so it was inevitable that Guy should be hovering about the place. His presence was a nuisance, but Barry didn't intend to stay long, and his business was with Lucy, anyway.

He looked at the three prints of Woodley High Street that she showed him. One was of very poor quality. The camera must have moved so that the picture was far too blurred, but the other two were quite promising.

'Not bad,' he said. 'Do you know when these were taken?'

'About nineteen-twenty, as far as I can gather. The man who took them died some time ago, but his son's quite happy for them to be reproduced.' She showed him the receipt she'd written. It included an amount for some books.

Barry traced the line of buildings down to his studio, which was indistinguishable from several other houses at the time, but his eye fell on a shop further down the street. 'I didn't know this place used to be a butcher's shop,' he remarked.

'Half of it was. The other half was the house next door, where the butcher's family lived. It's fascinating, isn't it? I'm afraid these pictures have suffered the ravages of time. Do you think you can do anything with them?' She looked doubtfully at him and then, for some reason, at Guy, who smirked patronisingly, but Barry said, 'No problem. This one's beyond help,' he said, indicating the blurred picture, 'but it always was. I can do a lot with these two, though.'

'Even the torn one?'

'Oh yes, it shouldn't be a problem.' He noticed that they both seemed surprised, but there was a great deal that could be done to hide that kind of damage. He suspected that Guy had been pronouncing inexpert judgement again.

Lucy slipped the pictures back into their envelope and handed it to Barry. 'That's excellent. How did the session with Fenella go?'

'It was very straightforward. Thanks for the introduction, by the way. I appreciate it.'

'It was no trouble.' Her smile was a fleeting reminder of better times. 'Oh, I've got a letter for you. The postman must have put it in the wrong bundle. It came this morning.' She gave him a small, blue, handwritten envelope.

'Thanks.' He peered at the postmark, but it had been smudged, and he certainly didn't recognise the writing. Just then, though, Guy said something to Lucy, and Barry took advantage of the interruption to open it. The address at the top was in Milnrow, Rochdale, and he realised the letter must be from the Fielden couple. He began to read it.

> *Dear Mr Craven*
> *I am sorry not to have written to you sooner to thank you*
> *for the lovely photographs. They are much appreciated.*

The letter went on to say how the pictures had been admired by friends and relations. He read on and blinked with surprise and dismay.

> *Arthur passed away only two weeks after we met you in*
> *Malham, so the photographs will always be a special*
> *reminder of that day. His health had been poor for some*
> *time, so it was not as big a shock as it might have been.*
> *He had a bad heart, you see. It had always been a problem*
> *since he came back from the Far East after the war. He*
> *always said he would see Lady's time out, but it wasn't to*
> *be. Do you remember Lady, our dog? She died three weeks*
> *after Arthur.*

Hell. He hadn't been all that old. Somehow, the worst things had to happen to the best of people. He looked at the letter again.

> *Lots of Arthur's old workmates came to the funeral and the*
> *Lancashire Fusiliers' Association gave him a very moving*
> *send-off.*
> *Anyhow, thank you again for your kindness, and I hope*
> *things are improving for you.*
> *Yours sincerely,*
> *Hilda Fielden*

He folded the letter and put it in his pocket, conscious that Lucy and Guy were looking in his direction.

Guy was grinning at him in the superior way he had. 'Do tell us why you were taken away in a police car the other day,' he said. 'I've been dying to know.'

Suddenly, Barry wanted to hit the grinning idiot. At least Lucy looked embarrassed. 'My car was off the road,' he told him simply. 'They needed me to do a job, so they came and fetched me.' Guy's look of disappointment was more than rewarding.

Lucy asked, 'So you're still working for them?'

'Yes, it makes sense for the time being.'

Guy was about to say something that was probably fatuous, but he was cut short by Lucy, who must have noticed that Barry was preoccupied. 'That letter,' she said, 'it's not bad news is it?'

'It is really,' he said. 'I haven't known these people long, in fact I only met them the last time I was in Yorkshire. It was a chance meeting in Malham, and it turned out to be their wedding anniversary, so I offered to take their photograph. Now, it seems, the man's died. He was only about sixty-five.'

'That's awful.'

He patted the letter in his pocket. 'His wife was very anxious to know that I wasn't using a Japanese camera. It was important to her, and now I know why.'

'There's a lot of silly prejudice about that kind of thing,' said Guy. 'Just out of interest, what were you using?'

'A Leica M3. She didn't mind that.'

'Huh.' The information seemed to amuse him, and he was very likely about to pursue the subject, no doubt in his usual sardonic way, when he remembered something that was presumably even more important to him than making sneering remarks. Taking a long, legal envelope from his briefcase, he said, 'I was going to deliver this by hand to Ellen Harper, the hairdresser, but I'm rather busy. Drop it in for me when you go, will you, Barry? There's a good chap.'

'I'm also rather busy,' Barry told him. 'You do it, Guy. There's a good chap.'

Barry was genuinely busy. He had to get back to his flat, because Belinda was taking the afternoon off to move her stuff in, and he would need to free up some drawer, cupboard and wardrobe space. At least, that was what he thought was needed. When she arrived, and he saw the bags and heaped clothes in her car, he wondered if he needed a bigger flat. He'd never understood how women had to have so many clothes. They had different things for this and that, and then, when an occasion cropped up, they had to go shopping again because they had nothing to wear. In that sense, Belinda was representative of her sex and, clearly, the space Barry had to offer was woefully inadequate. After filling all the available drawers and cupboards, there was still a massive pile of dresses, skirts, trousers and blouses to be accommodated. In the end, he got a length of steel tube from a plumbers' merchant in Elmston and mounted it on two old studio lighting stands. As a dress rail, it wasn't designer luxury, and it took up a lot of sitting room space, but it solved the problem.

By the end of the afternoon, they were both worn out, and Barry sat down to watch the six o'clock news while Belinda put the kettle on for tea. It was one of those news bulletins that made him wonder why he bothered to watch them. Inflation, he learned, was steady for the time being, at sixteen percent and, incredibly, that was relatively good news. The bad news was that the bank rate was set to rise to fifteen percent, and an increase in the price of petrol meant that it would soon cost eighty pence a gallon. Barry wondered for the umpteenth time if there was any point in being self-employed, except that it was employment of a kind, and that was more than many people were enjoying. Apparently, the government was to seek advice from the International Monetary Fund on ways to tackle the economic crisis, and the announcement had been meat and drink to Margaret Thatcher, who had used it to trounce the hapless Chancellor and Prime Minister. Barry wondered idly how things might be under her leadership. No one seemed to know very much about her, although she came over as hard and unfeeling, and she didn't appeal to him at all, but in his apolitical way, he just wanted to see a way out of the awful mess the country was in.

It was a relief when the national news gave way to the regional studios, but only until they came to an item about the murdered girl, and he began to give it his full attention. She had been identified as Pauline Francis, who was seventeen years old. They showed the most recent picture they had of her, in her school uniform at Douglas Fearnley Secondary School. It had been taken a little over a year before her death, but she looked much younger than he remembered her from the night on the marsh, when, as he recalled, she was wearing make-up.

She had left her home on the Morrison estate, telling her parents she was meeting friends, but none of the friends interviewed by the police remembered seeing her or having made any arrangement to meet her. Her parents were said to be too distressed to give an interview, and Barry was glad, at least, that they hadn't been pushed in front of the cameras in the way that so many bereaved relatives were. Instead, DCI Jackson, looking very uneasy in front of an army of reporters, gave a short statement to the effect that the police were actively pursuing a number of lines of enquiry. In other words, he hadn't a clue, and Barry felt sorry for him. Jackson had always treated him with a kind of civility that implied respect.

He realised that Belinda was standing beside him with a tray.

She asked, 'Is that the case you were on?'

'That's right. She was only seventeen.'

'I know,' she sighed, 'I caught that as I came in. It makes your blood boil, doesn't it? If they catch him, they'll give him a life sentence and then let him out after fifteen years to do it again.'

'I really don't know,' he said. 'All I know is that I'm sickened by it all.'

She sat down beside him. 'Is that why you've been out of sorts today?'

'Have I really? I suppose I have been thinking about it off and on, but I had some unpleasant news today as well.' He told her about Mrs Fielden's letter.

'That's an awful shame,' she agreed, 'but you didn't know them all that well, did you?'

'That's true, but I felt as if they'd done a lot for me.'

She frowned. 'What had they done?'

He told her about the state of mind he was in when he met them, and about how a few encouraging words from them had caused him to think differently about his predicament. 'I'm really glad I met them,' he told her, 'and then when I read the letter at the bookshop – it was delivered there by mistake – and I said something about it, I had to put up with a lot of sneering nonsense from that bumptious arse Guy.'

She nodded. 'He really gets to you, doesn't he?'

'That's an understatement. The fact is I can't stand him, although I don't suppose I'm alone in that. He treats everyone with his own special brand of disdain.'

'And he got to Lucy before you did,' she teased.

'Oh no, it's nothing to do with her.'

'I'm not so sure. If you ask me, it's a good thing I'm here now to keep an eye on things.' Her eyes were twinkling and she was obviously joking, but he couldn't help feeling that her need to be in control might become a little wearing after a while.

# 12

# Goosed

Things ran particularly smoothly over the next week or so. Having Belinda's belongings scattered everywhere took some getting used to, as did her assumption that reorganisation of Barry's way of life was not only necessary but long overdue. Her presence had its advantages though, and one in particular, so he went along with her quirky and unusual ways, as susceptible as ever. He felt a degree of unease that Jack seemed almost to have moved out, only appearing briefly on a nightly basis for supper, but he consoled himself with the thought that Belinda's stay was a temporary one. In any case, how could he allow a cat to influence his life?

Business, if not brisk, was reasonable as well. His reprints of the photographs Lucy had found had generated a good deal of interest before they were finally sold, so it seemed that the idea might be a good one after all. Things were coming together, and he was feeling pretty optimistic, right up to the moment of his injury. It was always the same; just as he thought he was on top of things, something happened to make him look like an habitual victim.

It happened when he took the proofs to Fenella Billingham's place. He drove into the farmyard, looking anxiously for signs of web-footed activity, but there wasn't a goose in sight, so he parked beside the farmhouse, checked the yard once more, and knocked on the door. There was no response at first, but after a second knock, he was joined outside by a man who appeared from one of the outbuildings.

'What can I do for you, young man?' He was heavily-built, about forty-five, and he spoke with the local accent that was rapidly disappearing.

'I'm looking for Mrs Billingham,' said Barry. 'I arranged to see her at ten o'clock.'

He looked as if he had suddenly remembered something. 'Oh, you'll be the photographer. Yes, she's expecting you, but she's in the paddock. I don't think she'll be long.'

'That's all right,' said Barry, 'I don't mind waiting.'

The man nodded his head in mock-solemnity. 'You'll spend all your life waiting for women. Might as well get used to it. Fenella's my wife, by the way.' He offered his hand and Barry shook it. 'Name's Dennis.'

'Barry.'

He nodded good-naturedly. 'Bloody horses. I don't hold with having animals on the place that don't earn their keep, but you know how it is with women. You say one thing to 'em and end up doing another. You married?'

'No.'

'Don't fall for it. Life's easier that way.' He pointed vaguely in the direction of the pasture. 'What about bulls? D' you photograph them, too?'

'I'm quite happy to,' he said. He was beginning to warm to Dennis, although he couldn't imagine what he and Fenella had in common.

'Good. I'll have a chat with you when I've seen these photos you've done for Fenella. I breed Sussex cattle, you see, and I've got a bull that's a real future champion. You can see him from here, see. Look.' He led the way to the fence. 'Over to the right here.' Barry followed where he was pointing, but couldn't quite see the animal, so he moved further to the right. He was uncomfortably close to the outbuilding where he'd last seen the geese, but he felt confident with Dennis there. He leaned over the fence and saw the bull. Even to Barry's untutored eye, he seemed a magnificent creature.

'Look at the arse on him,' Dennis enthused. 'That's what you want in a bull. He's a beauty, that one. Now, what I'd like is to get a good photo of him in the *Breeders' Gazette* before the shows—'

He broke off when Barry roared with pain. It was like violent stab in the scrotum and he was in the most appalling agony.

'Bloody bird!'

Through a red mist, Barry saw Dennis kick at something. That was before he collapsed against the fence, unable to breathe, see, hear, or feel anything except the unbearable pain in the area normally associated with pleasure.

He was vaguely aware of Dennis helping him into the house, and then the next thing he knew was Fenella arriving and reacting with alarm when she saw him slumped and moaning in a kitchen chair.

'It was that bloody gander,' Dennis told her. 'I'm going to get my gun and deal with the bugger now.'

'Don't be silly, Dennis. You know he's only like that when the geese are nesting. You should have looked out for him.'

'I should have known better than to let you keep the buggers in the first place,' he grumbled.

For Barry's part, he'd have been happy if Dennis had finished him off with his gun, as he leaned over the table, eyes watering and still breathing with difficulty. The pain had spread to his lower abdomen and he clutched himself in misery, longing for it to subside.

Fenella was standing over him, perhaps wondering what to do. In the end, she made a very sensible suggestion. 'Dennis, get Barry a drink.'

He shuffled off and reappeared in a moment with a very large whisky. The pain was ebbing slightly and Barry was able to drink some of it. He'd never been keen on whisky, and it burned his throat, but at least it was a distraction.

After a while, he was able to sit up and talk. Dennis had been outside again and found his envelope. It was covered in goose droppings but, fortunately, the photographs were untouched. Fenella was delighted with them, and spent some time selecting the ones she wanted enlarged.

'Look at these, Dennis,' she said. 'If you want a photograph of Auchinleck, this is the man to do it.'

'Auchinleck?' It was an odd name for a bull.

'He must have told you about his wonderful bull. He names them after generals,' she explained, 'and Auchinleck is his latest pride and joy. We've had Wellington, Kitchener, Gordon, Haigh, Wavell, Alexander, and goodness-knows who else.'

'Haigh was a dead loss,' said Dennis dispassionately, 'like his namesake. He got turned into beefburgers.'

Fenella asked, 'What are you doing for Christmas, Barry?'

'I don't know.' October seemed early to be thinking about Christmas. 'I suppose I'll go up home to my folks. I usually do.'

'Barry's from Yorkshire,' she explained for Dennis's benefit. 'Look, Barry, the least we can do after this is to give you a goose, if you can face one, that is.' She saw his look of horror, and laughed. 'No,' she assured him, 'one that's plucked and ready for the oven.'

He heard himself say, 'That's very kind of you.' He supposed it was.

⁓⧫⁓

Much later, he found himself lowering his pants in the doctor's surgery.

'Ah, so ye've been goosed,' said the doctor with a thin smile.

Barry didn't reckon much to his brand of Scottish humour. 'No,' he told him, 'I've been gelded. At least, that's how it feels.'

The doctor completed his examination. 'Any blood in your urine?'

'None that I've seen.'

'Ah.' He lifted his hands as a sign to Barry to pull up his trousers. 'Ye have a haematoma. Some wee blood vessels have burst, but it'll dissipate in a short while. I can give you a prescription for a support, but the NHS thing's a poor wee offering. Ye'd be better buying a jock strap from a sports outfitter.'

'Fine.'

'Oh, and try not to indulge in frivolities for a day or so.'

'Will it affect that?'

The doctor chuckled. 'Only psychologically. You could try it, but you might be disappointed.'

As Barry left the surgery, he was sure he heard the old boy laughing to himself. It was always the same after a personal injury. No one took them seriously. Even Belinda saw the funny side of it, although Barry wasn't aware there was one, and he had no need of Doc Nairn's warning, because carnal practice was the last thing on his mind.

# 13

# Misunderstanding

It was a wretched week, as upset led to catastrophe. First, there was the photograph of Michelle, which brought about a repeat performance by Belinda of an earlier scene. If she hadn't gone poking around in the darkroom she would never have seen it. Certainly, it had escaped Barry's notice, but she found it, and her reaction was less than reasonable.

'What's this?' She held up the print. 'Another bit of fun?'

'What are you talking about?' He took the picture from her. It was a portrait, little more than head and shoulders, with some kind of garment held up to obscure her bust, but she was in effect topless. He was a bit surprised as well as amused. He'd always imagined Wesley's thing with Michelle to be touchingly innocent, but it seemed that she was quite happy to doff her top for a picture. Still, the current problem had to be addressed. He asked, 'What's the matter with it?'

'It's the young girl from the cafe, isn't it? How well do you know her?' She was obviously accusing him of something, although he couldn't imagine what it was.

'It's Wesley's girlfriend,' he said. 'This is one of his pictures.'

'But Wesley's only a boy. How could he take a picture like that?'

'He's quite a talented lad.' He looked at the picture again.

'It's not bad, either. The highlights are a bit over-exposed, and there's too much reflection in her eyes, but other than that it's quite good.'

'I think it's indecent. She can only be about sixteen.'

'Seventeen actually, and what's indecent about it?'

'You both *know* her. It's not as if she's a professional model. It's just not right, not with someone you know.'

What could he say? 'I don't understand, Belinda. You're broad-minded enough, usually.'

Of course I am,' she snapped. 'What happens between you and me is one thing, but you seem unable to photograph anyone else unless she's stripped and ready for anything, and now, it seems, you're encouraging your assistant to do the same.'

He was beginning to see the problem, and it had nothing to do with prudishness, which was the last thing he would have expected from her, anyway. She was plainly jealous of any imagined intimacy he might have with anyone else, to the extent that she was taking umbrage at a picture not even taken by him, but taken in his studio by someone else. 'Look,' he said, 'this is what I do for a living. Most of the people I photograph are fully-clothed, but I occasionally photograph a nude. If you remember, I explained it to you earlier. There's always a good reason for it, and if a model poses for me in the buff, it doesn't mean that I'm going to indulge in sex with her before, during or afterwards. As far as I know, the same applies to Wesley and, for what it's worth, I'm not encouraging him to do anything he shouldn't. He uses the studio according to my rules, and that means no dirty raincoat pictures and certainly no porn, but if he wants to practise this kind of picture, it's fine by me.'

'It seems that anything's okay by you,' she said in an exaggeratedly sulky tone.

'Well, now you mention it, there is one thing that troubles me. What made you go into the darkroom anyway?'

Increasingly petulant, she said, 'I live here, don't I? I didn't realise it was out of bounds.'

'Don't be daft. The studio and the darkroom are work areas. They have nothing to do with my private life, and I just wondered why you were looking in there, that's all.'

Petulance gave way to haughtiness. 'Perhaps it's better if I don't, in future,' she said. 'Who knows what I might find?'

So it went on for the rest of the day. By night-time, she was in a less truculent mood, but Barry was left with serious doubts about their future together. Meanwhile, life had to go on. He had a session to do with Claret the following day, when, thankfully, Belinda would be at work.

By sheer coincidence, the subject of dodgy photographs cropped up the next morning, and it had nothing to do with Belinda or anyone else he knew. He was in the studio when he heard the bell on the outer door, so he went into the office to find a tall, well-dressed man in a smart, flared suit. He was fair-haired with an angular, neatly-trimmed moustache.

'Can I help you?'

'Mm,' he mused. It could have meant anything. He was stooping to look at the window display, which consisted of some pictures from the latest wedding and a couple of dressy shots from Claret's portfolio. 'Nice pictures,' he said eventually.

'Thank you. Are you looking to have some work done?'

He nodded slowly, as if trying to make up his mind about something. 'I think I could put some work your way.' His accent was North Kent, a kind of modified cockney, and having straightened up, he held himself very erect, accentuating his height.

'Really?'

He seemed to be sizing Barry up, because he obviously wasn't in a hurry to tell him what he had in mind. Instead, he asked, 'How's business?'

'Not bad, considering the way things are.'

He nodded again. 'Things are tough all right, especially in this trade.' He was looking directly at the work diary, which was open on the desk, and the blank spaces were all too obvious. Whilst things were no longer dire, Barry still felt some embarrassment that the man had noticed them.

'I'm doing all right,' he insisted, now quite suspicious of the visitor's intentions.

After all the preamble, the man suddenly came to the point. 'Have you ever done any glamour work?'

'No, it's not my kind of thing.'

'I could give you a lot of business,' he said.

'I've already told you I don't do tit and bum work.' He found the man particularly insistent, and when he spoke again, he confirmed Barry's suspicion.

'I'm talking about adult glamour. Specialised stuff.'

'Do you mean hard-core porn?'

'Call it what you like,' he said, 'it pays well. You wouldn't need to worry about this,' he indicated the work diary. 'I find myself short of a photographer and I'm looking for a talented chap who wants to earn some real money for a change. Do you do cine work as well?'

'Yes, but I'm not interested. As I said, I'm doing all right, and I don't want to get into porn of any kind.'

He seemed unperturbed and his flat expression remained unchanged. 'It's up to you,' he said. 'The offer's open. Give me a ring if you change your mind.' He reached for one of Barry's business cards and scribbled a name and a number on the back. Naturally, his wasn't the kind of business he wanted to advertise by having his own cards printed. Seeing, then, that one of Barry's desk drawers was open he slid the card across the desk and dropped it in. Barry found the familiarity of the gesture annoying, and he slammed the drawer shut before opening the outer door very pointedly. 'Good day to you,' he said, and the man walked out, expressionless as before and without a word. Barry returned to the studio to hang up the stuff from the costumiers for the afternoon session with Claret. The only details of size they'd been interested in had been 'size 10' and 'height 5ft 9ins', and he was a little concerned about the fit, so he quickly put the morning's visit out of his mind. It wasn't the first time he'd been approached in that way, and it could easily happen again. He turned his attention to the dresses and made notes about lighting.

Claret finished her coffee and put her cup down, ready to begin. 'What are we going to do, then?' Barry would always give her full marks for enthusiasm. She looked terrific, too, after her session with the hairdresser and the beautician. Her make-up was perfect for the Edwardian period, and her long, dark hair had been set in loose ringlets that bounced against her face, so that he could hardly wait to see her in costume.

'Let's try this one,' he said, taking her through to the changing room and showing her a dark green silk dress trimmed with lace.

She held the dress up to look at it and beamed with delight. 'This is lovely.' She was in such a hurry to put it on that she was half out of her jeans before he'd left the room.

She emerged after a few minutes, looking very much the part, but with the dress open at the back. 'Will you do me up, Barry? This thing's a sod to fiddle with. I don't know how they went on in them days.'

'I think the women who wore dresses like this had a maid to help them dress and undress,' he said, buttoning her up.

'I couldn't have done with that.'

'Oh, they were born to it.' He finished fastening her up and stood back to look at her. 'We'll have to pad your bust out, Claret,' he told her. 'Your kind of figure wasn't fashionable in those days.'

'What's wrong with it?'

'Nothing at all,' he laughed. 'It was *their* figures that were wrong. I suppose they had an unhealthy diet and no exercise, so they pulled themselves in with girdles, and that had the effect of pushing their bust upward. You'll be okay with a bit of padding.'

'Right.' She disappeared into the changing room and came out holding her shirt. 'Will this do?'

'I should think so.'

'Will you undo me again?'

He unfastened the buttons almost to the waist and she began to tuck the shirt into the front, smoothing it beneath her bust as she did so, and it occurred to him that, had Belinda been there, she would have been none too pleased.

Finally, satisfied with the effect, they started the session. Claret got straight into the part, posing in a creditably ladylike way, even if the mock-genteel accent with which she delivered her impromptu commentary lacked something. She was entertaining though, as she always was, and the afternoon passed quickly.

She posed for the last pictures in a white cotton dress stuffed with petticoats, and with a wide-brimmed hat. She carried a dainty parasol, and she was so taken with it that he had to ask her more than once to stop twirling it, so that he could take the picture. He'd unearthed an old backdrop that he'd never used. It was one of branches covered in white blossom, and it had always seemed too artificial for a normal portrait. He thought it might work in this sequence, but the more he looked at it the more contrived it seemed.

'I don't like it, Claret. I mean the backdrop. It's too sugary for words.'

'Oh!' Clearly, she was enjoying herself in the pose.

'If we use this costume, it needs to be outside.'

'When does it have to go back?'

'The costume? Don't worry about that. I'll come to an arrangement with them.'

She was happy again. 'That's all right then,' she agreed in her mock-posh accent. We'll do a session *ite*-side with it.' She gave the parasol an extra twirl and strutted back

119

and forth, waving a gloved hand and fluttering her lashes at him.

When the session was over, she came out of the changing room, looking strangely out of place again in her casual clothes and Edwardian make-up. 'I still haven't had any luck with the agencies,' she told him. 'Still, all I can do is keep on trying.'

'That's right.'

Regarding him seriously, she said, 'You've done an awful lot for me, Barry.'

'Oh no,' he assured her. 'It's a reciprocal arrangement.'

'I don't care if it *is* a repris... what you said... arrangement. You've done a lot for me.' She put her arms round him, kissing him extravagantly on the cheek just as the door opened and Belinda walked in. What had been a moment of innocence was about to become the focus of an all-out row.

It was a row that continued for a full hour. Each time he tried to explain the truth of the situation, Belinda shouted him down, refusing to listen, or at best, appearing to hear him out and then ignoring everything he'd said, so that there was little point in his saying anything at all. It was a fiasco, and he was only relieved that the shouting had started after Claret had gone. That way he was saved unnecessary embarrassment, except that she must have heard the initial explosion as she walked up the street. He was sure everyone else in the neighbourhood had. Then the whole thing was made worse by Jack coming in to be fed. He'd possibly been disturbed by the commotion, but at all events, he lost no time in launching himself into his characteristic 'This-one's-a-dead-loss-Barry-let's-dump-her' routine, fiercely arching his back, growling, and fixing her with his monocular glare. In fairness, he'd been carrying a lot of resentment lately over the usurping of his sleeping quarters, so no-one could blame him for wanting to add his two pennyworth. According to Belinda, however, his behaviour was the ultimate insult, and she stormed off to the bedroom and slammed the door behind her. Jack merely turned his attention to the contents of his bowl and, having eaten his fill, went out again. He was quite adept at switching his feelings on and off.

Much later, Barry found himself wondering why Belinda was in his bed and he was on the sofa, when he heard the bedroom door open quietly, followed by approaching footsteps. He steeled himself for yet more unpleasantness, but her touch on his shoulder was soft.

'Barry,' she whispered, 'come to bed.'

He hesitated, weighing up his options. The row was fresh in his mind, and he wasn't yet in the mood for reconciliation. On the other hand, the sofa was uncomfortable and he already had a stiff neck. 'All right,' he agreed, 'but no arguing. We can talk tomorrow.' There was no reply, so he assumed she was in agreement, and he got up from the sofa and followed her to bed.

He was lying there, wondering just what he was going to say in the morning, that he hadn't already said, when she moved against him, stroking and kissing him, as if the shouting and recrimination had never taken place. After all that had happened, he decided that it was best to go along with it, so he responded. At least, he responded as far as he could. The problem was that, despite Belinda's attentions, nothing was stirring. Each time he closed his eyes and concentrated on the matter in hand, all he could see was Jack baring his teeth and arching his back. Try as he would, he couldn't make the image disappear.

'Sorry,' he said finally, 'it's not going to happen.'

'Why not? Just because we've had a few words?'

'It's not that. I can't. It must have something to do with being bitten by that gander.' It seemed like a good enough excuse for the moment.

'But you haven't complained about it lately.'

Hell, she was arguing again. 'Let's just go to sleep,' he suggested.

She said nothing, but turned over abruptly and left him in comparative peace.

When Barry surfaced in the morning, she was already up. He staggered, half-asleep, into the sitting room and stumbled over a heavy suitcase. It seemed she had got up early to pack her belongings.

# 14

# Willing Hands

Apart from an *al fresco* session with Claret pencilled in for Wednesday afternoon, Barry had no appointments the following week. He'd left it so deliberately because he was on call again, and there was nothing worse than having to disappoint a client at short notice. Even so, he wasn't about to sit around brooding about the events of the past few days. Yet again, it seemed that fate had rescued him from another disastrous relationship. He decided to start the week in a positive way, by arranging a haircut, so he sauntered up the High Street to speak to Ellen, the hairdresser.

When he arrived, she was parking an elderly woman beneath a dryer, and the only other person in the salon was Alison, Ellen's niece. He knew her quite well from a couple of occasions when she'd stayed with Ellen, and she'd ended up at his place, doing odd jobs for him. She was thumbing her way absently through a magazine, and she looked thoroughly bored until she noticed him. It was likely that any familiar face would have been welcome. He had a few words with her before Ellen handed a magazine to the woman and turned to greet him.

'Barry! How did the session go?'

He gathered his thoughts. He'd almost forgotten about it with everything else that had happened. 'Really well, thanks, Ellen. You did a superb job on Claret's hair.'

123

'Thank you. She looked beautiful, didn't she? How's your girlfriend, by the way?'

It was funny that she should mention them in the same breath. 'No more, I'm afraid. She's gone.'

'Gone? Why?' It was typical of Ellen that if she wanted to know something, however personal, she simply asked.

'There was a misunderstanding that was never cleared up.'

'Oh dear.'

He decided to change the subject before she quizzed him further. 'I'd like to make an appointment,' he said.

'Right.' She made her way to the counter where she kept the book. 'When would you like it?' Thinking quickly, she said, 'Actually, if you're not busy, I can do you now while this lady's under the dryer.'

'Perfect.' He slipped his jacket off and sat with his back to a basin while she arranged a towel around his neck. Having his hair washed was always one of life's minor luxuries. Ellen performed an extremely thorough scalp massage, leaving it tingling and invigorated. Also, for her relatively slim figure, she had a generous bust, which delivered the ultimate face massage all the time she was rubbing the shampoo in. There was nothing erotic about it, really; it was just bosomy and pleasant. He submitted to this self-indulgence, revelling in the process. The radio was playing softly. Diana Ross and The Supremes were singing 'Baby Love', and he was almost purring when Ellen wrapped his hair up in a towel and led him to a chair across the room, where conversation was resumed.

As she combed his hair out, she asked, 'How's business?'

'Not too bad really. I'm on call this week so I haven't made any appointments, apart from Claret, that is, and she doesn't count as an appointment.'

'I know what you mean. Some jobs are family, aren't they? Speaking of family,' she went on, 'you can see I've got Alison again.' She waved her comb in the girl's direction.

'Yes, we had a chat when I arrived.' He looked at Alison in the mirror. She was a pathetic little thing, thin and freckled, with short, straight hair. From past conversations, he reckoned she would be nine or ten, but she looked younger.

'I'm looking after her this week because her mum's in hospital,' Ellen explained.

'Oh dear.'

'She'll be fine.' There was an exaggerated confidence in her voice that Barry assumed was for Alison's benefit. 'She's having a hysterectomy, and they're routine nowadays, aren't they?'

'Oh yes.' He hadn't the vaguest idea what a hysterectomy was, but he was happy to help play it down.

'Poor little soul, though,' Ellen pointed again at Alison's reflection in the mirror, 'she's going to have a boring time of it. I have to work, and she has no one to play with. It's half-term holidays this week, so she's stuck here all day. You haven't any jobs that need doing, have you, Barry?'

He'd suspected she was leading up to that. Still, she was right about the poor kid having a boring week ahead of her. 'Yes,' he said, 'I've got some jobs for her.' He could see the interest on Alison's face reflected in the mirror. She had enjoyed pottering around the studio before. 'What do you say, Alison? D'you fancy earning a few bob this week?'

She came over to his chair, the magazine forgotten. 'Can I?'

'Of course. I need an assistant, and Wesley won't be in until Saturday.' In truth, he welcomed the company. They both needed a diversion.

'You don't need to pay her, Barry,' said Ellen.

'Oh yes I do. I pay everyone who works for me.' Business wasn't exactly booming, but he reckoned a bit of pocket money wouldn't make much difference. 'The only problem I can see is that I may be called out by the police. If that happens, I'll have to send her back to you, but you're not far away.'

'No, that's fine. It's really good of you. Now,' said Ellen wielding her scissors, 'what's it to be? On the collar and just over the tops of your ears again?'

He'd actually intended for some time to give the dark-room a thorough cleaning. Dust was always to be avoided in developing and printing, and the weekly tidying session with Wesley only postponed the full treatment. However, with Alison there, he had no excuse. Also, it was safe to let her in now. Belinda's last discovery had led him to remove any material of a remotely questionable nature. He scrounged a pair of rubber gloves for her from Ellen, several sizes too large for her, but essential where chemicals had dripped, and set her on washing shelves and cupboards. She did the job well, too, despite being distracted by Jack who had mysteriously returned, following Belinda's departure. The distraction was that, for once, he behaved like a normal cat and insisted on checking all the newly-cleared spaces and interiors. That meant climbing into each cupboard as it was emptied and getting in the way of the cleaning. It presented Barry with an opportunity for a photograph, though, and with some black and white film left on a roll after the session with Claret, he was able to take advantage of it. It wasn't a distinguished profile, but a picture of two backsides: Alison's as she went down on all fours to mop out a floor-level cupboard, and Jack's, with his tail aloft as he stood beside her, peering inside. For a 'candid', it made a good picture, a bit of fun, and later, when he'd developed and printed it, he put it with the rest of the collection.

It was a useful day, made more pleasurable when Ellen phoned to tell Alison that her mum's operation had been performed, and that she would be able to visit her the next day. The rest of the week went extremely well, too, especially the afternoon with Claret, who made friends quite naturally with Alison. The weather held up and they were able to get some useful outdoor shots. By this time, Alison was taking her role as assistant seriously, insisting on taking light readings for him and helping to hold a sheet round Claret while she changed costumes. Seeing the two of them together, it occurred to Barry that it would be an excellent idea to find a second model. Individual photographs were fine for a while, but some variety was needed. He would have to think hard about it. In the meantime, Claret was doing an excellent job and, short of going through an agency and paying ridiculous fees, he couldn't imagine himself finding anyone to match her.

It wasn't just in modelling that she excelled either. Being on the late shift that Friday, she spent the morning with Alison and him at the zoo park at Bekesbourne. It was an example of Claret's generous and guileless nature, that he found totally appealing. She had helped to make the week enjoyable, undemanding and uncomplicated. It seemed right that they should round off their Friday morning out, as well as the week, by having lunch at the bookshop.

It was by far the pleasantest lunchtime Barry had spent there since before Jack's escapade. As Guy wasn't around, Lucy came through to join them, and the atmosphere quickly became reminiscent of the old days. It possibly helped, as well, that Barry was in a particularly good mood, something that Lucy noticed straight away.

'You're looking pleased with life, Barry.'

'Yes, we've just had a smashing time, taking photographs at the zoo park. In fact, it's been an excellent week, and I've only been called out twice. They were both traffic accidents, and there was nothing really horrible, so as you say, I'm pretty pleased.'

'And how's Belinda?'

'In the past, basically. We've gone our separate ways.' He saw Claret looking uncomfortable. She'd apologised several times since the unfortunate event, even though he'd insisted that it wasn't her fault, so he squeezed her hand under the table.

'I'm sorry to hear that,' said Lucy.

'Don't be,' he assured her, 'there was no future in it.'

Lucy was glancing oddly at Claret, no doubt noticing her embarrassment. She looked back at Barry, and he shook his head minutely. He was sure Claret hadn't noticed anything, and the conversation was interrupted, anyway, by Alison whispering in Claret's ear, and Claret pointing towards the door to the garden, where a sign said, 'Toilet to Rear of Garden.' It was an archaic feature of the place that Lucy found irritating. Claret waited until they were alone before explaining that Alison didn't read very well.

Barry asked, 'How do you know that?'

'She told me this morning at the zoo. There's a lot of reading to do at that place, you know.'

'I'd never thought about it.'

'Never mind. She enjoyed it just the same.' She checked quickly that Alison was still out of earshot and added, 'This is something different for her as well. She's only done this sort of thing when she's been with you.'

'Really?' He glanced at Lucy, who seemed as surprised as he was.

'Oh yes,' Claret went on, 'she told me before we came in. I don't think her mum and dad are all that well-off. You can tell by the way she's been this week. The way she's talked about it, you'd think she'd been in Majorca for a fortnight, she's enjoyed it so much.'

Lucy shook her head sadly. 'That makes me feel awful, Claret,' she said.

'Why?'

'Because I take so much for granted, and I never think that what I've got is all that special. I mean the reading thing alone is something I've never thought about.'

'There's a lot like her.'

'Numbers have always been my weakness,' said Barry. 'They still are, really.'

'If I could take pictures like you do, I wouldn't worry about sums,' said Claret.

'But Alison was taking readings for me this week.'

'That's numbers, isn't it? It's just things like *f* four and fractions of a second and that sort of thing. Maybe you should get her to do all your number work for you.'

They all laughed, and that was the end of the conversation, because Alison returned, and Michelle came to take their order. Lucy was still deeply thoughtful.

Claret steered Alison through the menu by suggesting various things in a way that showed remarkable tact for a girl of eighteen, and Michelle left with the order. Barry watched her go, and turned to Claret to say, 'How would you feel about working with another model on these period things, Claret?'

'It's fine by me.'

Lucy looked at him quizzically, so he explained. 'We need more variety in the pictures, and I think another face would give us that.'

She nodded and asked, 'Have you anyone in mind?'

'Yes, but I haven't asked her yet. Michelle photographs well. I've seen some work Wesley's done with her and I reckon she'd be ideal.'

'Right, go ahead and ask her.'

He did as soon as she was free, but she was uncertain.

'Go on,' he said, 'you'll be fine.'

'But I've never done it before.'

'Yes you have. I know you've done a sitting for Wesley and you did it well.' Remembering the nature of the photograph, he added cryptically, 'It'll all be ultra-respectable, buttoned-up-to-the-neck stuff. I'll bring Wesley in on it, and he can work on it as well.'

She hesitated for a moment, possibly embarrassed that he'd seen the picture Wesley had taken, and said, 'Okay, I'll give it a go.'

'Good girl.'

'You'll be fine,' Claret told her. 'Barry will tell you just what to do. It's easy.' That seemed to give her confidence because she looked much more relaxed, even when Alison regarded her with a professional eye, perhaps wondering how her blonde hair might look beneath the studio lights.

The rest of the meal passed as pleasantly as it had begun,

until Claret looked at her watch and groaned apologetically. 'I have to go to work. I wish I hadn't. This has been so nice.'

Alison looked up at her hurriedly. 'What time is it?'

'Nearly half past one. I have to go.'

'My Auntie said I had to be back by two o'clock. She's closing early to go to the hospital.'

'Don't leave now, Barry,' said Claret, getting up. 'I'll take Alison back. Honestly, it's no trouble.' She stood up, followed by Alison. 'Thanks for a lovely time.' She pushed Alison towards him, and he could see that the poor kid didn't want to go. Barry took out her money and gave it to her. 'There's your wages,' he told her. 'You've been a great help.' He meant it.

'Thanks, Barry.'

'Give him a kiss,' Claret urged her, 'he's earned it.' He leaned over to receive a peck on the cheek and then stood up as Claret inclined her cheek. It seemed to symbolise his topsy-turvy existence at the time. He watched them go together, Claret, tall, motherly and self-assured, and Alison, tiny and vulnerable. Lucy seemed to read his thoughts. 'Claret's rather special, isn't she?'

'Yes, she is,' he agreed, 'but there's nothing in it.'

'No?' Clearly, she wasn't convinced.

'No, she's very young.'

'But she has qualities ahead of her years.'

'True,' he agreed. 'I think of her as precociously immature, but in the nicest way. It may be because she had responsibilities thrust upon her early in life.' He told her about Claret's demanding father and brothers.

'How awful.' Guiltily, she glanced at her watch. 'The doorbell hasn't gone once, but I should really get back to the shop. Bring your coffee and join me if you like.'

He did, and they continued to chat. At one stage, Lucy said, 'Autumn's upon us already. You know, I really think the dining room would benefit from having some bright, summery pictures on the walls before the weather grows colder. My mother used to hang paintings by a local artist, but he's long since died, I'm afraid.'

'I could let you have some of my pictures from the Dales,' said Barry. 'It's anybody's guess what the locals will make of them, but they might at least brighten the place up.'

'I'm inclined to agree. Thank you, Barry.'

He had to go home eventually and, when he stood up, Lucy came with him to the door. He suspected that she, too, had gained something from the day, and he felt that an old wound, albeit a superficial one, was almost healed.

⌇⌇⌇❖⌇⌇⌇

Some weeks later, he came across DCI Jackson and, naturally, he asked him about the Pauline Francis case.

'It's a familiar scene,' he told him. 'All the leads we thought we had have led us nowhere. Between ourselves, we have no suspects, and the only evidence we have confirms our suspicion that she was on the game.' He saw Barry's expression and smiled knowingly. 'Yes, it seems she wasn't as innocent as we thought, although God knows the poor girl didn't deserve what she got. We're still hoping someone will remember something, but experience makes me pessimistic.' He shook his head. 'This kind of thing's not unusual.'

# 15

## January 1977

# The Bleak Mid-Winter

G oing home for Christmas was very pleasant. Barry was able to spend time with his family without the rush associated with his usual flying visits, and he returned to Kent in a relaxed and optimistic frame of mind. He also left with an expanded waistline and a car full of cakes and other offerings. It would be a good start to the New Year for Wesley. The holiday hadn't been without some drama, however, and he was incredulous when his mother informed him that his father had 'put his back out with the wrestling.' His father? Wrestling? But it turned out that he'd sustained the injury at his own fireside and in front of the television set. In a moment of triumphant euphoria he'd leapt up and immediately been seized with pain. He spent the whole of Christmas at an attitude of ninety degrees. Of course, it hadn't diminished his passion for the entertainment, and Barry had to hear the story of how that brute Bruno Elrington had finally encountered justice, being knocked out cold in the fourth round by that honest sportsman Tibor Szakacs. The problem was that every time Barry's father excited himself at the memory of it, his back twinged again, causing him to gasp with pain, so that everyone laughed involuntarily and he was offended.

It was still good to be back at the flat, though, and he was particularly pleased that Lucy had insisted on feeding

Jack in his absence, despite his earlier indiscretion. It meant that they were friends again, and likely to remain so, as Jack had behaved himself this time, at least according to his own unique standards. There was other good news too. Lucy had sold several of the period prints and some of his Dales pictures as well, so that they were most of the way towards covering their outlay.

Barry's portrait business was less healthy, so he was particularly grateful for the police work. It was regular, quite well paid and, with one exception, the cases hadn't been too horrendous. He still thought about Pauline Francis occasionally. It wasn't surprising, as her case was as difficult to forget as it was to understand.

About a week after his return, things came to a halt, quite literally, as the country was hit by blizzards. The weather was unusually severe in the south-east and, in that little corner of Kent, there were snowdrifts seven or eight feet deep in places. It wasn't too long before one of the local farmers made a single track through Woodley High Street, but there was still a lot of clearing to be done and, being accustomed to the more severe winters in the north of England, Barry was impatient about the time it was taking. Even so, he was comparatively mobile. With the advantage of a sack of building sand in his boot, courtesy of Gavin Peckett, he was able to make whatever journeys he needed. In general, however, people were staying at home, and that meant no business. One frequent visitor however, was Claret who had taken to dropping in at odd times whether or not there was work to be done, simply for coffee and a chat. He suspected, also, that she felt in need of support. She'd had no luck at all with the agencies she'd tried so far and, in consequence, she was feeling worn down. As Barry saw it, she was aiming too high. He'd looked at the names she'd tried, that numbered among the top agencies in the country, and he'd warned her against being over-ambitious at that early stage, but it seemed he'd made no impression. She wanted to become the new face of Chanel overnight. He could have used his limited influence on her behalf with some of the agencies who handled work of a more modest nature, but he knew that she'd prefer to achieve what she could by her own efforts. He was saddened to see her disappointed, but there was a limit to what he could do.

It was after one such visit from her that he decided to brave the sub-zero winds and cross the road to The Three Tuns, where, as he'd expected, he found Gavin Peckett. He was unsure whether Gavin was propping up the bar, as usual, or whether it was supporting him. Either way, he looked exhausted, and judging from the grubby state of his tartan shirt and disreputable jeans, Barry got the impression that he'd come straight from work.

'I'm absolutely knackered,' Gary told him after he'd bought him a pint. 'This weather's good for trade but I'm mending bursts in my sleep.'

'It's no good for *my* trade,' Barry told him.

'Take up plumbing, my son,' he said, yawning. 'You could do it as a seasonal thing.'

'If you're so tired,' Barry asked him, 'why don't you crash out at home like a normal person?'

'I will,' he said, 'just as soon as I've received payment for services rendered.' He indicated the landlord, who responded with an eyes-to-the-ceiling expression. 'I did an emergency job for Harry this morning, a burst in the cellar, and he said that the next time I came in, I needn't buy a drink all night.' He grinned mischievously. 'So I'm collecting tonight, before the tight old sod forgets he said it.'

'It makes sense,' Barry agreed.

Gavin turned to the landlord and raised his eyelids and his empty glass. Harry took down two fresh glasses and said, 'Barry's is to pay for, Gavin.'

'No problem.' He counted out loose change and pushed it

across the bar. 'I'll tell you what else I did today, Barry. 'I mended a burst for your friend at the bookshop. What a job that was.'

'Why?'

He took the two pints and handed one to Barry. 'Oh, she was all right. It was Lord Snooty who got on my wick, that smooth sod who's knocking her off. He was there.'

'Yes, he goes in there a lot.'

'Well it's a shame he's got nothing better to do, the prat.' He made a gesture of disgust. 'Standing there, making clever remarks all the time about what I was doing and giving me the usual grief about plumbers always leaving their tools behind. I'm not kidding, Barry, I'd made an effort to fit the job in and I was rushed off my feet, so you can imagine what sort of mood I was in.'

'I can. I know he's tested my patience a few times.'

'Well he didn't test mine for long. I said to him, "Listen, mate, if you're so fuckin' clever why don't you get a bag of tools and join me? I've got enough work for both of us." That stopped him.'

'Good for you.' Barry found the picture pleasing. 'I've never taken him head-on, like that, but your way sounds fine.'

'I'm surprised you haven't told him what's what before now. He's not one of your favourite people, is he?'

'No, he's not,' Barry agreed, 'but I must admit I felt a bit sorry for him before I went away.'

Gavin gave him a strange look before draining his glass. 'You felt sorry for him? You must be off your nut, Barry. I reckon you'd have felt sorry for Hitler if he couldn't find a bob for the gas.'

'Maybe I'm wrong,' Barry insisted, 'but I felt sorry for him because he has very little substance. Look at what he's got. He has a good job that pays well, there's that BMW he drives, he has... well, other things as well but, in reality, he's quite insecure.'

'How d'you make that out?' He signalled Harry again in his usual effortless way.

'I had to judge a competition at the local camera club before Christmas. Actually I did it along with the manager of Fotokit, who donated the prize, but I was brought in as the professional.' He paid for the drinks and took his. 'Before the entries went in, I suggested that each one was numbered so that we didn't know whose work we were looking at, and that the only information we needed was the film type and speed, the exposure, the focal length of the lens, and anything that was unusual about the way they'd taken the shot.'

'The what length?'

'Whether it was long, short or medium,' he explained.

'Right.'

'Now, every single entry was marked with those details, but most of them had included the make and model of the camera as well, and that told its own story.'

'You've lost me.'

'I'm coming to it. The equipment was too important to them.'

'Yes,' Gavin agreed, 'a hammer's only a hammer, when all's said and done.'

'Exactly. I must say there were some excellent pictures, some quite good ones, and a few that, well, let's say the people who took them had a lot to learn. The title was *As Time Goes By*, and, as you can imagine there were some interesting interpretations.'

'I wouldn't have known where to start.'

'You would if you thought about it. Someone took a shot of the old part of Elmston and the new part side by side, which was quite good, I suppose. Then another one took a multiple exposure shot of Big Ben to make it look as if it was marching across the page. He was trying to be clever, and he cocked it up. For one thing, he hadn't used a tripod, so the images weren't level, and they weren't the same distance apart either. As well as that, the idea was totally naff. The winner, however, who turned out to be a girl of sixteen, took a picture of her grandma.'

'Her nan,' Gavin corrected him with the local dialect word.

'Sorry, I'll get the hang of the language one day. It was a picture of her nan, sitting in a fireside chair with a cup of tea, and basically staring into space. The girl had made sure that everything that needed to be was in focus, and you could see pictures from the past on the mantelpiece, obviously very important to her. The ornaments, too, looked as if they'd been there a long time, but it was the old girl's expression that was most important. She was remembering.'

'How d'you know?' Gavin could be infuriatingly hard headed.

'Because the other things in the picture suggested it.'

Gavin narrowed his eyes for a moment. 'How d'you know it was tea she was drinking, and not coffee?'

'Because an old lady in her situation, with all those things around her would be drinking tea.'

'All right.'

'Now, that picture was taken with a simple camera, bought about ten years ago for less than ten quid. If she'd used an expensive camera she might possibly have got a sharper image, but the picture would have been the same, just as good, no better and no worse. I explained that to the competitors, and I hope they remembered it. I had to give a talk at the presentation, and I was all set to talk about The Changing Scene of Photography, or some such thing, but having seen what I had, I changed it and talked about the essence of photography, how it boils down to using the imagination and seeing a picture, composition and timing, and that sort of thing. It's not about having the latest gadgets. I told them that there's many a time I've done a session and I've just not thought about my camera until I've needed to reload it. It's simply a tool. Getting hooked on the latest bits of technology for their own sake leads to gimmickry, and that's worthless. At that point, I saw Guy in the audience with his nephew. The boy was indignant, but Guy simply looked deflated. It was only afterwards I discovered that the horrible picture of Big Ben had been taken by Guy's nephew, doubtless with his uncle's help.'

Gavin looked at him flatly. 'I still don't see why you felt sorry for him.'

'Never mind,' Barry told him, 'let's have another drink.' In fact, they had several, and as it so often happened when serious talk was combined with drinking, they were both considerably the worse for it by the end of the evening.

'I'm going for a leak,' declared Gavin, none too clearly.

'I'll join you.'

Gavin seized Barry's arm and whispered loudly, 'We mustn't use the wrong bog.' He paused to burp discreetly. 'You see, I've started work on the inside ones, but all this,' he said, waving vaguely in the direction of outside, 'has inter... inperr... got in the way of it, so we have t' go outside.'

He needn't have bothered telling Barry; there was a big sign outside the door, explaining the problem, and inebriated though he was, he could still read it. They made their way outside to the old urinal and Gavin stopped him. 'Barry,' he said, 'ho... how long is it since you wrote your name in the snow?'

'I can't remember.'

'I'm going t' do it now. I'm going t' write *Gavin Peckett, Plumber and Heating Eng'neer, Registered Gas Install...*, no,' he reflected, 'I'll stop there at *Engineer*. I need a leak, but not that badly.'

'Why don't you write, *Meh...Meni...Mechanical Services Contractor?*' At least, that was what Barry thought he said.

Gavin looked at him as scathingly as he could with the impediment of drooping eyelids and said, 'Don' be silly, Barry. If you can' even say it, how the fuck d' you expect me t' spell it?' He lurched past the urinal, fumbled with his fly, and began his uro-calligraphy on the unbroken snow. He was doing quite well, but he never quite managed *Heating Engineer*. It was a good try though.

'Your turn, Barry.' he said.

Concentration wasn't easy in that state, but Barry made a conscious effort and wrote, *Barry J Craven*. Then, with a rush of bravado, framed it. 'How's that, Gavin?' There was no answer, because he was fast asleep, leaning against the wall. With some difficulty, Barry scuffed out the writing. They said it paid to advertise, but he also had his reputation to consider.

✦

He'd been thinking about his entry for the competition for some time, and it seemed to him that a large number of other photographers would be giving equal thought to theirs. He needed something that would be sufficiently unusual and original to stand out from the rest, and it seemed to him that, whilst tinted prints were hardly an original idea, his treatment of them was. It wasn't just in the way he set up the poses. He'd experimented with the printing and toning processes as well, so as to get a range of effects that gave him extra scope for creating atmosphere, mood and so on. He made up his own toner solution, and found that by varying the amount of sodium hydroxide in the mix, he could produce subtle variations of shade. It took a great deal of trial and error at first, and much of his earlier work found its way into the rubbish bin, but soon he found himself increasingly in control. His idea for generating business with period pictures was to be the basis of his entry. Of course, he'd need to get Claret and possibly Michelle in for some extra sessions, but that was easy enough.

On the business side of things, the old landscape prints were proving quite popular with Lucy's customers as well and, as long as the original photographs kept coming in, he would be able to copy and retouch them. He had the copy camera set up permanently in one corner of the darkroom, for that purpose alone. However, he couldn't say that the portrait business was thriving. Whilst people were prepared to buy odd pictures from the shop, they were reluctant to spend money on a portrait session. It was a thoroughly bad time for anyone in a luxury or leisure business and, the sooner he could win

139

some kind of acclaim and draw clients from further afield, the easier things would be.

Even so, there was a lot about life at the time that was pleasant. Claret and he had taken to calling into the bookshop quite regularly, and when things were quiet, Lucy and sometimes Michelle would join them. On Saturdays, of course, Wesley was there, too, and there was a closeness about the group that he was sure everyone felt without ever alluding to it.

Inevitably, Guy would appear for a while, but his presence wasn't the irritant it had been. His attitude had mellowed to some extent, for whatever reason. Barry couldn't imagine that his embarrassment at the photo competition was the only reason for it. Possibly he could see that Lucy enjoyed being part of a gathering that wasn't of his making, and in which he felt less than central. At all events, he was no longer a problem, and Barry continued to feel some sympathy for him, at least, until the day of the accident.

# 16

# Blues and Twos

That Saturday, Barry had been out to photograph one of Dennis Billingham's bulls, and the afternoon had been surprisingly uneventful, mainly because the geese were no more. Apparently, one of them had been found to have gizzard worm and, as it was something that was passed rapidly on to the rest, the whole flock had been destroyed. Naturally, Barry tried to sound sympathetic.

Fenella had been busy on his behalf, showing the pictures he'd taken of Mandy to her equestrian friends, and she assured him that his services would soon be in demand. By that time, Mandy was heavily in foal and he was looking forward to seeing the two of them after the foaling.

He was thinking about that when he drove into Woodley High Street, and he was surprised to see Lucy standing outside the studio, looking unusually agitated. He parked beside her and dropped the passenger window.

'Barry,' she said, sounding breathless, 'Jack's been hit by a car. Ellen's got him in the salon.'

'Jump in.'

She joined him in the car and they drove the short distance to the salon, to be met by Ellen, who was also in a state of anxiety.

'I'd have taken him to a vet,' she told him, 'but I've got clients until five-thirty. Lucy's car's off the road and she's not insured to drive mine. She was going to call a taxi if you hadn't come soon.'

'It was good of you to take him in, Ellen. Where is he?' He was anxious too. His first thought when Lucy met him was that Jack had been killed, but that obviously wasn't the case, and he wanted to get him to a vet as soon as he could.

'In the rest room.' She apologised to the woman whose hair she'd been cutting, and took them through to the tiny room she used for brewing tea and coffee. Jack was lying on a towel on the floor. He was alive – Barry could see him breathing laboriously and, every now and again, he gave a very feeble attempt at a *miaow* – but his face was a mess of blood and saliva. It was almost a re-run of the night he'd arrived at Barry's flat, except that, on that occasion, Barry had simply been moved by pity. This time, he was dealing with the little character who had been ordering his life for a year, for good or ill, and to whom he'd grown very much attached. It was horrible to see him like that. He asked Ellen if he could use her phone.

"Course you can. Do you need the phone book?'

'Yes, please.'

He followed her into the salon and found the vet's number in the directory. The girl who answered had a reassuring voice. She told Barry to bring him in straight away. As he came off the phone, he found both Ellen and her client looking at him expectantly.

'I'm taking him to the vet in Marsden,' he told them. 'It shouldn't take long, even at this time.' It was just turned five. The road would be fairly busy, but Marsden was only a few miles away.

'Let me know when you can,' said Ellen.

The woman in the chair added, 'Oh yes, I do hope he's all right.'

Barry turned to find Lucy in the doorway. She was holding Jack wrapped in the towel. 'I'll carry him while you drive,' she said.

'What about the shop?'

'Esme and Michelle are going to lock up. It's nearly closing time anyway.'

'Oh, thanks. That'll be a great help.' He turned to Ellen and thanked her again, but she just said, 'Chuck the towel away when you've finished with it. It's an old one anyway.'

Lucy slid into the passenger seat, holding Jack like a baby and talking softly to him while Barry started the engine and drove off.

'I saw it happen,' she told him. 'I don't think the driver of the car even realised he'd hit him. Poor old boy.' She stroked him, talking to him again. An emergency ambulance came tearing towards them, and Barry prayed that there hadn't been an accident on the Marsden road.

They joined the main road and he picked up speed. Then, almost immediately, the police sign, familiar to him by then, loomed in front of them. *Slow Down, Accident Ahead.* He cursed. It was just what they didn't need and, as they rounded the next bend, they saw a policeman holding up the traffic just two cars in front of them. It seemed they'd narrowly missed their turn, and would have to wait for a line of traffic to pass in the opposite direction. Lucy said nothing, but Barry saw her close her eyes in a gesture of hopelessness. He couldn't let this happen. He leapt out and secured the attention of the policeman, who was talking into his mobile radio. He recognised Barry and spoke again into the set before turning back to him. 'We'll just let these few through, Mr Craven, and then you can get in. It's been bloody madness here, but at least we've got the injured driver away.'

Barry stared at him for a moment before realising he must have mistaken him for the rota photographer. At all events, it was his mistake and Barry was going to take advantage of it. He rejoined Lucy in the car, and when the officer came forward and beckoned to him, he took off. Out of the corner of his eye, he saw Lucy staring in surprise, but there was no time to explain. They reached the scene of the accident, and he dropped his window to speak to the senior officer. Immediately, he recognised Inspector Charnley, who gave him an odd look.

'This isn't your week, is it?'

'No, I'm sorry, Inspector. I'm sure the rota man will be along soon, but this is an emergency. I'm taking my cat to the vet in Marsden High Street.'

Charnley stared at him, and then looked into the car and saw Jack. It was then that Barry realised he was human after all.

'Poor little thing. All right then, off you go. No, just a minute.' He spoke to the driver of one of the traffic cars and then said to Barry. 'All right, you've got an escort.'

They followed the police car, with its lights and sirens going, and reached the vet's surgery in no time, where a nurse took Jack into a treatment room. Barry and Lucy sat nervously and helplessly in the waiting room.

When Jack had been examined and x-rayed, the vet returned to the waiting room to speak to them.

'I don't think there's any internal injury,' he said, 'but his lower jaw's badly fractured and there are some dental problems. If you want me to go ahead I'll operate on him after surgery.'

Barry agreed, and the vet went to speak to a colleague, leaving him with Jack. He was relieved by what the vet had told him, but Jack was still in a dreadful state. Barry stroked him and spoke to him softly. 'Jack, little mate, you can't give up now. Not after all we've been through together. You've got to come out of your corner fighting.'

Suddenly, he was aware of a hand on his arm, and he looked round. The vet had left the door open and Lucy had come in. 'He'll be all right,' he told her, trying to exude more confidence than he felt. 'They're going to operate on him tonight.' He put an arm round her, and she laid her face against his. He wasn't sure who needed the comfort more, but it did plenty for him.

Eventually a nurse came to take Jack away. 'Don't worry,' she said, 'he'll be okay now. Give us a ring after nine o'clock tomorrow morning, and we'll tell you when you can come in and see him.'

They walked back to the car in silence. Eventually, Lucy asked, 'What time is it? My watch has stopped.'

'A quarter to seven.'

'As late as that?'

'Yes, I was just thinking, as neither of us has eaten yet, shall we call in for something on the way back?'

She looked at him doubtfully. 'I'm afraid I'm not terribly good company tonight.'

'Neither am I, so why don't we go and eat somewhere? If we're both miserable it's not going to make any difference.'

'All right,' she agreed, 'but not The Three Tuns, please.'

'Fine.' It seemed odd, considering she spent so many evenings there, but it wasn't the place Barry had in mind anyway. 'The King's Head's just up the road from here. D'you know it?'

'I don't think so.'

'It's okay.'

'Let's go there then.'

The King's Head was very ordinary. It served basic stodge, and the beer was no worse than in most places, but it was always cheerful. It was a welcoming place and, on that night, it was the ideal place to be. Lucy had been withdrawn at first, and he naturally put it down to her having seen the accident and endured the nail-biting wait for his return. He'd never known her so quiet, and he found it unnerving, but she began to relax a little after a while, to the extent of making conversation.

She asked, 'What is it about this beer that you don't like?'

'It's weak, tasteless, and it has an excuse for a head that has all the substance of a politician's promise.'

She gave a thin smile. 'You're a typical northerner, Barry.' Then, leaving aside his feelings about the local ale, she said, 'I look at your pictures and I think I'd like to go there one day.'

'You should.'

'Maybe I shall.' She smiled weakly again and it seemed to him she was still preoccupied.

'I'm terribly grateful for what you did tonight, Lucy,' he said.

'It's nothing. I mean, Jack's rather special, isn't he?'

'He is, but even so, I've been amazed at what people have done. You, of course, but Esme and Michelle looking after the shop, Ellen taking Jack in when she had a client, and as for old Charnley giving us an escort....'

'Yes, there are *some* genuine people about.'

'What do you mean?'

She took a deep breath and exhaled loudly before she spoke. 'When the accident happened, the first person I contacted was Guy. With my car off the road, I thought he might just do the decent thing. I checked first that he wasn't with a client. Had he been, I couldn't have expected him to help, but no, he was free all right. He simply didn't want to know about it. All that concerned him was that we were due to go out for the evening, and anything else might make us late.' Her tone was flat and without emotion.

'You were supposed to be out with him this evening?'

'Yes, but I can safely say that I shan't be going anywhere with him, ever again. We're finished.'

So that was it. He regarded her with some curiosity. 'Surely that wasn't because of Jack?'

'No,' she smiled grimly. 'It had been going to happen for some time. Today was just the last straw.' She pushed her plate away. 'I'll tell you about it, but not tonight, Barry. If you don't mind, I'd just like to go home.'

They drove home almost in silence, When they arrived, he dropped her outside the bookshop and thanked her again. She touched his hand and said, 'Let me know about Jack.'

Barry was wide-awake by seven-thirty and he lay in bed watching the first hint of weak, January sunlight creep between the curtains, giving the room a grey, sombre character. Images of the previous night and mainly of Jack returned, and he slid out of bed to pull the curtains aside. The effect was still gloomy, so he switched on the room light. That made it marginally better. He'd been encouraged to some extent by what the vet had told him. At least, it seemed, there was no damage to Jack's internal organs, but he'd looked pretty awful all the same. He rubbed his eyes and went into the kitchen to put the kettle on. He could never have believed that he'd be so concerned about a cat. They'd kept them at home, but none of them had ever been a major concern for him. Jack, though, was somehow different. Lucy had been right when she said that he was special. He lit a cigarette and inhaled the smoke gratefully. Having abstained for three days, he'd gone into The Three Tuns and bought a packet from the machine as soon as he'd dropped Lucy at the bookshop.

That was something else, the end of her and Guy. It had taken him completely by surprise, although, for him at least, the news had been eclipsed by the trauma of Jack's accident.

He emerged eventually from the shower, and shaved, feeling slightly more human. He put it down to the tea and the cigarette, so he put the kettle on again and lit another cigarette. It was a little after eight, which meant that he could phone the surgery in another hour. He took the tea into his bedroom and began to dress.

The hands of the clock seemed almost to have stopped turning but, eventually, he was able to pick up the phone and dial the number of the surgery. It seemed to ring for ages, and he remembered it was Sunday. There would probably only be one or two people there. He was about to put the phone down to try again later when someone answered. It was a girl's voice, possibly a nurse. He told her who he was and made his enquiry.

'Oh, Jack,' she said, 'he's fine. I looked at him a few minutes ago and he was asleep, but that's a good thing.'

147

'He's really all right?' He felt that he had to have it confirmed, to be absolutely sure.

'Yes, Mr Davis operated on him last night. He had to wire his jaw but it was quite straightforward.'

'He wired his jaw? What does that mean?' He had visions of Jack's head encaged in a wire harness.

'It's to fasten the bones together,' she explained, 'to help them knit. You won't be able to tell the difference.'

'Oh thank you,' he breathed, 'thank you very much. That's such a relief.'

'There's nothing to worry about,' she told him. 'We'll need to keep an eye on him for a few hours, and Mr Davis will look at him later on, but you should be able to take him home tonight. You can come in and see him this morning if you like. It's up to you.'

'That's wonderful. Thank you again.' He replaced the phone and sat back in relief. He had to tell Ellen and Lucy but, just for the moment, he sat there enjoying the knowledge that there was no longer anything to worry about. He lit another cigarette, his third that day, and he'd normally have been plagued with guilt, but he didn't care. He strode across the room and looked outside. Guy's car was parked outside the bookshop, and he decided to phone Ellen first. It wouldn't surprise him to learn that Guy had cobbled up some kind of reconciliation with Lucy, in which case she wouldn't want to be disturbed just then.

He managed to contact Ellen, who sounded almost as relieved as he was. She hadn't had much to do with Jack apart from seeing him about the place, but she'd been very concerned. He thanked her again for taking him in, gave her the news and then rang off. Now it was Lucy's turn. He looked through the window again and saw that Guy's car had gone. Possibly she'd gone somewhere with him. There was no way of knowing, short of calling on her. After a moment's thought, he decided to phone her instead. If she was upset, for whatever reason, it would be easier that way for both of them. He'd have left it until later, but she'd made a point of asking him to let her know, so he had to. He found the number in the book. It wasn't one that he'd needed in the past, but to delay making the call, he transferred it to his diary. He hesitated again, and then dialled the number. She answered almost immediately.

'Lucy, it's Barry. I haven't caught you at a bad time, have I?'

'No, no, not at all.'

He wasn't convinced, but once started, he had to continue. 'I phoned the surgery,' he told her, 'and Jack's okay. They said I could go in and see him this morning, and I'll probably be allowed to bring him home tonight. Isn't that amazing?'

'Lovely. You must be terribly relieved.'

'Oh, I am.'

'When are you going?'

'Any time now, I suppose.'

'Wait for me, will you? I'd like to come with you if you don't mind. I'll be with you in a few minutes.'

She hadn't sounded exactly full of life, so it seemed that Barry's earlier interpretation of Guy's visit might have been wide of the mark, in which case he was surprised that she could even think about going to the surgery with him. It was very odd, but he had no doubt he'd find out more quite soon.

In fact, they were well on their way to Marsden when she brought up the subject of Guy's visit. She'd been very quiet, and he'd been reluctant to mention the matter. She was bound to have a lot on her mind.

'I'm sorry I wasn't very sociable last night,' she said.

'Don't be. It's quite understandable, and I wasn't in the mood for a party either.'

She gave a sigh of impatience. 'He came round this morning.'

'I know,' he said, 'I saw the car.'

'He said he was calling to find out if I wanted him to take me to the cash and carry tomorrow.'

'That was a bit lame, wasn't it?'

'Oh, it was his feeble way of trying to patch things up.'

'And did you?'

'Absolutely not. It had gone way beyond that. I told him I had no intention of seeing him again.'

He glanced across quickly and noted that the engagement ring was missing from her finger. She obviously meant it. 'I'm sorry,' he said, 'for your sake, that is.'

'Thank you.' She touched his arm lightly.

They continued in silence for a few minutes, and then he said, 'You know, if you do need a lift to the cash and carry, I'm quite happy to do it.'

'Oh, would you? That would be a real help. Thank you.' Suddenly, unaccountably, she began to laugh quietly so that he looked at her in alarm.

She smiled at him and said, 'That brings the conversation down to earth, doesn't it?'

'I'm sorry.'

'No, no, it's just what I needed.' They went on their way in a lighter mood.

The nurse led them into a room full of cages containing animals of various species. Barry looked around, unable to see Jack at first, but the nurse unfastened one of the cages at floor level and lifted him out. He was still a mess, but a healthier mess. His chin had been shaved for the operation and it bore a line of ugly black stitches. Most prominent of all though, was a wide, conical, protective collar, which left Barry undecided whether he resembled an unlikely saint or a novelty table lamp, but whatever the effect, he was glad to see him. He took him from the nurse and stroked him. His *miaow*

was a pathetic affair, but it was probably painful for him to open his mouth too wide.

'He'll be uncomfortable for a few days,' said the nurse, 'and he'll need liquidised food. We had to extract his upper fangs because they were broken, but the most painful thing will be his jaw.'

Barry handed him to Lucy and watched as he tried to hook his forepaws over her shoulders. His plastic collar kept getting in the way, and in the end, he settled for eye contact. It must have satisfied him, because he was purring. It was a welcome sound.

Eventually they put him back into his cage and Barry made arrangements to collect him at the end of the day. On the way to the car, Lucy said, 'I won't come with you tonight if you don't mind. I just wanted to see him. I've got people coming over this afternoon so I'll be quite busy.'

'Fine. You've done plenty already.'

After a little thought, she said, 'I really think you should let me look after Jack for the next few days. I mean, I'll be around all the time, and if he has to have liquidised food, where better for him to be than in a place that has a kitchen with a blender?' It made sense, and he had to agree.

He had an unexpected visit from Claret that afternoon. He'd called at Sainsbury's on the way back from the surgery with Lucy, and Claret wasn't there, so he assumed she was having a day off. She was horrified when he told her about Jack and, having heard the whole story, insisted on going with him to collect him. It was quite surprising. For a free-spirited bundle of fur and bad habits, he'd made a remarkable number of friends. Not everyone could have known that, though, and Barry got an old-fashioned look from the veterinary nurse when he arrived with Claret instead of Lucy.

Mr Davis, the vet, was in the surgery, so Barry had an opportunity to thank him properly.

'He'll be just fine,' he said. 'Give him food in liquid form for a week and then bring him back to have his stitches out. He'll be all right with solids after that.'

'Even with his fangs missing?'

'Oh yes, he'll manage. They always do. It takes a lot for a cat to starve to death, believe me. The only slight problem could be that his jaws may not always come together as neatly as they did, and he could have the appearance at times of having a hare lip.'

It was a shame. He looked odd already with his missing eye, but at least he would be well again. 'I see,' he said. 'A friend of mine's going to look after him for a few days. She keeps a teashop, and she'll be on hand to see to him, so there's no problem with the feeding.'

'It sounds to me as if he's going to live like a king.'

'He always does. It's his second home, and I can't blame him for adopting it. When you live over a photographer's studio and there's a teashop almost next door, where do you go to eat?'

Mr Davis looked at him sharply. 'Are you a photographer?'

'Yes.'

'Have you done any medical photography?'

'Yes, I do forensic photography for the police, and that involves some pathological work.'

'Excellent,' he said, 'I may be able to offer you some work of a different kind if you're interested.'

Business-hungry as ever, Barry was certainly interested as well as surprised. It was an ill wind, but best of all, he still had Jack.

# 17

# Recuperation

In the week that followed, Barry naturally called at the bookshop every day to see Jack, and he was rewarded before long with signs of his recovery. He imagined at first that Jack might be frustrated by his temporary loss of independence. He was a macho tom, and being fed liquids with a dropper wasn't part of his image but, surprisingly, he seemed to enjoy the pampering. After a couple of days he was able to have his collar off for a short spell so that he could lap from a bowl, but it had to be a very short spell indeed, allowing some post-prandial washing but preventing the ultimate DIY. In fact, he seemed determined to remove his stitches, so it was a relief when they were able to take him to the surgery and have it done professionally. The visit passed without any incident, except for the look Barry got from the nurse when he turned up with Lucy again. He was developing a reputation he'd done nothing to earn.

Lucy became less preoccupied and more inclined towards her old self during that week, too. Looking after Jack had somehow been good for her, and now that he was free of his stitches and home again, they had something to celebrate, so Barry invited her over to the flat for a drink.

When she arrived, he was a little taken aback. He'd been used to seeing her regularly in the shop, where she always dressed carefully and in a businesslike way. She often wore trousers or a neat skirt, and there was never a suggestion in her appearance of anything but smart respectability. Not that she'd gone to extremes that night; it was only a casual drink between friends, and she'd found the balance exactly. It was the feminine way she looked that made such an impression on him. Her make-up was very light, and it was right as well. Being a photographer, he noticed that immediately. He also noticed her hair, which she wore loose, rather than tied back, as it so often was, and it looked softer somehow. There was nothing overtly sexy about the blue trouser suit; it didn't cling particularly and, of course, it wasn't at all revealing, but it was perfect on that occasion.

'You look good.' he told her.

'Thank you. I thought it was time I made an effort.'

'And you have.' Actually, he was conscious of his own lack of style. He'd finally forsaken the wretched flares in favour of some very ordinary panel-fronted trousers in a nondescript shade of beige and, inevitably, a patterned shirt with long, rounded collar points.

If Lucy had noticed anything, she gave no sign, but peered instead along the passage. 'You know,' she said, 'in all the time I've known you I've never been into the place where you work.'

'I'll show you around if you like.'

'Oh, please.'

As she seemed so genuinely interested, he began the tour. 'This passage is just a storage space. I keep all my film in the fridge there.'

'In a fridge?'

'Yes, professional film has to be kept cool. It doesn't have much of a shelf life as it is, but it wouldn't last two minutes anywhere else.'

'I see.'

'And this is the darkroom.' He opened the door for her. 'Everything I need for developing and printing's in here, and this,' he told her, pointing towards the far end of the bench, 'is the copy camera I use to reproduce the old prints you send me.'

'Fascinating.' It really was too. He could tell she wasn't simply being polite.

He pushed open the studio door and switched on the main light. 'Just a second.' He went into the passage and took some cut film from the fridge before joining her. She seemed mesmerised by the lights and reflectors, so he invited her to sit on the chaise longue while he arranged them around her. When he'd finished, he handed her a mirror and switched off the main light.

'That's amazing,' she said.

'Oh, there are lots of ways of doing it. This one simply highlights your face and keeps the background in darkness.' He loaded the camera and framed her head. She half-smiled at him, suspecting what he was going to do, and he took the shot.

'That was sneaky.'

'I know, but you get the picture free of charge.'

'Lovely.' She pointed to the Corfield. 'D'you always use this for portraits?'

'Not always. It depends on what people want. This one takes large format film, so I can make big enlargements without losing quality.' He opened the safe and took out the Mamiya. 'This one's a medium format camera,' he explained. 'It takes a film half the size of the portrait camera, and I use it for weddings among other things. This one,' he said, showing her the Pentax, 'takes the usual thirty-five millimetre film, and it's good for getting in close and shooting sequences.' He switched on the motor drive and pressed the shutter for a few imaginary frames.

'Claret told me about that.' She looked at him coyly. 'She says it turns her on.'

'Really?' He knew it could have that effect on some girls, but he hadn't associated Claret with it. 'I've never thought of her in that way.'

'She's not as innocent as you might imagine.' She turned back to the safe. 'Which is the one Guy wasn't impressed with?'

'I suppose he might react that way to any of my equipment,

but this is the one that earned the "humph".' He handed the Leica to her.

'It looks all right to me, not that I'm an expert. What's wrong with it?'

'Nothing. It's beautifully built, it'll last at least a lifetime, it has a lens system unrivalled by anything else in this studio, and listen to this.' He cocked the shutter and pressed the release button.

'I could hardly hear it.'

'Exactly, and that's what makes it so useful with nervous subjects. You'd be surprised how many of them blink when the shutter goes off. Anyway,' he said, putting the cameras away and locking the safe, 'let's go upstairs and have that drink.'

They went up to the flat and heard Jack scratching at the door.

'He must have heard you arrive.' As if to confirm that, he made straight for Lucy as soon as Barry opened the door. 'There are times when I feel truly neglected,' he said.

'Nonsense,' she said, picking him up, 'he's just being an attentive host.'

'Do you always see the best in people?'

'Usually, for a while at least.' It wasn't difficult to see what was on her mind.

'What would you like to drink?'

'Have you any red wine?'

'I certainly have. Take a seat.' She sat on the sofa while he opened a bottle of claret and filled two glasses. Handing one to her, he took the armchair opposite her.

'You explain things very simply, Barry.'

'It's because I'm used to doing it. Clients sometimes want to know about these things and there's no point in confusing them with a lot of jargon and technicalities.'

'I think another reason is that you don't feel the need to impress.' Clearly, she had some instance in mind, and she confirmed it by saying, 'You were angry, that day that Guy sneered at your camera, and I never understood what it was about.'

'It wasn't that, although I don't welcome uninformed criticism. It was what he said about people being prejudiced about Japanese goods that angered me. He wasn't to know, but the person who'd written to me had every reason to take the line she did. She mentioned her husband being in the Far East during the war, and later she referred to the Lancashire Fusiliers' Association being at his funeral. The regiment was at the fall of Singapore, and the survivors were taken prisoner. I remember reading about it in the papers when they were campaigning for compensation. Considering the way they were treated, it's no wonder the poor devil came back with a heart condition. He said something to me about getting over disappointments and disasters, and he certainly knew about that. Still,' he shrugged, 'as I said, Guy wasn't to know that.'

'It wouldn't have made any difference. Casual callousness was part of his facade. He thought it was manly.'

'Good Lord.'

'Oh yes, he was full of hang-ups. That was the problem.' She took a sip of her wine and nodded her appreciation. 'He was terribly upset after the camera club competition, you know.'

'Because his nephew didn't win?'

'Basically, yes. He badly wanted you to be impressed with Jonathan's picture because, naturally, he'd helped him with it. He was going to follow it up by showing you some of his own.'

'We didn't know the identity of the contestants until after the judging.' He thought it was important that she knew that.

'I know.'

'And my talk wasn't aimed specifically at him. It was meant as a piece of advice to them all.'

'I understand that, Barry, but he took it very much to heart.'

He found that very surprising. 'What I don't understand,' he said, 'is why he saw me as a challenge. I don't think I've ever been a threat to anyone.'

'I'm sure you haven't, but look at it this way. You've done

an awful lot in a short time, and everything you've achieved has been by your own efforts. On the other hand, Guy has achieved very little. He went to an expensive school because his father was there before him and because his parents could afford it. He got a pass degree from a third rate university and then went into the family firm and struggled. He was bound to feel challenged by someone with real ability.'

'I thought there was something missing from his life, but I didn't realise it was as bad as that.'

'No, he hid it well. At least he hid it from me for a while.' She stared at her glass.

He'd asked her over to give her a diversion, but they'd happened on to the subject he'd meant to avoid. He looked around for inspiration and found it in the unlikely shape of the wine bottle.

'I've been meaning to ask you this. Do you know how Claret got her name?'

'No, I have to say I've wondered.'

He told her the story of the naming of Claret, Bailey and Cliff, and watched with satisfaction as her smile widened.

'At least they're unusual names,' she said 'Well, two of them are. As you can imagine, I went through school being called "Lucy Locket". Did you have a nickname?'

'Not really. I never attracted much attention at school.' He took the bottle and refilled both glasses.

'I can't imagine why.'

'Oh, well. I suppose anonymity is better than notoriety.' He opened another bottle and left it to breathe. 'Tell me about your school,' he suggested.

'I was at Bedgebury. Have you heard of it?'

'Yes, I take the school photographs every year.'

'Really? It's a pity they didn't have someone like you when I was there. The photographer who came in those days had dandruff and a horrible leer. He used to letch at us all the time.'

'I do that,' he said, 'but I'm discrete about it.'

'No you don't. I won't believe it.'

'You're a kind soul, Lucy. Anyway, did you enjoy being there?'

'Yes I did, but I don't think my schooldays were as eventful as yours. Tell me, did you go on getting into trouble because of Jack what's-his-name?'

'Rushworth. Well, yes, there was him and there were others. Taking the side of the underdog has been a lifelong weakness, and I can't seem to get away from it. I live in a world that's ideal, in which every story ends with romantic music and rolling credits as Fred Astaire and Ginger Rogers dance happily up a wide staircase.'

She smiled broadly. 'I'd gathered that, but it's not such a bad fault. As far as I'm concerned, you're a hero. You've been positively chivalrous to me this week.'

That made no sense to him. 'I haven't done anything.'

'Yes you have. You've been the best company I could have had, you've entertained me, and you've never once dripped platitudes or treated me like a casualty. You've just been yourself, and very sensitive, too. You invited me here because you thought I might feel awkward about being asked out somewhere, as if I were a lame duck who needed a treat, and that was very considerate of you. Promise me you'll never change, Barry.'

By that time, he was fairly glowing with the things she'd said about him, but he couldn't help feeling a little awkward as well. It wasn't the first time Lucy had read his mind. 'All right,' he said, 'I don't think I could change anyway. It's just a cross I have to bear.'

'Scout's honour?'

''Fraid not. I was never in the scouts.'

They got through more than two bottles of wine that night, and when he saw Lucy home, they were both in a state of mild anaesthesia. He didn't think either of them was used to drinking quite so much, but it had probably done them both some good.

'Good night, Barry,' she said, 'and thank you for a lovely evening.' She offered her cheek, and he kissed her lightly, which was very nice. He felt he could congratulate himself on a job well carried out. As for anything else that might happen, he just had to wait and see.

# 18

# Just Being Sociable

Barry and Lucy went about together quite a lot after that. They spent time in each other's place, chatting and drinking, although not in the same quantity as they had that night. They went out to various things as well. On one occasion, Lucy took Barry to a ballet in London. He'd seen an opera and been to a few concerts when he was at school, but he'd never seen a ballet and he hardly knew what to expect. It was *Coppélia* by Delibes, and he found everything about it quite magical, the music, the dancing and the story itself. Apparently, Guy had refused to go with her in the past because he thought the male dancers were all gay, and he was afraid that as a member of the audience he might arouse similar suspicion, so it was a pleasant change for her, too.

She didn't mention him just as often as she had in the first few weeks, and she was much happier altogether, but Barry was conscious of a growing frustration. Whilst he'd never have admitted it, his early interest in her had never really waned, and he'd still thought of her, in between his unfortunate interludes, in a guarded but special way. He really couldn't remember a time when he'd been slow to make a move, but in this situation, it just wasn't right. She'd never shown any indication that she was interested in more than casual friendship, and he was convinced that taking any initiative might easily ruin things between them. The feeling of constraint was acute at times. Fortunately, there were diversions, and he was recovering from one of them as he prepared to go with her to a dinner party at Dennis and Fenella Billingham's place.

The incident came about through Fenella, who had been as good as her word in mentioning Barry to her friends, although he suspected she might have made this particular recommendation with her tongue in her cheek. Her last words to him were, 'You'll need a chaperone.' Barry thought she was joking.

When he arrived at the address, he was greeted by an exceptionally tall, ruggedly-built woman of around forty. Apparently, she was very active in organising the local pony club, and he imagined her voice must have developed its huskiness through years of bellowing at little girls across wind-blown pastures. He found her quite daunting at first. She took him inside and offered him tea, over which she insisted on hearing the story of his life, squeezing his thigh occasionally to make an interjection. He decided then that she was more than exceptionally friendly and, with that worrying thought in mind, he allowed her to lead him to the paddock. The subject of the session was a liver chestnut gelding of much the same conformation as Fenella's Mandy, but rather larger. He gave Barry no problems at all, however, unlike his owner, who seemed incapable of communicating with him whilst daylight shone between them. She was probably six feet tall, and his nose came up to her chin. Her third shirt button lay carelessly undone and, each time she wheeled him round in half a bear hug to suggest a different camera angle, he found himself staring into her considerable cleavage. Eventually, he persuaded her to stand beside the horse and let him photograph them together. After that, he began a strategic withdrawal, during which he received the beefy right arm treatment again and had his bottom squeezed as a bonus. His heart was still pounding five miles down the road.

He and Lucy arrived at the farm some time after seven, to find, somewhat embarrassingly, that they were the first. He'd always tried to avoid that, because it made him feel like a spare part, but Dennis and Fenella sat them down with a drink and it wasn't long before Barry forgot any awkwardness their early arrival might have caused.

Lucy asked, 'Who else is coming?'

'Just Gwenan and Tom,' Fenella told her. 'I don't think you've met them. Tom's a policeman, quite a character.'

'Most of 'em are,' said Dennis, 'but Tom's all right. Gwenan's nice too.'

They chatted until the doorbell rang, and Dennis went to answer it. He reappeared with a pleasant-looking woman, quite tall and darkly attractive, and Barry looked up in surprise as DCI Jackson followed her into the room. He greeted Barry heartily, and the introductions were made. Then Fenella looked at the two of them in amusement and said, 'I gather you two know each other already.'

'That's right,' said Tom, 'Barry and I see each other occasionally in the course of work.'

Gwenan asked Barry, 'You too?' In the light of Tom's explanation, it probably seemed a reasonable presumption that they were in the same profession.

'No,' he said, 'I'm a photographer.'

'It was Barry who took all those beautiful pictures of Mandy,' said Fenella.

'Really?' Gwenan sounded impressed, and while Dennis busied himself getting drinks, and Lucy and Tom were in discussion, she turned to him to ask, 'What do you do apart from scene-of-crime work and photographing horses?' She had the faintest Welsh accent, which he found quite pleasing.

'I do people pictures really,' he explained, 'but for the time being, I take most kinds of work. I've done quite a lot of work recently at a vet's practice.'

'How unusual.'

'I suppose it is. The vet has pioneered a new surgical

process that he wants to promote, so I've been taking pictures during some of his operations.'

'It sounds a bit gory, but I imagine you're used to that.'

'That's right, and it gives me an opportunity to take other pictures too, pleasanter, more cheerful ones that people might want to look at.'

Fenella came in at the end of the conversation and said, 'Barry was on an equestrian assignment this afternoon, weren't you, Barry?' Her eyes twinkled as she said it. 'I'm ready to serve now, so would you all like to come through?'

Barry looked around the table. Gwenan was next to him, quiet but friendly; there was Dennis, bucolic and unreserved, Lucy, now completely relaxed, her eyes shining with fun, and Tom, whose massive frame and ebullient nature dominated the gathering. Then there was Fenella, vivacious and irreverent as ever. It promised to be a good evening, although it was just a shame that Fenella had to embarrass him.

'I've been dying to hear about Barry's experience this afternoon,' she told everyone. 'I recommended him to an acquaintance of mine and, on reflection, I think I should have given him a little more warning of what to expect.'

'A little more warning? You dropped me right in it.'

'If you remember, I did suggest a chaperone.'

Everyone was looking in Barry's direction, so there was no backing out. 'What I really needed,' he told them, 'was a bodyguard.'

Dennis asked him mischievously, 'Did you escape with your honour intact?'

'Please, Dennis,' Fenella admonished him, although she knew how the conversation would go.

'Well, that's what she's like,' he protested. 'Each time I see her, I feel as if I'm being mentally rogered.'

'How lucky can you get?' The thought apparently appealed to Tom.

Dennis snorted. 'You haven't seen her. I wish I could breed some of what she's got into my stock, I'll tell you, including that backside of hers—' He was silenced by a glance from

Fenella, and Barry knew he had to tell the story. Lucy, who knew nothing about it was smiling at him expectantly across the table, so he went ahead, describing the experience as tastefully as he could. When he was finished, Dennis picked up the wine and said, 'Poor devil, you need a drink after all that. I told Fenella it was a rotten trick, sending you out there.'

'No,' said Barry, 'it was business, and I suppose there are hazards in every job.'

Fenella narrowed her eyes and grinned at him. 'I thought the two of you would get along beautifully,' she said.

As they began the main course the conversation ran naturally into relationships, with Tom and Dennis taking a playful, misogynist line, and Lucy saying, 'Well, having recently broken off an engagement I can honestly say that it'll be a long time before I'll get involved with anyone else.' Everyone looked towards her. It was possibly the first intimation as far as Tom and Gwenan were concerned that Lucy and Barry were not necessarily an item, but the momentary awkwardness was dispelled by Fenella, who said, 'Oh, Lucy, Guy was a dead loss. Even you have to admit that you'd given your brain the day off when you took up with him. You can't live like a nun just because you got it wrong once.'

'I know, but all the same....'

It was clearly an awkward subject for her, even though she was the one who'd mentioned it in the first place, but Barry felt he should ease her embarrassment by drawing the attention away from her. 'I've given up on that sort of thing too,' he announced, gratified when everyone turned like spectators at a tennis match to look at him.

'Surely not,' said Gwenan, 'you're a young man with everything to look forward to.'

'I don't know,' he said. 'I've got it wrong more times than I care to remember.'

'This is becoming a competition,' Dennis observed.

'No,' insisted Barry, 'where my track record's concerned, all bets are off.'

'Come on then,' Tom challenged him, beaming around the

table, 'put your record where your mouth is. We want to hear everything.'

'All right,' he said, 'let's just take the last few months as a sample.' He began to count on his fingers. 'First, I got involved with a girl who turned out to be hopelessly insecure, so that she needed constant reassurance. That one hit the bottom of the bin pretty quickly. Then I had a brief thing with a PE mistress.' There were affected moans from Tom and Dennis, but he continued. 'I should say she was a PE mistress for whom I could get nothing right apart from, well, one or two things.' He didn't want anyone to get the wrong idea. 'Thirdly, I formed a ridiculous first-sight infatuation with someone who, when I met her again, almost accused me of being a bourgeois materialist and dealer in the fashion cattle market.' By this time, he was confident that he'd removed the glare of attention from Lucy, but he completed his catalogue. 'Fourthly, I found myself a very attractive girl, and that lasted several weeks. Unfortunately she turned out to be jealously possessive and a power freak into the bargain.'

'And that's just in a few months,' Gwenan commented. 'Barry, when do you find time for work?'

'That's not a problem. These things never last very long.'

'It's just as well,' said Dennis. 'I think you should leave all that until you retire. Then you can concentrate on getting it right.'

'I don't think I ever will,' he said. 'I reckon there's something strange about me that makes these things happen.'

'I don't think so,' said Gwenan. It may be that you're impulsive. Possibly, if you didn't rush into these things you might save yourself a lot of trouble. What do you think, Tom?'

'No, it's just as he says. There's something strange about him.'

'How do you know?'

'I don't. I just think there is.' He was smiling gleefully, and Barry knew it was a leg-pull, but Gwenan wanted to argue.

'You call yourself a detective, and you jump to a conclusion like that?'

'I'm off-duty,' he said, 'so I'm allowed to. Anyway, we do sometimes jump to conclusions. We're all human,' he added, 'and we often do it for lack of substantial evidence.'

'Well I don't,' she said, 'and I don't think there's anything strange about him. He'll sort his love life out.' She turned towards Lucy who had been quietly following the conversation. 'So will you, Lucy. It's only a matter of time.'

***

The night was mild for early March, and they travelled home with the windows part-way down. Barry watched the wind ruffle Lucy's hair as she drove. Apparently deep in thought, she seemed unaware of it, and of the fact that her dress had fallen open at the split. He ached within, as he so often did.

# 19

# They Call it 'Glamour'

When the doorbell rang, he thought it might be Lucy, although he wasn't expecting her for another half-hour. A couple of days after the dinner party, he'd suggested that she came over for a drink, and she'd naturally agreed.

He opened the front door to find Claret there. He hadn't seen her for a while, and it was obvious to him that she wasn't entirely happy, but he waited until they were in the flat before asking her what was troubling her.

She hesitated, possibly wondering where to begin, so he opened a bottle of wine and filled two glasses.

She sat on the sofa, gazing down at the carpet and then lifted her eyes to look at him. 'It's just not happening, Barry,' she said. 'I keep trying these bleedin' agencies and every time it's the same.' She began to cry quietly.

He moved over and sat beside her, putting his arm round her. 'What sort of rejection have you had? Is it something one of the agencies has said?' Rejections were usually quite cryptic. They often said that their books were full, or that the applicant wasn't quite what they were looking for, but they were seldom hurtful, principally because there was nothing to be gained by it.

'It's not that,' she sniffed. It wasn't going to come quickly so he waited. Eventually she blew her nose on a tissue and

168

began to speak. 'I really thought I was getting somewhere. I answered an advert in the local paper. It said they were looking for models, so I wrote off to this box number. All you had to do was send measurements, your age and a photograph. They didn't want a portfolio or anything like that.' By this time, he was way ahead of her, but he let her go on, in the hope that talking about it might somehow be good for her.

'They phoned me and gave me an address to go to. It was one of them big houses in—' She was interrupted by the doorbell and she made to get up.

'No, no, don't worry,' he said, 'it's only Lucy.'

'If Lucy's coming I'd better go. I don't want to be in the way.'

'You're not in the way and I don't want you to go. It's nothing like that. She's only coming for a drink, nothing important.' He went downstairs to open the door.

Lucy came in and saw his expression immediately. She asked, 'What's the matter?'

'Claret's upstairs, in a bit of a state. Apparently, she fell for a dodgy advertisement for models. She's just telling me about it, and I think having you here might make it easier for her.'

She followed him upstairs, where, to her credit, she said nothing but simply sat beside Claret, holding her hand. Barry filled another glass and sat on Claret's other side. He asked, 'Where was this place, Claret?'

'It was one of them houses off Birchley Road.'

That made sense. It was on the older, sometime residential, side of Elmston. Many of the larger Victorian houses had been converted into flats and, in an area where anonymity was accepted, girls would come and go almost unnoticed. He asked, 'Why didn't you tell me about this appointment?'

'I thought you'd be mad at me 'cause I hadn't done it the way you said.'

'I see. Go on.'

She hesitated and looked at Lucy, who squeezed her hand. 'I had to talk to this bloke who asked me what I'd done, so I told

169

him I'd done some sessions with a photographer, and then he showed me some pictures. They were horrible, just pictures of women showing their... you know... their bits an' pieces.'

'Did he show you anything else?'

'No, that was enough for me. He told me they paid good money for it but I didn't want to know, so I legged it.' She started to cry again on Lucy's shoulder. In the absence of anything more helpful to do, he filled up Claret's glass and his. Lucy hadn't touched hers. Presently Claret calmed down. She was no longer sobbing, but her breath was coming in shudders, so that her speech was barely coherent. 'I really thought I was... getting... somewhere and all I did... was make a fool of myself.'

'No, you didn't,' said Lucy. 'You just learned the hard way. We've all done that at some time.'

'I wasn't... going to tell... anybody.'

'Well we're glad you did. Now come on, have a drink and you'll feel better.'

'I only came round to ask Barry... if he could talk to... somebody in the trade.'

He waited until she was more settled and coherent before asking, 'What did this man look like, Claret?'

She thought about it. 'He was fairly tall, taller than me, about six foot, and he had one of them moustaches like Benny's in ABBA, but he didn't have a beard, just a moustache. He had fair hair, not blonde, but about the same shade as Lucy's, only not as nice.'

'How was he dressed?'

'I can't remember, but he was smart. He was wearing a suit and all that. He looked respectable, and it wasn't until he showed me the pictures that I realised what a dirty sod he was.'

'Can you remember the address?'

'No.' If she could, she wasn't going to tell him. 'I don't want any trouble. I've had enough.'

'I know, Claret, but can you tell me which end of Birchley Gardens it was?'

'No, I just want to forget it.'

Lucy was looking questioningly at Barry, but he shook his head. He would talk to her later. The important thing was to get Claret into a happier frame of mind. It took a while, but they got there eventually.

'So there it is,' he said. 'You've had a bad experience, but you've lost nothing, apart from your gullibility I suppose.'

'What's that?'

'Being too easily taken in.'

'Yeah, it won't happen again.'

'I know it won't,' he told her, 'and I'm surprised that you want to face a camera after this, but if you're serious about wanting me to put a word in for you with the trade, I will. You won't be working for Chanel but I can promise you that the most revealing thing you'll have to model will be a bikini or a set of underwear.'

She brightened immediately. 'Oh, that's all right. I don't mind that.'

'Okay then, I'll get on to it.'

'Thanks, Barry. You're fantastic.'

He sighed discreetly. It had taken time, but she'd finally accepted his advice.

She looked at her watch. 'I have to get back.'

'All right,' he said, 'you'd better freshen yourself up. You know where the bathroom is, don't you?'

When she'd gone, he went back upstairs with Lucy, and they sat down again. 'I need a cigarette,' he said, almost guiltily.

'Go ahead,' she said, 'you've earned it.'

He lit one and inhaled the smoke luxuriously. 'I'm glad you were here. It helped. I felt somehow inadequate with her, as a bloke.'

She shrugged. 'I don't know about that, but if I did any good at all I'm glad.' She eyed him curiously and asked, 'What was all that about the man's appearance?'

'I'm pretty sure it was the same person who called on me some time ago. He was looking for a photographer.'

'Really?' She made a gesture of distaste. 'It sounds like a dignified title for someone who'd do that sort of thing.'

'And the rest.'

'What do you mean?'

'The stuff he showed Claret was soft porn, the kind of thing you'll find in most newsagents, albeit on a top shelf. They call it "glamour", but we know the truth.'

'I've seen it. It's foul.'

He wondered, for a minute, how she'd come to see anything of that kind, but he decided not to pursue it. Instead, he filled the glasses. 'That was just the thin end,' he said. 'I imagine the idea was to make her believe that what he showed her was all she'd have to do. The rest would come later when she'd become involved.'

'How do you know this?'

'He told me that they do what he called "specialised stuff".'

'You mean it gets stronger than that?' Horrified though she was, she was no less keen to know.

'It certainly does. These people produce anything to fill a demand, and it doesn't touch the newsagents' shelves because it's illegal to sell it. It's distributed by mail order, although there are places in London where it can be bought over the counter. Soho's full of them. They don't care what they have to portray as long as it sells.'

'I don't think I want to know about the details. It just sounds like a horrible business.'

'It is. I don't know that most of the material's particularly harmful in itself. It's amazing what's sold on the open market in Scandinavian countries, and I suppose if it keeps a lot of inadequate soloists happy, there's no harm done. It's what these people do to the likes of Claret that sickens me.'

'Me too, but what can you tell the police if Claret can't give them the address?'

He thought about that. 'Not much, I'm afraid. They could get an address from the phone number I've got, or from the box number in the paper. Other than that, I've got a name and some things I've been told, which doesn't amount to very much. I suppose they could search the place for evidence. It would be up to them.'

'Are you going to contact them?'

'I certainly am. I'll phone Tom Jackson in the morning.'

It was actually late in the morning when he managed to speak to him. He'd had to leave a message, earlier, asking Tom to call back, and when he heard Barry's story, his response wasn't encouraging. He basically shrugged the whole business off.

'We can't do a thing without real evidence, Barry.' It was just as he'd feared, and when he heard Tom's argument, it made depressing sense. A man had offered him work of a dubious nature, he'd hinted that the subject matter went beyond magazine glamour, but he hadn't told him anything specific. As Tom had said, there was no point in applying for a search warrant because there was simply no evidence to justify one. It was too frustrating for words.

Having brooded about it for some time, Barry turned his attention to Claret's on-going problem, and the next telephone conversation he had was much more positive.

'So all she has to do is to phone them for an appointment?' Lucy was agreeably surprised.

'That's all.'

'I didn't think it would be as easy as that.'

'Easy' wasn't the word Barry would have chosen, but it would certainly be less difficult than what Claret had been doing. 'They have to satisfy themselves that she's suitable. I've known the proprietor of the agency for a couple of years. I did some work for them before I came here, mainly portfolios, and they were very impressed when I told them what Claret had been doing for me, so that gets her off to a flying start.'

'What sort of work would she get?'

'Mail order catalogues and in-store fashion shows, basically. It would be a good grounding for her. I still think she has a future as a photographic model, but she has to start somewhere.'

'That's true.' Lucy was toying with the sugar spoon and it was clear to Barry that her thoughts had wandered. After a while, she said, 'It's an awful shame the police can't do anything about those people. You'd think suspicion alone would be sufficient grounds for a search warrant.'

'Apparently it's not, and according to Tom, an unsuccessful search would only prompt them to change their location and be extra careful. What the police need is one piece of hard evidence of obscene publication. That's all.'

'And there's none to be had.'

'There might be.' He'd been thinking about it, and he had a half-formed idea.

Lucy regarded him suspiciously. 'Barry,' she said, 'I don't know what you have in mind, but I think you should forget whatever it is. I've got an awful feeling about this.'

'I'm not going to do anything dangerous. I'll just make a harmless enquiry. There's nothing to worry about.' He smiled to reassure her, but without success.

'You've got that look about you that worries me,' she said.

'I'm not taking any chances,' he assured her. 'Don't worry, it'll be all right.'

'Barry, for goodness' sake, be careful.' She took his hand and gripped it across the table, and he was surprised by the depth of her concern. He was taking a bit of a risk. He knew that, but he also knew he was doing the right thing.

# 20

# Concealment and Disclosure

Barry emptied the contents of his desk drawer, fearing at first that he might have lost the card, but he eventually found it among the jumble of pencils, pens, boxes of staples and various clutter that had inevitably found its way in there. The name 'Ken' was scribbled over the number. It didn't give much away, which wasn't surprising, and the phone number was disappointing. The first two digits suggested the Kingsford area, which was nowhere near the location Claret had described, and then it occurred to him that he'd been somewhat naïve to expect anyone actually to inhabit and offer the phone number of a place that was being used for illegal purposes. However, he would find out where that was in due course; at least, he hoped he would. It was dependent on the offer still being open. Since his visit, he might easily have found someone to do the job permanently. The fact that he was advertising for models suggested that business was still being transacted.

He dialled the number. It rang several times, and he was about to put the receiver down, when the line clicked open and a recorded message began to play. As far as Barry could remember, the voice sounded like that of the man who'd called, but the message was anonymous, merely stating the fact that the speaker was unavailable, and inviting the caller to leave a message. He waited for the signal and said, 'This

Barry Craven, the photographer in Woodley. You called on me some time ago. If your offer's still open, I might be interested.' Then he paused. If he wasn't careful, the next bit might sound phoney, although he'd rehearsed it countless times. 'I'd be very interested to see a few examples of the kind of work you do.' He left his phone number and rang off. He could only wait. Everything depended on the man being sufficiently interested to phone back and to allow him a few minutes to look at the stuff he was peddling.

Nothing happened for the next two days. He kept checking the answering machine for a message but, as usual, there was a scarcity of anything, let alone a reply to his message. He began to suspect that he'd found someone to do the work regularly, in which case there was no point in his returning the call. When he shared his suspicion with Lucy, she was relieved, but he felt completely frustrated. The only bright spot of the week came when Claret phoned him in high spirits to tell him that the agency had given her an appointment to see them the following week. It had taken a most unpleasant experience to persuade her, and now she was full of enthusiasm.

He was about to close for the day, that Thursday afternoon, when the man phoned.

'It's Ken. I got your message. I'll come and see you tomorrow morning if you're free.'

'I'm usually free.'

'That's what I thought. I'll be there around ten. You've got a loupe, I suppose?'

'Of course.'

'Okay, I'll see you then.' He rang off.

Barry couldn't believe it. Not only was he interested, he was bringing some examples as well. He went into the darkroom to find the magnifying loupe and to load the copy camera.

Finding himself alone for the evening, and in the absence of anything of interest on television, he decided to spend a pleasant few hours with Wally Brand, Alf Tupper, The Hon Piers Mornington and some more of his boyhood heroes. It had been some time since he'd looked at any of his old *Rover* 'adventure papers', as the publishers called them to distinguish them from comics.

He sorted through the pile and took out some of the 1958 issues, which were among his favourites, poured a glass of wine, a perk that came with being a grown-up schoolboy, and sat down to read them. He read about Sergeant Pilot Matt Braddock VC, testing a wonderful new aircraft that was sure to win the war, except that no other pilot could handle it without crashing it, and went on to be reminded of how Wally Brand discovered that his boots had been tampered with, just in time to save Melchester United, who were four goals down at half-time. He wondered, not for the first time, if Piers Mornington, *alias* The Light Blue Streak, ever attended any lectures at Cambridge. He always seemed to be on the running track, and it struck Barry, in his ignorance of such matters, that it was an awful waste of a university place. Then he found one of the regular real-life stories. This one was about Allan Pinkerton, founder of the famous detective agency. There were anecdotes about some of his agents; in particular, one who pursued a criminal right across America. It took several months, and he suffered gunshot wounds before bringing his man to justice. At that point, Barry stopped reading. As real-life stories went, that one was perhaps a little too vivid at such a time.

He'd often thought that moments of crisis should come as a complete surprise. There would be less pressure on the heart and the adrenal glands, at least, and it would probably lengthen life considerably. By ten o'clock, he was nervous beyond his worst imaginings, and he wondered why he'd put himself in that situation. He stopped just short of questioning his sanity. He kept checking the time, wondering if the man would show up, suspecting that part of him would be relieved if he didn't.

At about ten past ten, the door opened and he came in. He was much as Barry remembered him, smartly dressed and upright. If anything, he looked a little friendlier as he extended his hand. Barry offered him a seat and asked, 'Would you like coffee? I've got some on.'

He nodded. 'That would be nice. Milk and two sugars for me.'

Barry fetched the coffee things in on a tray and set them down on the desk.

'So business isn't too good after all?'

'It could be better,' Barry admitted. 'That's the reason I called you.'

'I know.'

'Look,' said Barry, 'I told you I *might* be interested. The thing is, I've always had a respectable business, and frankly, I wouldn't even consider this if things were better.'

'I know you wouldn't. You and a lot of others.' The corners of his mouth turned up slightly in what passed for a smile. 'For what it's worth, my business isn't all that different from yours. I supply a need, just like any other service. The difference is that not everybody sees it that way. That's how I look at it, anyway.' He shook his head when Barry offered him a cigarette, saying, 'No thanks, I'll stick with these.' He took out a packet of Capstan Full Strength and accepted a light. 'Cheers.'

Barry lit a cigarette, hoping his hands wouldn't shake as he did it. 'It's a big step,' he said. 'That's all I'm saying.'

The man gazed at Barry without blinking. 'Say we used

178

fifteen frames a session - it's sometimes more than that –
and you got twenty quid a frame. Multiply that by say, three
sessions a week. How long does it take you to make that kind
of money, doing what you call respectable business?'

Barry made a gesture of hopelessness. It was true. He
made nothing like that.

'Then there's the cine work. You've got the necessary
equipment, I take it?'

'Yes.'

'Good, because a fifteen-minute film would earn you a
"bullseye".'

Fifty pounds for a fifteen-minute clip was ridiculous.
It was little wonder the man could persuade struggling
photographers to work for him.

Ken continued. 'No-one would know it was you who'd done
it. You could go on being respectable. What have you got to
lose?' He took out a long envelope and passed it to Barry. 'You
asked to see some of what we do,' he said. 'Shove them under
a loupe and tell me you couldn't do the same for a just reward.'

Barry took the envelope and opened it to find several strips
of unmounted transparencies. Dry-mouthed, he said, 'Okay,
I'll have a look.' Pointing to the percolator, he said, 'Feel free
to help yourself to more coffee if you want it. I'll look at these
under a good light.'

Ken nodded again. He didn't waste words.

Barry took the envelope into the darkroom and closed the
door behind him. His heart was beating violently as he took
the loupe and examined the first strip, forcing himself to
concentrate. It was the kind of rubbish he'd expected, badly
posed, and photographed by someone with limited skill, or
none at all. The lighting was inadequate and poorly used.
It was possibly no more than unsophisticated on-camera
flash, and the focusing wasn't too good either, but it was
what Barry was looking for. He took the next strip and found
more of the same, plus a few that were truly sickening. He
could only guess at the ages of some of the subjects. Still, he
continued to examine them, and came to one that would have

won no prizes, and he doubted that it would have sold many copies either. It was a close-up of something tame compared with the rest, but it was just as contrived. Presumably the genitalia were supposed to be the focal point, but neither his nor hers was in focus. From what he could assess, the picture had been shot through possibly an eighty-five millimetre lens, at a wide aperture. That would be because of the shambolic lighting, but it also meant that there was very little depth of field. Basically, not a lot of it was in focus. He could only imagine that whoever had taken the picture had either focused hurriedly, or he'd gone back just a few inches, so that only part of the girl's leg was sharp. There was something else as well, a slight discoloration that contrasted with her natural flesh tone. He thought at first that it might be a skin disorder, but the effect was less random than that. It was more like an artificial pattern. He polished his glasses and hurriedly put them on again. As he stared at it, he realised what it was and, suddenly, his blood felt like ice. He took the strip of film over to the copy camera, listening for sounds of movement outside. So far, there was nothing, so he inserted the transparencies into the slide carrier and set the exposure. Praying that he'd got everything right, he squeezed the shutter release cable, feeding the strip through and repeating the process until he had a copy of each frame and of one in particular. When he'd finished, he gathered the transparencies together and replaced them in the envelope. Then, breathing as normally and calmly as he could, he took them back to the office where Ken was waiting. He felt that he'd been ages in the darkroom, but Ken seemed unperturbed. Half-smiling again, he asked Barry what he thought of the pictures.

'The quality's not brilliant,' he told him.

'Agreed, but photographers have always been a problem. My last one left some time ago, just disappeared with no warning, so I've been doing it myself since then. I've got someone to do the developing and printing, but nothing else. It'll be four, no, five months now. It was about the end of

September. I'm no great shakes with a camera, so the sooner I can find a good photographer the better.'

Barry passed the envelope to him, asking, 'Did you take these?'

'No, they were taken by the chap I told you about, the one who left me in the lurch.' He eyed Barry curiously. 'Why do you ask?'

'After what you just said, I thought you might have, but it seems he wasn't much of a hand with a camera either.'

He nodded. 'But you are, so what d'you say?'

'I don't know. I really have to think about it a bit longer.'

'What's there to think about? You'll be quids-in, and it'll be completely separate from what you do here, so there's no risk. I've got a discrete little basement all set up at the quiet end of Birchley Gardens. All you have to do is turn up and snap away.'

'Don't press me,' said Barry. 'Give me a few days, and I'll make a decision.'

He sighed heavily. 'All right, but don't leave it too long, or you might miss the boat.'

After he'd gone, Barry poured some coffee and sat in the office, smoking and generally gathering his wits. He was sure Ken suspected nothing, and why should he? He wouldn't expect a photographer to be gathering evidence. He finished his cigarette and returned to the darkroom.

'You must be out of your mind, Barry. Did you realise the risk you were taking?' Tom Jackson sat at Barry's desk and waited for him to hand him the prints.

'Never mind that, Tom. Look at these.' He passed him the envelope containing the photographs.

Tom took them out and looked at the first one. He said, 'Oh my God!'

'Pretty horrible, isn't it?'

'Definitely not to be viewed on a full stomach.'

'No, but you wanted grounds for a search warrant, and here they are.' He let him look at all but one of the prints he'd made. 'There,' he said, 'every sexual activity known to man, and most horrible of all, I wouldn't like to guess at the ages of some of these youngsters. I'd forgotten about that when I told someone recently that I couldn't see this sort of thing doing much harm. Frankly, I can't think of an appropriate punishment for what they do to these kids.'

'I know. Fair enough, Barry, you've made your point. Now, you say you've got a location?'

'Sort of. It's a basement at what he called "the quiet end of Birchley Gardens". I don't know the number and, obviously, I didn't want to press him on it, but there aren't all that many houses to go at.'

'That's right. We've got a phone number to trace, presumably for his home address, and a description for surveillance. Having seen him again recently, is there anything you can add to the description?'

Barry thought hard. 'Not really, he made quite an impression the first time.'

Tom read from his notebook. ' "At least six feet tall, smartly dressed in fashionable clothes, fair haired, chevron moustache".'

'Very upright stance.' Barry had just remembered it.

'Military bearing, would you say?'

'Yes, that sort of thing.'

'Good.' He scribbled a note and put his book away.

'Wait,' said Barry. 'There's more. Look at this last print.'

'Do I have to? What's so special about it?'

Barry joined him on the other side of the desk to look at the image. 'Forget what they're doing and look here,' he said, pointing to the discoloration on the girl's thigh. 'I last saw something like that when I caught my assistant in the changing room, trying to hide his acne with concealer - it's a sort of cosmetic correction fluid – and he'd made a mess of it. That,' he said, pointing again to the thigh, 'is concealer that's been applied by someone who doesn't know how to do it properly.'

Tom looked at him blankly. 'You've lost me. What are you trying to say?'

'Last Saturday evening you said something about detectives jumping to conclusions when the evidence was thin. Do you remember the conversation?'

'Yes, it was just a bit of silliness.'

'I know, but it struck a chord with me at the time. I remember you telling me how you suspected that Pauline Francis, the girl whose body was found on the Marsh, was on the game, and I've been meaning to ask you what made you suspect that.'

'Oh well.' He thought for a minute, 'Let's see, the family had been having a tough time with unemployment and they were struggling to make ends meet. Apparently, they'd been heavily in debt, but they said that Pauline had found a job waitressing and she was earning good money. Enough, it seemed, to pay off most of their debts. Naturally, we had to talk to her employer and workmates as part of the investigation, and that's when we found that no one at the restaurant she'd claimed to be working at had heard of her. We checked all the restaurants in the area in case there'd been a mistake, and drew a complete blank. The money was coming from somewhere else. The other bit of evidence was the bra she was wearing when her body was discovered, and the knickers that we found nearby. You didn't see them, did you?'

'No.'

'Well, they certainly weren't the kind of underwear most girls of her age would wear. The knickers were something else entirely.'

'The sort of thing you might expect to see in one of these?' Barry pointed to the pictures on his desk.

'Frankly, yes, but what's the connection?'

'She may have been engaged in the sex industry, Tom, but it wasn't prostitution. From what you've just told me, I reckon she'd just done a porn session.'

'That's guesswork, and where does the concealer come into it?' He stopped and thought. 'She did have a nasty scar on her thigh, but I wonder how many girls there are with a similar disfigurement. We can't see her face on this, more's the pity, because it would be prettier than the bit we can see.'

'The pattern the concealer makes suggests a large, very nasty scar to me,' said Barry, 'similar to the one on Pauline's body.'

'But you can't know that. It was months ago.'

'I can. You have to remember, Tom, it's my business noticing these things. I spend my life photographing the beautiful, the acceptable, the ill-favoured and everything between. I see the images enhanced through a lens, and these things register. Also, I have to say that the image of that poor kid's body has haunted me. It's not something I'll forget quickly. I reckon that if you compare the line of the concealer in that picture with the scar on the mortuary photographs you'll see that what I'm saying is right. An extensive scar is the most difficult thing in the world to camouflage for any length of time because the tissue's so shiny. There's nothing to key the stuff into, you see and, considering it was so badly applied, it could easily have been rubbed off by her skirt by the time she was murdered.'

Tom hunched forward, studying the transparency. 'I don't know,' he said. 'Can you be sure this stuff is what you say it is?'

'Wait there.' He went through to the changing room and found three sticks of concealer which he put in front of Tom. 'There it is. There's light and medium, and this one's for covering strongly-coloured marks, such as red veins and the like. A make-up artist or beautician would be careful to clean the area to be treated first. Then she'd mix the shades to match the flesh tone. She'd smear it on in thin layers and work it outward to break up any outline, because it can't be done all at once. Finally, for a facial job, she'd go over it with foundation cream, but in this case she'd apply a powder which would fix the concealer and disguise any tiny difference in colour that remained. Okay?'

'Right.'

'Give me your hand. I'd say your flesh tone's medium, so I'll take the medium stick and just cover part of it, like this.' He smeared the stuff on. 'I'd guess that's how it was done in the picture, without preparation, blending or powdering. Now compare your other hand with it.'

He peered from one to the other. 'You know, I think you may be right. I'm not convinced about your being able to identify the scar after all these months, but you never know what else we might find in that place.' He stood up to go. 'Just two things, Barry. Having done what you have, stay out of it from now on. There's an awful lot at stake in organised crime of this kind, and these people don't fight with feather pillows. If this chap contacts you again, tell him you've thought better of it. Then tell us.'

'Okay, that's one thing. What's the other?'

'Do you think I might wash this stuff off before I go? It would be bad for my image if everyone at the station thought I'd taken to wearing make-up.'

# 21

# Unwelcome Attention

He didn't expect to hear from Tom for several days at least, so he was in a pretty relaxed mood over the weekend. That Friday had been a day of indescribable tension, and the feeling of relief was intoxicating. There was always the chance that Ken would phone him or call at the studio again, but he felt able to cope with that after all that had happened.

Wesley arrived as usual on Saturday morning, and they spent some time planning the next two weeks' work. He was going to be there full-time for industrial experience, and Barry wanted him to take full advantage of it. They would concentrate on lighting, camera angles and printing processes, all of which gave them a great deal to do in the coming fortnight, and they were both looking forward to it.

On Sunday evening, Barry enticed Lucy into the lounge bar of The Three Tuns. She'd been in the restaurant countless times with Guy, but the lounge bar was a new experience for her, and so was Gavin Peckett. She'd met him before, of course, when he mended the burst pipe in the bookshop, but that had been entirely different. Barry had wondered at first whether she'd resented or been amused by his reaction to Guy's interference on that occasion, but if she remembered the incident, she showed no sign of it. She actually said very little that night, and there was no need for Barry to say much because, typically, Gavin did most of the talking, with Lucy teasing him good-naturedly from time to time. Barry was content merely to listen to the conversation, putting in an occasional comment every now and again. He was more at ease than he'd been for a while, and he felt no need to challenge or endorse Gavin's arbitrary observations. At one stage, he and Lucy were broadly in agreement on the subject of cats and dogs in relation to their human counterparts, both of them singling out well-known personalities for attribution.

'Margaret Thatcher,' said Gavin, 'is undoubtedly a cat. You know what she wants, but she goes for it in her own good time, and if you offered it to her at any other time she'd tell you to get stuffed.'

A young chap, tall and with close-cropped hair and a neat moustache, whom Barry never seen before was being served at the bar. He lingered long enough to listen to Gavin and hear some of the conversation, and returned, apparently baffled by it to his friend, who was momentarily concealed in a corner by the door. Barry noticed him particularly, because they didn't usually get many strangers in there.

'Now, if Barry was an animal,' Gavin went on, 'he'd be a dog, because you always know where you are with him.'

Lucy asked, 'What kind of dog?'

Gavin thought briefly and said, 'A Labrador.'

'Why a Labrador?'

'Because he's steady, but much too soft-hearted for his own good.'

'I don't know.' Lucy considered the point and regarded Barry thoughtfully, as if checking that she hadn't missed something. 'I know what you mean, but I see him more as a bulldog.'

Gavin spluttered and put his glass down. 'A bulldog?' He seemed to find the notion laughable. 'But there's nothing fierce about him.'

'Bulldogs aren't necessarily fierce, either. Many people think they are because they've had bad press at some time, but they're actually very loyal and affectionate, and they see a job, every so often, that has to be done, and they won't leave it alone until they've worried it to death.'

'Like killing a rat,' suggested Gavin.

'No, not necessarily. I'll give you an example, because we had one at home when I was a little girl. His name was William, and he was a gentle soul, not remotely fierce. Anyway, one Easter holiday, I was riding my bike when I skidded on some gravel and came off. I didn't break anything, but I had lots of cuts and bruises and I was quite shaken. When I was cleaned up, patched and bandaged, but feeling miserable, William got up to sit next to me. He wasn't allowed on furniture, but I let him stay because I wanted him there, and he just lay with his chin on my bandaged leg while I stroked him. It made me feel better, and you know, for the rest of that holiday he never left me alone. He felt that he had to guard me all the time so that nothing else could happen to me.'

'A protective bulldog,' Gavin mused.

'And a sympathetic one.'

'That's him all right. Barry's a bulldog,' he conceded, and then added, 'crossed with a Labrador.'

Barry never heard the rest of the conversation because, aware of a pressing need to visit Gavin's newly-installed and much celebrated plumbing, he excused himself at that point. He made his way through the crowded room and pushed open the door to find the gents full, so he continued outside. The old facilities had been good enough those past several years, and the matter was now quite urgent.

A minute later, he stood outside, relieved, smoking peacefully and looking at the spot where Gavin and he had written their autographs. At least Gavin hadn't regaled Lucy with that story. Not yet, anyway.

He decided he liked being a bulldog, with or without Labrador connections. There was something straightforward and unassuming about the breed that he could recognise, and a suggestion of fallibility that was familiar as well. He remembered being pleased by that thought, because it was the last coherent one he had before his arms were wrenched back and a dark shape moved in front of him. He struggled to free his arms and lashed out with his feet, but then he was paralysed by a blow to the solar plexus, followed by several more to the face. Soon, he was lying helpless on the ground, struggling for breath and taking kick after agonising kick until the lights went out and the world ceased to exist.

## 22

# The Agony and the Evidence

He was aware of several things happening at various times. A light was being shone into his eyes, and he could hear voices, but he couldn't make out what they were saying. At other times, he was being moved from one room to another, seemingly without purpose. Most of all, he was aware of the unbearable pain in every part of his anatomy.

It was still there when he woke up in bed. He could feel it in his head, stomach, back, legs, arms and groin, but, most of all, in his chest. With each breath, he felt that he was being stabbed. It was a while before his eyes focused and he saw the nurse who was standing beside his bed.

'Take it easy,' she said. 'Just lie still and rest. I'll give you a drink, now you're awake.' Her voice was quiet and soothing. She picked up a funny little thing like a miniature teapot with its spout at right-angles to the handle, and offered it to him. He tried to move his hand to take it, but stopped when the pain shot through his chest.

'No,' she said, 'let me do it.' She put the spout in his mouth and let him drink. It tasted unpleasantly of peppermint, but he drank it because he was so dry. At some stage, he had to pee into a bottle, and that simple manoeuvre was agonising, but he felt so relieved after it that he drifted back into sleep again.

⌒⌒⌒◈⌒⌒⌒

'Were you able to see your assailant, Mr Craven?' The constable sat by his bed, notebook in hand and clearly impressed by the extent of his injuries.

'No, but there were two of them.' He tried to recall the incident, but the pain that seemed to affect the whole of his body also clouded his memory. 'There may have been more. It's difficult to say. At least two, anyway.'

The constable wrote that down. 'Have you any idea who they might have been? Somebody with a grudge, perhaps?'

He had a pretty good idea. 'I can't give you a full name or address,' he told him, 'but DCI Jackson probably can.'

'DCI Jackson?'

'Yes, I gave him some information about a beaver merchant who's under investigation. He must have had something to do with it. I reckon it was either him or some of his mates.'

'Right, sir, I'll speak to CID about it. There's just one other thing. Do you possess a cigarette lighter, one of those Tommy lighters that have a reserve petrol tank?'

'No, I use a gas lighter. Why?'

The constable looked at his notes. 'I didn't think it would be yours, sir. A lighter of that type and with a regimental insignia enamelled on it was found at the scene of the assault. We think one of your attackers may have dropped it.'

'I don't recall ever seeing one like that,' he told him.

He closed his notebook. 'You'll let us know if you remember anything else, won't you, sir?'

'Of course.'

He stood up to go. 'I hope you're better soon, and I'll speak to CID about that matter. Goodbye, sir.'

'Goodbye.' He was leaving the ward when the man in the next bed spoke.

191

'That's nice, isn't it? You wake up feelin' horrible, and the first visit you get's from the law. You been mugged or something?'

Barry's neighbour was a grey, wizened man who sat on the side of his bed. Barry didn't really feel like talking, but his neighbour was being friendly, so he responded. 'Something like that. It was just a straightforward beating-up.'

'They made a good job of it,' he said, like a connoisseur admiring a piece of fine craftsmanship. 'What you got under there?' He pointed to the wire cage that provided protection from the weight of the bedclothes.

'The same as you, but I don't think mine will ever work again.'

He shrugged. 'I don't use mine nowadays, but I suppose you're still young.'

'I can't even think about it just now,' said Barry.

He appeared to give the remark some consideration before getting up and hobbling over to take the seat vacated by the policeman. 'I'm Ted,' he said, extending a hand. 'I'm in for observation 'cause of me circulation an' various things.'

'Barry. I can't shake hands, it hurts too much.'

'Fine, Barry, I'd better introduce the others. Over there, by the door, there's Adam. It's not his real name. It's Indian and no-one can pronounce it, but he was here before any of us, so we call him Adam. God knows what he's got. The kid next to him is Brett. Bloody silly name. He plays football and he's having his cartilages done. Next to him is "The Padre". He's a Jock, and he belongs to some funny church that doesn't approve of people enjoying themselves. He had a go at me about swearing, the day he came in, the miserable bugger. They think he might have gout, but they're not sure. Him across from you we call "The Musician". We don't know his name, but he's lost his marbles anyway.'

'What does he play?'

'The bedpan. He calls for the bloody thing every night just at visiting time. You'll hear him tonight. It's like the bloody proms.'

Their conversation was interrupted by the arrival of the dinner trolley. Barry couldn't have eaten for almost twenty-four hours, but he wasn't at all hungry. Even so, he found himself being fed by a plump, Irish nursing auxiliary, who went about the job with maternal strictness.

'Nurse,' he asked between compulsory mouthfuls, 'is it possible to get a message to someone?'

'Sure it is, and someone's left a message for you. She called just a half-hour ago. Just a minute.' She fumbled in her pocket and produced a piece of paper, which she unfolded. 'It's from a Miss Hart. She says you're not to worry about Jack. He moved in this morning.'

'Oh, that's good. Thank you.'

'Who d'you want to send a message to?'

'It's all right,' he said. 'It was about Jack.'

She shovelled another forkful of shepherd's pie into his mouth and asked, 'Would Jack be your little boy then?'

'No, he's my cat.'

She gave him an impatient look and delved again with the fork.

The ward began to fill up with visitors, and soon all the beds were surrounded by friends and relations. The low hum of conversation made Barry feel sleepy, and he was about to close his eyes when Wesley and Michelle arrived.

'We brought you these,' said Michelle, depositing a paper bag on the bedside table. 'They're grapes.' She peered anxiously at his swollen face. 'I hope you can manage them.'

'I'll try,' he promised. 'Thank you.'

Wesley eyed the hump of bedclothes with obvious interest. 'Where does it hurt, Barry?'

'Everywhere. My chest, mainly. I've got some cracked ribs and the rest is bruising, but I know what it's like now to be run over by a steam roller. I've been kicked everywhere, including the usual place.'

Wesley grimaced. 'That's nasty. Dangerous too.'

'Thanks, Wesley, I'm encouraged by that.'

He looked uncomfortable, but Michelle leaned forward and spoke sympathetically. 'It'll probably be all right if you rest it, Barry. Just don't use it for a while.' It wasn't the kind of wisdom he would have expected from a girl of seventeen, but she meant it in a kindly way.

A nurse appeared with a bedpan under a towel and drew the curtains around The Musician's bed. The concert was about to begin. Oblivious, Wesley said, 'I've been in the studio all day.'

Barry had forgotten all about his industrial experience. 'Of course,' he said, 'what have you been doing?'

A heroic blast, amplified by the stainless steel bedpan, came from within the curtains opposite. Michelle looked embarrassed, and Wesley bit his lip, trying not to laugh. 'Just holding the fart— fort,' he said. 'When you didn't open up, I got the key from Lucy and she told me you were in hospital.'

'She's coming later,' said Michelle. 'It's her night for going to the cash and carry.'

'A bloke rang up wanting some passport and visa pictures,' Wesley continued, 'so I told him you were ill. He said he wanted them in a hurry, so I offered to do them. That's all right, isn't it?' He looked down, pretending not to have heard the latest salvo of postern reports.

'Fine,' said Barry.

'Right, so he's coming tomorrow. I looked in the book to see what you charged for the last passport job and quoted him double because of the visas. He was happy enough.'

'Well done.' He'd charged over the odds, but there was no harm done.

'A lady rang up as well. She wanted a picture of her dog with her four puppies. She's a friend of Mrs Billingham's.

Three of the puppies are going this week, so she couldn't wait for you to come home.'

'That's too bad.' Barry was distracted by The Padre trying to attract the nurse's attention.

'Norrse,' he called, 'could ye no' open a window here? Some fresh air is orrgently required.' It must have been worse on his side of the ward.

'No, it's all right,' said Wesley, concentrating hard. 'She brought them in this afternoon and I did it. I used studio flash, so it wouldn't matter if they moved a bit.'

'Quite right.' Barry was stunned.

'I charged her for a family sitting. The pictures are good. I developed them after she'd gone, so she can have 'em any time.'

Barry closed his eyes in disbelief. He'd been battered half to death, and he felt worse than he had in the whole of his life, but something had gone right. In spite of the acne, chronic kack-handedness and awkwardness of recent memory, Wesley had come of age, and ahead of time. All he could say was, 'Well done, Wesley. Good lad.'

Michelle regarded him proudly, but Wesley looked distinctly embarrassed, so maybe that was the best moment for Lucy to arrive. Barry noted gratefully that The Musician's curtains had been reopened, and a nurse was carrying the offending bedpan away.

Lucy waited until Wesley and Michelle were gone, then she leaned over to kiss Barry carefully on a part that wasn't bruised, bloodied or swollen. She regarded him ruefully. 'Oh, Barry' she sighed, 'what are we going to do with you? I know I asked you never to change, but you've got to keep these crusades within bounds.'

<hr>

He had a number of other visitors in the next few days, including Ellen, Gavin, and Fenella Creswell. It felt good to be popular, especially at that time. He had a visit from Claret as well. She came on the afternoon before he was due to go home, followed by the stares of The Padre, Brett the footballer, a young doctor and an electrician who was cleaning the light fittings at the time. It wasn't entirely surprising; she looked pretty fabulous with her hair down, and in a dark red, almost knee-length dress. Taking the chair by Barry's bed, she kissed him lightly on his unscathed forehead and took his hand anxiously.

'Barry,' she said, 'this is terrible. I didn't know 'til I saw Wesley at the studio. What have they done to you?'

'I'll be all right,' he told her nervously, 'but please don't press down where your hand is. I've got a couple of cracked ribs and they hurt like hell.'

'Right, sorry.' She released his hand and sat back, carelessly crossing her legs, oblivious to the clatter as the electrician fought to regain his balance on the ladder. 'I could have died when Wesley told me about it. You didn't get involved with those people just because of me, did you?'

'Well,' he prevaricated, 'they needed sorting out anyway.'

She didn't seem convinced, but said simply, 'They ought to hang the buggers by their... dangly bits.'

'I'll vote for that.' It was time for him to steer the conversation towards something more pleasant. 'Are you looking forward to going to the agency? Friday, isn't it?'

'Yes, I'm a bit nervous though, and I wanted to ask you about my portfolio. The binder's starting to look a bit rough and I wondered if you had another one I could take.'

'Of course. I should be home before you go, but if I'm not, just ask Wesley and he'll find you one.'

'Oh, thanks.'

They chatted about how agencies work, what she could be asked and the questions she should ask of them, until she looked at her watch and groaned. 'I've got to go, Barry. I'm on the late shift, but I'll see you later.'

'That's fine. Thank you for coming, but before you go, Claret....'

'What?'

'Will you do me a favour?'

''Course I will. What is it?'

'Don't look now,' he told her, 'but there's a chap across the ward who's been mentally undressing you ever since you arrived. He's a sort of alternative vicar.'

'The dirty bugger.'

'I just want to see what he does when he gets really excited. Will you pretend to kiss me, slowly and passionately?'

She grinned mischievously. 'No trouble. Just think, he might blow a gasket.' She stood and bent over him so that her hair fell on the pillow, enclosing him with her scent, and delivered a gentle, lingering kiss on his lips. It caused him no discomfort at all; in fact, he was aware of at least one area of growing recovery.

'Thanks, Claret,' he whispered.

'You're welcome,' she whispered back. Then she straightened up and said in a louder voice, ''Bye, darling. See you soon.'

He let her reach the exit, and called across the ward, 'You okay, Padre?'

'Och yes, thank you,' he answered loftily. 'I'm just re-tying my pyjama cord. It seems to have become undone somehow.' There had to be some fun in being in hospital.

It was an anti-climax when Tom Jackson walked in, but Barry was still pleased to see him.

'What a mess, Barry,' he sympathised, 'but I've got some news for you. We searched the house in Birchley Gardens and found labels, packaging materials and all the evidence we need. We've also made a couple of arrests.'

'Oh, perfect.' In the pain and turmoil of the past few days, he'd given little thought to the enquiry.

'By the way, your friend Kenneth Hyman didn't do this.' He waved a hand over the bed. 'At the time the attack took place he had the best alibi of all. He was locked in a cell, charged with various offences under the Obscene Publications Acts, nineteen-fifty-nine and nineteen-sixty-four, among others. He can't have done it.'

'Then he must have got someone else to do it.'

'I don't know, unless he suspected something before he was arrested, but the whole thing did take him rather by surprise. I've no doubt we'll find a connection, but let me tell you the big news. You were right about that scar. Forensic checked the photo you gave me against the photographs from the mortuary, and the similarity was too great to be ignored. Also, I looked at the pathology report again, and sure enough, traces of a cosmetic substance were found in the region of the scar and on the skirt. You were right about that too.'

'I was convinced, but it's still good to know.'

'Yes, you surprised me.' He leaned forward eagerly. 'Best of all, in examining the confiscated material from Hyman's place we found pictures of Pauline Francis that included her face this time. She *had* been working there.'

'Brilliant. So do you think…. What did you say his surname was?'

'Hyman.'

'D'you think he killed her?'

'It's possible, but I'm not at all sure. He has to be a suspect for now, but we're very keen to find the missing photographer.'

# 23

# Stymied

He wasn't sorry to go home that Thursday morning. Three days and four nights in that place were as much as he could take without protest. In any case, protest wasn't allowed. The snoring and other natural emissions had kept him annoyingly awake at night, so that he usually fell asleep at about five o'clock in the morning, one hour before being woken again by the staff for ablutions and breakfast. After that, sleep was either impossible or forbidden. He'd been told-off twice for dozing off during consultants' rounds, and whilst he was grateful for the care they'd taken of him, he was heartily sick of the regimentation.

The pain in his chest had receded to some extent, but he had to dress very carefully, all the same. Fortunately Lucy had brought him an old, roomy jacket that he hadn't worn for ages and, with a bit of help from one of the nurses, he managed to get it on without swearing too much. Finally dressed, he shook hands with Ted, exchanged 'Goodbye' for '*Alvida*' with Adam, was given some advice on street brawling by Brett the footballer, received a blessing from The Padre, and was favoured with a toothless smile by The Musician. All that remained was to thank the staff and get a taxi.

He asked to be dropped at the bookshop. Wesley had been coping magnificently, and he saw no reason to take over straight away, but mainly, he wanted to see Lucy. She was

199

serving a customer when he arrived, but Jack came out from behind the counter and greeted him with a rare display of fondness.

'He's missed you,' said Lucy as soon as her customer had gone. 'We all have.' She accepted a peck, which was safer by then, because the cuts on his face were healing and, whilst it was still a horrible sight, the bruising was much less painful. 'Come and have supper here tonight,' she offered. 'You can't possibly look after yourself yet.'

'Thank you. That would be nice. I really wanted to take you somewhere after all you've done, but I look an awful sight and I can't get into any decent clothes yet with my chest strapped up.'

'Don't worry, I don't mind being seen with you like that, but there's no rush.' Looking at his worn old jacket, she remembered something. 'Oh yes, when I took your clothes from the hospital, I washed what was washable, including your trousers, but there was no point in sending your suede jacket to the cleaners, because it's so badly damaged. It's still here, but I don't think you'll want to keep it.'

'Thanks, that was kind of you. It's a shame about the jacket. It was my lucky one.'

'That takes some believing after what happened on Sunday night,' she said.

'I know, but it was my pulling jacket. It seldom failed.'

'Think of all the disasters you've pulled recently, Barry. Maybe it's as well.'

'All the same,' he sighed, 'I may never pull again.'

Wesley showed him the pictures of the bitch and her puppies. They were extremely good, considering his lack of experience with animals.

'They were very well-behaved,' he said, apparently surprised by the discovery.

He had some printing of his own to do, so Barry made a start at putting his competition folder together. It was a pleasing thing to do after all the horrors of the past week, and he was as satisfied as he ever could be with the pictures. He was fortunate to have Claret as a model. She was incredibly photogenic, and her hair colouring and skin tone were complemented beautifully by those of Michelle. They made an excellent pair. After much thought, he made the final selection and, as lunch beckoned, he placed the prints, negatives and transparencies together in a 15 x 22 inch envelope which he placed on his desk. He would do the mounting and final presentation over the weekend.

He spent the rest of the day helping Wesley with his contribution to the college exhibition. Considering the excellent way he'd stood in while Barry was in hospital, he felt he owed it to him, and he was delighted when his tutor called to see him and complemented him on his work, and especially on running the place single-handedly for three days. It had been a good day, and Barry was feeling human again.

⚜

He'd showered with some difficulty, and was recovering from the ordeal of fastening his trousers, when the doorbell rang. He went downstairs to find Claret on the step, excited and nervous about the next day.

'I'll get something wrong, I know I will,' she said.

'It'll be perfectly straightforward,' he assured her.

'I've actually come about that binder.' She produced her old one which was showing signs of frequent handling.

'Just remember what I told you yesterday, keep calm and you'll be all right. They're good people to deal with.' He found her a new binder in the cupboard and brought it through to the office. 'Get yourself one of those big envelopes,' he said, pointing to the stack of 15 x 22 inch envelopes on the shelf.

'It'll keep it clean on the train tomorrow. You can dump the old one here if you like.'

She took an envelope and inserted the new binder, taking the pictures and their transparent sleeves from the old one and sliding them in with it. 'Thanks, Barry. I'll let you know what happens.' She turned to go.

'Just a minute, before you go, would you mind helping me with my shirt buttons? It still hurts to do anything like that, and it's difficult anyway, with all this strapping in the way.'

"Course I will.' She put the envelope on his desk and fastened him up, With a naughty grin, she asked, 'D'you want me to tuck it into your trousers?'

'No thanks,' he said, remembering how he'd been affected by her attentions in hospital, 'I'll manage that.'

'Okay then, see you later.' She picked up the envelope from the desk and opened the door.

'Good luck.' He locked the door behind her and looked at his watch. He was due at Lucy's place very shortly, so he made his way stiffly upstairs again to finish dressing.

Despite spending so much time in the bookshop and tea room, it was only about the second time he'd actually been in Lucy's flat. It was much more comfortably furnished than his. He put that down to the woman's touch, and the likelihood that she'd inherited a lot of furniture and bits and pieces from her mother. There were two things she hadn't inherited, though. One was Jack, who was there when he arrived, and the other was one of his pictures. It was a view from Storiths in Upper Wharfedale.

'I bought that as soon as I saw it,' she said. 'It looks like such a beautiful place, I'd love to go there some time.' She was wearing a dress he hadn't seen before, in a deeper shade of blue than the trouser suit, and the hem was a little higher than she usually wore them. He felt clumsy, strapped and ill-dressed in his 'comfortable' clothes, and he was more than ever conscious of his cuts and bruises.

'I'm going there again, soon,' he said. I need a break after the week I've had.'

'Yes,' she said, 'you need a tonic.'

He hadn't been thinking about it particularly. The words just came out. 'Why don't you come with me? I mean I'm not suggesting, you know....'

'I know,' she smiled, 'you're suggesting a *platonic* tonic.' She looked away in thought for a moment and he felt awkward. It had been a ridiculous thing to say anyway, and he was trying to think of a way of changing the subject when she said, 'You know, it's not a bad idea. I was just thinking that if Esme and Michelle kept the tea room going I'd only need to close the bookshop, and they'd look after Jack as well. They could have their time off later, or before, whenever they want it. Yes, let's do that. When were you thinking of going?'

'Next month, I thought, when spring's out.' He still couldn't believe she was serious about it.

'It's already begun.'

'Down here it has,' he corrected her, 'but it's still winter in the Dales.'

'Is it really? Let me serve up and then you can tell me about it.' She went into the kitchen and came back with a creative thing she'd done with avocados and prawns, and then produced a bottle of Chablis. 'Now, you sit here,' she said, pointing to a chair under the picture of Upper Wharfedale, 'and tell me about this place while I look at the picture. I've skinned the avocado, by the way, so that you don't have to wrestle with it.'

'Thanks, I appreciate that. This is lovely.'

'It's your first night at home, so enjoy it. Right, I'm listening. You were talking about spring in the Dales.'

'It's incredible,' he told her. 'All the winter it's been sleeping, dark and brooding, and the hillsides are barren. Then the first leaf buds begin to open and the grass takes on a new, fresh greenness. The Craven Fault – no connection

– that runs through Wharfedale is a limestone fault, and the grass that grows over it is lighter, fresher green than it is anywhere else. There's a new scent about the place, as well.'

'Wonderful, and what sort of places would we visit?'

'Let me see, I think I'd go for contrast to begin with. We could start by looking at something well-known, like Bolton Abbey.'

'Yes, I've heard of that.'

'And then possibly the Valley of Desolation. Then there's Trollers' Gill.'

'Why's it called that?'

'Because Trolls used to live there when it was a cave.'

'As in The Three Billy-Goats?'

'The same.' Thinking again, he said, 'I think I'd take you to Aysgarth Falls. It's wonderful when the ice has thawed and the water comes over like solid sheets. There's Malham too, the Faeries' Glen, the Cove and Gordale Scar. They're all worth seeing.'

'Wasn't that where you met those people? The man who died and his wife?'

'That's right.'

'They made an impression on you, didn't they?'

'Yes, they did. I was down in the dumps because business was so bad, and because of other things that had happened, and those people really made me begin to look outward again. It's difficult to explain, but they made me see things in a different way. They'd spent all their lives working hard for very little, but they had pride to spare, and I realised that I was aiming from the wrong end. At odd times, when I feel impatient that I'm not doing vastly expensive portraits for the rich and famous, I think of something the old man said and then I start to look at the job sensibly again.'

'I see.' She reached for his empty plate. 'We're having Dover Sole. I'll take it off the bone for you. At a pinch, you could eat it with a fork.'

'That sounds lovely, but I'll make an effort.'

She took the plates away and came back with the sole

surrounded by mushrooms. 'Bear with me, and I'll get the vegetables.' She reappeared with new potatoes, courgettes and peas. 'Feel free to scoop the peas. You're a special case.'

'I'll try to be civilised.'

She helped him to vegetables and refilled the wine glasses, which was just as well, because any unusual movement caused twinges of pain in his chest.

'It's better if I'm not away over the Easter holiday,' she said. 'It's always a busy time at the shop.'

'We'll miss that. It's not a problem.'

'Oh good. I was talking to Ellen while you were in hospital, by the way. She told me Alison's going to be around again. I don't know what the problem is this time, but Ellen's got her for the bank holiday weekend.'

He laughed. 'What's the betting she ends up at the studio?'

'I shouldn't be surprised. You know, I envied you and Claret that day you brought her into the shop.'

'Why?'

'It's silly, I suppose, but you'd all had a lovely time together that day, taking photographs and going to the zoo, and I knew that I could never have done something like that and talked about it afterwards with Guy. He would never have understood how people could enjoy themselves in that kind of way. Also, I remember hoping at the time that, if I had children, I would never have a girl, because she wouldn't stand a chance with Guy. I'd seen him with his nephew and niece. He was only ever interested in Jonathan.'

'I think it was the same with his brother,' said Barry. 'I've never seen a child so shoved into the background as that little girl.'

'Yes, they're very much alike.' She paused and pushed her plate to one side. 'That day, when you and Claret were discussing Alison's reading problem, I knew that if Guy had been there he would have sneered. That was when I first started to have serious doubts about what I was getting into.'

'You said earlier that he could be cynical.'

'Yes, he was particularly scathing the night you and

Belinda came into the restaurant. You know they saw each other briefly, don't you?'

'She told me that, yes.'

'He said he gave you two or three days at the most. He reckoned she was a nymphomaniac.'

'She wasn't,' he laughed. 'She was quite normal.'

'Anyway, you lasted a lot longer than he did.'

'Yes, she told me that, too,' he said, adding hurriedly, 'I mean that their relationship was short-lived.'

She smiled. 'Don't worry.' She waved her hand as if to be rid of the subject. 'Now, I've got ice cream.'

'Thank you, but honestly I couldn't eat anything else.'

'Neither could I. Shall I make coffee?'

'Yes please.'

'Good. You find a comfortable seat and I'll be with you shortly. Would you like a cognac?'

'Oh, yes please.' He watched her go into the kitchen, and eased himself away from the table and into an armchair. The wine had relaxed him, possibly because it was the first drink he'd had since Sunday, and he sank gratefully back into the cushions. They were another refinement that was lacking in his flat. Suddenly Lucy appeared at his elbow with a tray containing the coffee things and two glasses of cognac.

He asked, 'How did you know?'

'Intuition,' she said, smiling, 'and the half-empty bottle in your flat. As you live alone, I couldn't imagine anyone else being responsible.' She set the tray down and poured the coffee, putting his on a small table by his chair. He was reminded of the incident when Jack had thrown wine over Guy's suit, and his eyes went naturally to where Jack was sleeping on the sofa beside Lucy.

'That was the table,' she confirmed, 'but I don't think he'll repeat the performance tonight.' She'd read his mind again, but he was used to it by then.

'I feel so guilty,' she said. 'Whenever we get together I seem to talk about the Guy thing, and you must be tired of hearing his name.'

'Not at all. You've got to get him out of your system.'

'I already have. I told you it had been coming for some time. I think it's just a bad habit I've developed. You must stop me when I do it.'

'I wouldn't dream of it,' he said, 'and it really doesn't bother me.' The cognac after the wine had lulled him into a state in which he might have accepted anything without protest. 'I'm glad you're happy again.'

'That's nice. Thank you.' She tucked her legs beneath her on the sofa and Jack stirred briefly before resuming his sleep. They continued to chat about all kinds of things whilst, all the time, he was conscious of wanting her badly. It wasn't just a physical thing, although that was seldom far from his thoughts. He wanted everything that Guy had come by so easily, and which was still beyond his reach.

After a while, she said, 'Barry, you're not going to manage those stairs. Why don't you sleep in my spare room?'

It wasn't the most exciting of invitations, but it was a sensible one, and he accepted it. At his modest request, she unfastened his shirt and wished him a good night. He finished undressing, turned out the light and lay in the darkness, trying not to think of her in the next room. A little later, he heard the door swing open, and became aware of a movement at the foot of the bed. It didn't excite him, because he was used to it. Soon the purring began. Jack was happy enough with the situation, but what did *he* know?

Wesley had already opened up when Barry got to the studio, which was embarrassing because he insisted on favouring his employer with knowing looks, whistling at odd times. His brief moment of responsibility had given him confidence, and Barry could only pretend not to be irritated by the teasing. It was a while before normal working was resumed.

As they were depressingly free for the day, Barry took him

through some lighting set-ups and left him to experiment, using the dummy that had lain unused in the changing room since he first moved in. It was a relic of the days when he used to set his lighting meticulously before a sitting so as not to waste the client's time, but he'd gradually discarded it as experience took over. However, it was perfect for Wesley, who could treat it as a surrogate client, talking to it and answering its imaginary questions without embarrassment, at least until he realised Barry was watching him and listening. There was no more mickey-taking after that.

He was upstairs in the flat, sorting out some clothes he could wear without a lot of struggling and buttoning, when he heard a tap on the door. It struck him as odd, because Wesley never felt the need for such niceties. He knew where Barry kept his mother's baking, and he usually helped himself. He turned from what he was doing, and was surprised to see Claret in the doorway. He wondered for a second if her appointment had been postponed for some urgent reason, but when he saw her face crumple, he knew something was badly wrong. He drew her over to the sofa and sat her down, waiting for her to make sense. It was a situation that was disturbingly familiar.

After some time the sobs subsided, and he made some coffee while she gathered herself.

'I can't go, Barry.'

'Why not?'

'I can't, I just can't.'

'Tell me why you can't.' He was being as patient as he could be, but his ribs were hurting and his shirt was wet with her tears.

'I had a massive row with my dad last night. He went bloody mad, shouting and swearing. It was horrible. He was making out that what I was doing was wrong.'

'But you haven't done anything wrong.'

'I know, but try telling him that. He said it was as bad as whoring, parading my body like that.'

'How can he say that?'

She began to cry again, and he resigned himself to another wait.

Eventually she was ready to talk once more. 'I know what it is. He's scared I'll leave home and I won't be there to run around after him all the time while he shouts at me. My mum left 'cause she couldn't stand it, and I know how she felt.'

'I could speak to him for you.'

'Hell no, Barry. You don't know what he's like, and you've had enough happen to you already.' She continued to sob.

'Come on, Claret, please don't start that again.'

She bit her lip and stared downwards. 'He burned my bloody portfolio. He didn't even take it out of the fucking envelope and look at it, he just shoved the whole lot on the fire.'

'I can always print the pictures again.'

'But you don't understand. He'll never let me do it. He was horrible. Then me brothers came in and they started an' all. They said they'd taken care of things already, and I didn't know what they were talking about. I thought they were just mouthing off, 'cause they're always doing it, and then I remembered. Last Sunday I was tidying up and I found another of them dirty books. I told you I'd found one before, didn't I? Well, after what happened to me, it made me livid. I was so mad, I said something about that place I'd been to and how disgusting it was. I didn't think they'd do anything, but last night they were bragging to my dad about how they'd followed this bloke from his house across the road to the pub, and they'd waited 'til he went to the gents and they'd done him over, and I realised they were talking about you. It was them that did it, Lame Brain and Thickhead. They couldn't even get the right man. They must have heard me talk about you and they thought you were the porn man. I told 'em they'd got the wrong man an' they just laughed it off. My bleedin' brothers, 'cept I wish they weren't. I'd rather belong to any family but mine.' She began to cry quietly, and he let her. He needed time to think before he said anything to her, and he was still coming to terms with what she'd told him. He poured cognac into two glasses and gave one to her, downing the other one himself. It wasn't yet eleven-thirty, but they both needed it. His first impulse was to go to the police, and no-one could have criticised him for that. He'd had half a week in hospital and was still enduring the effects of what those bastards had done to him. On the other hand, despite what Claret had said about them, he suspected that there might come a time when she would resent his handing them over, especially if it resulted in a prison sentence for them. He doubted it would come to that, but he'd no knowledge of such things. There was also the fact that it would be of no help to Claret in her current situation. He turned the problem over and over before reaching a decision.

'Claret,' he asked, 'did you tell me your brothers were in the Army?'

'Yes, and I wish they'd get posted to Hong Kong and stay there.'

'So they're at home on leave now?'

'No, they're on an urban warfare training course at Lydd, so they're at home quite a lot. I wish they'd sod off. I'd be happy if I never saw 'em again.'

'Listen, has one of them got a cigarette lighter with a regimental badge on it?'

'They both have. Why?'

'Never mind, but tell me this. When are they likely to be at home again?'

She thought for a few seconds, trying to remember. 'Tomorrow lunchtime until Sunday night.' She grabbed at him in alarm, making him wince at the pain. 'Barry, don't come round. You mustn't!'

It wasn't until after lunch that he felt sufficiently composed to do anything constructive. He'd decided not to tell Lucy about the morning's visit until he'd got something sorted out, but he'd noticed her looking at him strangely. Although he was trying to disguise his preoccupation, she knew he had something on his mind, as she always would, but she hadn't tried to probe. He was thankful for that.

Wesley was in the studio, happily experimenting with various camera angles, and he was likely to be occupied for some time, so Barry decided to start mounting the photographs for the competition. He took some black card and the other things he needed into the office and picked up the envelope of pictures, which seemed remarkably stiff and heavy. He knew then that something was wrong. He tipped the contents on to the desk and stared in utter dismay. Instead of the neat bundle of photographs and transparencies he'd left there, all he could see was a black binder and a pile of plastic sleeves containing pictures of Claret. With his heart somewhere between his knees, he realised that she must have taken the wrong envelope the night before, leaving her stuff on his desk, and that meant that her father hadn't burnt her portfolio after all. It was Barry's competition entry he'd destroyed.

He hadn't been in Lucy's flat very long before she asked, 'What is it, Barry? You look as if the world's about to end.'

'Lost a quid and found a tanner,' he muttered.

'What?'

'My entry for the competition, I've lost it. It's gone, and so have my chances of any real advertising and publicity for another year.' He told her about Claret's visit, carefully avoiding any reference to her brothers and the earlier incident. 'And then,' he concluded, 'when I found that Claret had picked up the wrong packet, I knew my work had been destroyed.'

'But haven't you still got the negatives?'

'No, it was stupid of me, but I put everything in there to keep it all together. It's all gone.'

She sat beside him on the sofa and rested her hand on his. 'When did the entry have to be in?'

'Two weeks from today.'

'So there's still time to do something.'

He shook his head. 'Some of those pictures were shot on location and in costume.'

'Like the ones we've been selling in the shop?'

'No, they were different pictures. There was a theme to it, you see, a historical parallel. I can't shoot it all again. For one thing I need Claret, and she's hardly in the right frame of mind just now.'

'Could you do it with Michelle?'

'Not really. She's very good, but her main quality is that she's a natural contrast to Claret. She wouldn't be the same on her own. I could hire a model, but again, it wouldn't be the same. In addition to that, there just isn't the time to do it properly. It's typical, I suppose but, having had time to spare for ages, I find I've got a busy week and weekend coming up, and it wouldn't be right to leave much more to Wesley. He's done an excellent job so far, but he's still only half-trained, and he's only seventeen, too. It's easy to forget that.'

'It is,' she agreed. I suppose there's no chance of putting something together from all those pictures you told me about, the ones you've kept from way back?'

'Not a chance, I'm afraid. There has to be a theme, you see. No, there's only one thing to do, and that's to carry on working away at the job as I've been doing, building the business up gradually with whatever work comes my way. Beggars can't be buggers. At least I've got the police work, and I can enter the competition again next year, or find a different one. It's the most awful shame though, because the portrait competition is something special.'

'You said there was only one thing to do, and you've just mentioned three things, so you're on the way already.' She added gently, 'I suppose it just wasn't meant to happen this time.'

He managed a weak smile. 'You're right,' he agreed. She was too, but it was a bugger all the same. Once again, not an awful lot in his life was going right. In fact, the only thing he had to look forward to in the short term was a phone call the next day.

# 24

# A Deal

It was a young man's voice that answered the phone.
Barry asked, 'Is Mr Humby in?'
'Yeah, who wants him?'
'My name's Craven, and I want to speak to all three of you before the police do, and believe me, that could be very soon. I'm coming over now.' He put the phone down abruptly, because, at that moment, he considered politeness an unnecessary extravagance. Two of them had landed him in hospital, and the other had just ruined his chances of giving his career a considerable boost, so he reckoned he owed them nothing.

He left the studio in Wesley's charge and set off for the Humby household with Claret's portfolio under his arm. The house was in one of the tiny streets off the bottom end of the High Street and, even in his bruise-stiffened state, he was there within ten minutes.

The door was opened by a tall, middle-aged man whom he took to be Claret's father. He regarded Barry with a mixture of unsureness and truculence.

'You'd better let me in,' he told him curtly. 'You'll find it's in your interest.'

He stood aside and let Barry into a small, well-furnished, but cluttered room. Two young men dressed in casual clothes sat on a sofa. One was holding a Sunday tabloid, although he seemed to have little interest in it. The other, who looked

214

up sharply when Barry entered the room, he identified as the character who had been at the bar of The Three Tuns on the night he was attacked. They both wore neatly-trimmed moustaches and the extremely short hair that marked them out as servicemen. He waited for Claret's father to join them.

'What's this about the police?' he demanded.

'You mean you've no idea? The fact is, you're all in big trouble, all three of you, and as you haven't much time, you'd better listen.' He turned to Mr Humby. 'I'll start with you. Yours is the lesser offence, because you're not facing a prison sentence like these two,' he said, indicating the hapless twins, who were now looking extremely rattled, 'but you could easily find yourself with a fine, not to mention a law suit.'

'What am I supposed to have done?'

'You'll be charged,' Barry told him, 'with wilful destruction, the destruction of my property, to be precise.'

'What are you talking about?'

'You burned a number of valuable pictures belonging to me.'

Realisation dawned on his face, and he said defiantly. 'They were Claret's pictures I burned.'

'No, they weren't.' He held up the binder to show him. 'These are Claret's pictures. The ones you destroyed were mine. She'd taken the wrong envelope.'

His jaw dropped. 'I wasn't to know that, was I?'

'I wonder how many magistrates have heard that excuse. You were in a rage at the time, so why shouldn't you destroy my property? Plead as hard as you like, you'll still be charged with it, and I can't see you getting away with it.' He let that penetrate and then continued. 'Now, Claret tells me you object to what she's been doing. I think you'd better sit down, because I'm going to show you exactly what she's been up to.' He opened the binder and showed him the first picture, one of Claret in her favourite red dress. 'Do you find that disgusting?' He turned the pages one by one. There were poses in various items of clothing and one in which she was simply holding Jack in her lap. He remembered taking it as a hand shot. He

215

turned and showed it to the twins. 'Look at that. It's not the kind of pussy picture you two like to look at, is it? He returned to Mr Humby and opened the binder at the picture which had first prompted him to try a sepia print. 'That's as nude as she gets. Look, she's showing no more than she would in a bikini.' He snapped it shut. 'You've got a dirty mind, haven't you? I'll tell you what the problem is. You don't want Claret to move away because you don't want to lose your house slave. That's right, isn't it? You can't face having to look after yourself, and because of that, you're prepared to deny her a chance of earning a good, decent living, doing what she enjoys. You make me bloody sick.' He hadn't been feeling particularly intrepid when he arrived at the house, but his anger was feeding on itself and, if he were honest, he was beginning to enjoy himself. He turned his attention to the twins, who, to his delight, were looking increasingly apprehensive. One had taken out a cigarette and was reaching for a box of matches.

'Pity about the lighter, wasn't it?' Barry flicked his, and the young man looked at him foolishly, his hand shaking as he accepted the light. 'Don't worry, it's been handed in to the police,' he told him, 'by the police, as it happens. Unfortunately for you, it's got your fingerprints all over it. Also, there was a witness. He was too terrified to do anything at the time, but his conscience has led him to contact the police.' That was lie number one, but they weren't to know that. 'Yes,' said Barry, 'you stand the same chance as I did when you found me outside the pub. I don't know what you'll be charged with. Assault and battery, I suppose, and the fact that you attacked the wrong man won't make a scrap of difference. It's got to be worth three months minimum.' He'd no idea what they could be charged with, or what sentence they might expect, but according to Claret, bullshit was their first language. Barry was only speaking in a way they understood. 'If your father has a dirty mind,' he went on, 'then you've both inherited it, but you're very confused. You don't want Claret to be photographed wearing beautiful clothes, but you're more than happy to enjoy pictures of other people's sisters. Not their faces or their clothes, just their boobs and their bits and pieces. That's right, isn't it? That's the kind of rubbish you keep in your bedroom and, presumably, in your service quarters.' Two white faces stared at him. 'Now, this is the score,' he said. 'The police are only like any other profession, in that they look after their own, whether they happen to be police officers, canteen workers or cleaners. They even look after scene-of-crime photographers,' he said, pointing his thumb at himself, 'and they've given me a chance to speak to you before I prefer charges. Your arrest is only a phone call away from happening, so why shouldn't I tell them to go ahead? You all bloody-well deserve it.' He paused, and the silence was richer than gold. His second lie had found its mark. The twins looked to each other, and then to their father for support, and finding none, gazed abjectly at the carpet.

'It's time someone in this house,' said Barry, looking at Mr Humby, 'learned some basic cooking and cleaning skills, because, either, you give me your guarantee that Claret will be allowed to follow the career she wants, or there'll be blue lamps flashing outside this house within the hour.'

Needless to say, Gavin thought he'd been too soft with them. 'You went to all that trouble, Barry,' he said, 'and I could have taken a few mates round there. We wouldn't have left any evidence either. I'd have done it. Don't forget it was me that found you lying in the mud.'

'I know, and I appreciate the thought, but I've had enough of blood and toughery to last me a lifetime.'

'I suppose you have,' he conceded. 'Anyway, how are you getting on with Lucy?'

'Much the same. Good friends, but nothing more than that. She's looked after me since I came home, though, feeding me and that sort of thing, but there's nothing doing.'

'Funny, that.' He scratched his head and called for two

more pints. 'When we went to the hospital she was wetting herself with the worry of it. In fact, she stayed there all night, waiting for you to come round. I went home because I had a full day to do, the next day.'

'What?'

'Well, I've got a living to earn.'

'No, not that. You said she stayed at the hospital all night?'

'Yes, she rang me in the morning. It was a good thing she did, too. I'd slept through the alarm. It was all your fault.'

'I didn't know that.'

'Look, mate,' he treated me to the kind of pitying look he normally reserved for the hard of thinking, 'if I hadn't thought there was something between you, I'd have made a play for her meself, wouldn't I? I mean, she's a bit tasty.'

'But it doesn't add up.'

'What doesn't?'

'Any of it. She's fed me, put me up in her spare room, listened to all my moans and still come back for more, but I know that if I make a move, I'll come up against a brick wall.'

'So what was she like before all this happened? I mean since she parted with Dozy Pillock?'

'Just friendly. You know, very helpful with Jack after his accident and, well, amiable I suppose.'

'It seems to me,' he said, 'that she's trying to make her mind up about something.'

Gavin was like that. He always thought he had the answer, but Barry was more than ever drawn to the conclusion that he'd lost his touch. Even worse, he no longer had his suede jacket, and that seemed to say everything. He was doomed to a life of unrequited... anything that was worth requiting, really.

# 25

# An Unexpected Offer

B arry and Wesley were kept busy throughout the following week, and one way and another it turned out to be an excellent spell of industrial experience for him. For Barry's part, he was simply grateful for the work. Foreign holidays were still very popular, despite the economic difficulties of the time, and one hundred pound charter flights to the USA were the most recent excitement, so they found themselves in demand for passport and visa photographs. The passport business had been eroded to some extent by the photo booths, but they couldn't provide visa pictures in the size demanded by the US Immigration Department, and Barry was only too happy to fill the need.

They also spent one day at Lucy's old school, taking class and individual photographs so that the girls could take them home for the Easter holiday. The job involved lots of group sittings, including hockey teams and the like in their kit, and there were times when Barry thought he might have to send Wesley for a cold shower. He nearly passed out when Barry told him they would be called upon later in the year to do the team pictures for the summer games. Whilst all this was happening, he found myself imagining Lucy in a harmless way, back in her schooldays in the various uniforms and strips that were paraded in front of them. It did him no good at all, so he put all thoughts of her from his mind and concentrated on what he had to do. He was very conscious of his appearance as well. The strapping on his chest had been reduced, so that he was able to wear a suit again, and the cuts on his lips were healing nicely, but the bruises were turning to a sickly shade of yellow, giving him a jaundiced look that couldn't have been pleasant. No-one said anything, of course, but he still felt awkward and somehow less than respectable.

He thought about Claret from time to time. He hadn't seen her since that morning at his flat when she told him about the row with her father, and he was anxious to hear about the aftermath of his visit. As much as anything else, he wanted to know that it hadn't been in vain. He was to be kept waiting, however, because the next time he saw her was when he called into Sainsbury's after a reassuringly uneventful wedding that Saturday. The place was heaving, as it usually was at weekends, so it had to be a very quick word. He asked her how things were at home.

'It's amazing, Barry,' she said. 'I can't believe you went round there, but it did the trick, at least as far as my dad's concerned. The Dozy Duo have gone back now, but even they were quiet.'

'That's good. I thought they might be.' He started packing his things into carriers. 'Have you made another appointment with the agency?'

She looked down, shamefaced. 'I couldn't, not after I let them down.'

'It's all right. I phoned them on Monday and told them you had a tummy bug. They're expecting to hear from you.'

'Really? Oh thanks, Barry. I thought I'd blown it.'

He heard a querulous voice beside him say, 'Are you two going to talk all day? I've got to get home and feed my family.'

He apologised and paid for his shopping. 'Come and see me, Claret,' he said. 'I'm at home for the rest of the weekend.'

He poured the drinks and handed one to Claret, thinking how good she looked. She was wearing a deep blue shift dress and her long hair was loose, resting on her shoulders.

He asked, 'Are you on your way to something?'

'No, why?'

'The dress and the make-up.' Claret's casual garb usually consisted of jeans and a blouse or tee shirt, depending on the time of year.

'No, I just thought I'd make myself look nice to come here.'

That struck him as unusual, but he said, 'I'm glad you did.' He sat on the sofa and was surprised when, instead of taking the armchair, she came and joined him.

'My dad told me he'd burned your stuff by mistake,' she said. 'It was my fault for taking the wrong envelope. You can print it again though, can't you?'

'No, the transparencies were in there too.' He tried to wave the subject aside. He didn't want to go into all that again.

Her eyes filled with horror. 'Oh, no. That's terrible.'

'Just bad luck, and it wasn't your fault. You were excited about going to the agency, and I was in a hurry to go out, so we both had our minds on other things at the time.'

'All the same, I feel responsible.'

'You mustn't. It's done now, and there really is nothing I can do about it.'

She was wretchedly silent for a minute, and then she asked, 'What did you say to my dad?'

'What did he tell you?'

'He just told me about burning your pictures. He said it was my fault. Then he said you'd explained what modelling was all about and how there was nothing wrong with it. You must have explained it well, because he told me he'd decided to let me carry on and do what I want.'

'That's about right. Once I'd convinced him that it had nothing to do with the beaver trade he saw my point.'

'The what trade?'

'The porn business.'

'Right. I've never heard it called that, before.' Returning to the domestic situation, she said, 'The Dopey Duo weren't so full of themselves, either. What did you say to them?'

'Not much. I just told them they were lucky not to be arrested for what they did.'

'They were an' all. You're too good-natured sometimes, Barry.'

He accepted that, although it wasn't how he would have described his feelings when he met her family. He reached for the wine bottle and topped up both glasses.

'You're getting me into bad habits,' she said. 'I didn't used to drink much at all.' Nevertheless, she took it readily enough and downed half a glass before saying, 'I've been meaning to ask you something.'

'Ask away.'

'Are you going out with Lucy?'

'No, not in the usual sense.' The direct question had taken him by surprise, but she merely nodded. 'I thought you weren't.' She turned fully towards him, one arm hooked over the back of the sofa, and regarded him gravely. Eventually she asked, 'Does your chest still hurt?'

'Not as much as it did. I have to be careful, but it's very much better.'

'That's good.' She drained her glass and put it down, shaking her head when he reached for the bottle. She was quiet again and he looked at her enquiringly.

'I've been doing some thinking, Barry.'

'Oh, yes?'

'Yeah.' She seemed to be nerving herself to tell him something. Eventually, she said, 'Some horrible things have happened to you, an' they're all my fault.'

'We've been through that, Claret. It really wasn't your fault that you took the wrong envelope.'

She turned to look him in the face, absently causing her skirt to ride up tantalisingly as she did so, although she seemed oblivious to the fact. 'You've been really good to me, Barry, and I don't deserve it.' She leaned towards him and kissed him softly on the lips, as she had in hospital, except that, on that occasion, it had been a game. This time, it felt incredibly as if she meant it.

Mindful of her feelings, he allowed it to continue, but only for a minute or so, after which he said gently, 'Claret, this can't happen.' He was unable to say more, because she kissed him again, this time with total conviction, and he was rendered temporarily helpless by the compelling feel of her body, her lips on his, and the mesmeric effect of her perfume. With an effort, he said, 'You mustn't do this, Claret, even if you feel guilty.'

'You got beaten up because of me, and now you've lost your pictures, an' whatever you say, that was my fault too.' She kissed him again.

'No, it wasn't. I keep telling you.'

'It was, because none of it would have happened if you hadn't been helping me. You lost your girlfriend as well.'

'Belinda? That wasn't your fault. It was going to happen anyway and, believe me, she was no loss.'

'It was my fault,' she persisted, 'because it was seeing you with me that made her flip the way she did. I could hear her shouting when I was outside, in the street.'

'That's just it,' he said. 'She was incredibly jealous. She'd have gone mad if she'd caught me kissing my maiden aunt. As relationships go, that one was well into a nose-dive, so you've nothing to blame yourself for.'

It was as if she hadn't heard him. 'I feel bad that I've caused you all this trouble, and I thought, as you hadn't had anybody since Belinda, you might be feeling the draught. I just feel that I want to do something to make up for it all.'

He was incredulous. She was prepared to offer herself to him out of guilt, and imagined guilt at that. 'Oh, Claret,' he sighed, 'you've no need to do that.'

'Don't you fancy me, then?'

'No one in his right mind could fail to fancy you, but you see, it's just not right in this case.'

'I'm not a virgin, if that's what's bothering you.'

'No, that's not the problem. You see, feeling guilty is no basis for what you had in mind.'

'I've made a fool of myself, haven't I?' She was picking at the hem of her dress in embarrassment.

'No, you haven't.' He took her hand away from her dress and said, 'We're friends, and you can't make a fool of yourself between friends.' He wondered quite how to go on. 'That's the point, you know,' he said. 'We're friends, and we should go on being friends for a long time, but if we made it something different, sooner or later the new thing would be over, and where would that leave our friendship?'

She nodded, accepting the argument. 'So you're not mad with me?'

'Of course not.' If anything, he felt desperately sorry for her. She was a young girl making her way in life without the benefit of a stable, supportive home or sensible guidance. It was little wonder she was behaving recklessly.

'I do like you a lot,' she said. 'It wasn't *just* what I said.'

'I know, but you're not hurt, are you?'

'No, not now. Well, not really, anyway.'

If only everyone could be as uncomplicated and direct as she was. 'Good,' he said, 'let's have another drink.'

She was back to her old self by the time she left, even to the chaste kiss, and he was immensely relieved.

# 26

# Corn in Egypt

'Are you all right, lifting that with your ribs?' Lucy watched him load a case of mineral water onto the trolley. It was at his suggestion that he'd gone with her that night to the cash and carry. He needed tea, coffee and sugar, and it seemed churlish to let her get them for him without lending a hand.

'I'm not lifting it with my ribs.'

'You know what I mean.'

'Yes, I do.' He stood back and waited for the pain to subside. 'Perhaps you're right.'

'I can do it,' she said. 'You pick up the bits and pieces and I'll do the labouring.'

He settled for it, a little surprised at himself. At one time, he'd have found the situation deeply emasculating, but much had changed in the past two weeks or so, and he was philosophical about it. He watched as she flicked her hair absently behind her ear and ticked the item off her list. Although he couldn't understand why, there was something familiarly engaging about watching her carry out the most basic, everyday tasks. She crouched, smoothing her skirt beneath her, to pick up a case of olives. There was nothing at all special about that, but he found it pleasing. He put it down to the unsettling effect of his weakened condition, but he'd always been adept at deluding himself.

Eventually, they loaded everything into Lucy's estate car and set off home.

'Gavin told me you stayed at the hospital all night,' he remarked.

'Well,' she said, 'you know how these things happen. By the time they'd examined you and got the results of the x-rays, it was too late to go home to bed.'

It wasn't the kind of answer he'd hoped for, but what could he expect? 'I'm grateful anyway,' he said.

'There's no need.' She pulled up at some traffic lights and looked at him squarely. 'It was worrying though. You were an awful mess, and then when I heard that you'd been to see Claret's father and those thugs, I could hardly believe it.' She stopped and her expression relaxed. 'It was just you being quixotic again. You can't help it, can you?'

'How did you know about that?' He had a pretty good idea.

'Gavin told me. He came in for a coffee break one morning.' The lights changed and she moved off. 'Claret's a lovely girl,' she said, 'but doesn't it seem to you that her destiny is to complicate your life?'

'I don't know. It could be, but she's done plenty for me, as well.' Naturally, he made no mention of Saturday evening. Even so, he noticed the merest lift of her eyebrows, and he took some encouragement from it. He said, 'She's given me a great deal of professional satisfaction, and she's very rewarding to work with.'

'She's a very pretty girl. Have you never been tempted to stray from the professional path?'

Again, he thought about Saturday evening, opting for the whitest of lies. 'No, I haven't. You see, I still think of her as very young. My heart just wouldn't be in it.'

'I didn't think men needed to take that into account,' she said dryly.

'You must have known some unscrupulous men.'

She nodded slowly. 'I think I have.'

'Apart from anything else,' said Barry, 'she and I are friends, and I really believe it would harm our friendship.'

There was a line of traffic coming towards them on the main road, and they had to wait before turning into Woodley. She looked thoughtful for a second and said, 'I think you were right about the friendship thing. It wouldn't a good idea to jeopardise that.' There was a break in the traffic, so she drove into the High Street and pulled up outside the bookshop.

After they'd unloaded the car and stacked things in the kitchen, they went up to her flat for a drink. They talked about the trip to Yorkshire, and he was quite surprised that she was still keen to go ahead with it.

'You usually stay with your parents, don't you?'

'Yes,' he said, 'but I shan't this time.'

'Won't they mind?'

'No, as long as I put in an appearance during the week, they'll be happy. It wouldn't be a good idea for us to stay there.'

'I wouldn't dream of imposing on them.'

'It's not that. They really wouldn't mind. The problem would be my mother and her match-making. She's famous for it.'

She smiled. 'Mothers do that, don't they? I know mine did whenever she had an opportunity.'

'Did you give her many?'

'Not really. I tried to keep that side of things away from home. It was the casual friendships she usually seized on. That sometimes made life difficult. I was reminded of it when we had that conversation on the way here.'

'Really?'

She refilled his glass and sat down again. 'Yes. You know, being a boarder in a girls' school I saw very few boys, naturally, apart from in the holidays, and they were just people to play with. They were always there when I came home, and whilst I had to take some good-natured banter about being at a posh school, we always got on well. That was when I was very young, of course. There was a time, during adolescence when things began to change.' She stopped and laughed. 'Obviously they did, I know, but I mean relationships changed. One of the boys I'd almost grown up with began to see me in a

227

different way, and it was all very sad because it was just as you told Claret. In this case, it was an innocent thing, which made it so much more of a shame that, when it ended, so did our friendship.' Remembering again, she said, 'I knew lots of chaps at university of course, but there was always a division between those who were friends and those with whom I got involved. It was as if there were two distinct races of people. D'you see what I mean?'

'Yes, I do.' He wasn't sure where this conversation was going, but it was touching uncomfortably on the problem with which he was currently more than preoccupied. 'Do you think that's always the case, that friendships are bound to suffer when two people get involved?'

'I don't know,' she said frankly. 'Some people make it work. Take Fenella and Dennis as an example. They knew each other for ages and got on well before things became serious, and they still describe themselves as good friends. On the other hand, you see cases in which every aspect of the relationship has turned sour. It's impossible to see a pattern. Don't you agree?'

'I suppose so. I went out with a girl for a whole year, before I came here.'

'A whole year? That must be a record for you,' she laughed.

'I haven't always had the same problem.'

'Of course not.'

'Anyway, that came out of a friendship and we parted amicably enough, so no, there doesn't seem to be a pattern that I can see.'

'Having agreed on that,' she said brightly, 'I'm going to change the subject. We haven't eaten yet.'

'Neither has Jack. I'm going to be very unpopular.'

'You're not having a lot of luck just now, are you?' she mocked. 'I'm sorry, I shouldn't say that. You've had a rotten time, and it's the greatest shame about the competition.' She smiled sympathetically. 'The closing date's this weekend, isn't it?'

'No, I got it wrong, being disorganised as usual. It's not for another week, but I still couldn't have done it properly in the time.'

'I think you're just disheartened, although no-one could criticise you for that. Mind you, I'm not convinced that you couldn't patch something together from all your old pictures.'

'I don't think I could, and it's all mixed up anyway, the people pictures with the rest.'

'You don't *think* you could? That means you're not sure.'

'You never give up, do you?'

'Perish the thought. Listen, let me pick up some food, and we'll take it to your flat. I'll feed Jack and cook something for us while you empty your drawers or wherever you keep the stuff. Then I'll help you sort it. How's that?'

They sat together at the table in Barry's kitchen with a huge pile of prints and transparencies in front of them.

'I told you they were all mixed up,' he said.

'Yes, you didn't exaggerate, did you? Is this a viewer?' She pointed to the loupe.

'Sort of. You just use it like a magnifying glass.'

She placed a strip beneath the loupe and exclaimed, 'Wow, I've got a big picture now!'

'That's a relief.'

She slapped his wrist playfully. 'Clever Clogs. Now, shall I pass over any people pictures and keep the rest over here?'

'Fine.'

'Good. I like playing with this thing.'

He continued to sort through the prints while Lucy examined strip after strip of slides through the loupe and, although the pile had seemed mountainous, they seemed to be getting through them very quickly. Unfortunately, whilst there was some good stuff in there, he still couldn't see a theme worth considering. Lucy, however, was determined not to give up.

'There's got to be something in this lot that'll give you an idea,' she insisted.

'Honestly, I think you're wasting your time.' He opened a second bottle of wine and filled two glasses. 'Most of those slides are the ones I took in Yorkshire. They're all landscapes.'

'No they're not,' she said. 'What about this? It's a lovely picture. It tells a story in itself.'

'Let me look.' He peered over her shoulder and saw one of the pictures of the Fielden couple outside The Listers Arms in Malham. 'Those are the people I told you about,' he said, sitting down again.

'There's another one here.'

'It'll be much the same.'

'No, it's not. It's a picture of their dog almost asleep on their feet. It's really good.'

He smiled to himself. The exercise had been in vain, but with Lucy's enthusiasm for his work, at least his ego was receiving a boost.

'Barry?'

'Mm?'

'This competition, does it have to be people pictures only?'

'No, there are three classes. There's Portraits, Landscapes and Animals.'

'My goodness.'

'What is it?'

'I've had an idea. All this time you've been preparing pictures of people, and I have to say you're excellent at it, but you may have been missing something even better.'

'Not animal pictures?'

'Yes.'

He shook his head. 'I only do those for my own interest, apart from the ones that I'm paid for, of course.'

'But look at these.' She picked up a pile of discarded prints from his side of the table and began to leaf through them. 'I've been watching you throw these away, and it's a crying shame, because you've got an amazing flair for it. You can capture an animal's expression when no one else would ever notice it.' She continued to look through them. 'You must have hundreds of animal pictures and there's bound to be a theme there. Come on, let's start again.'

So they began the process once more, and soon he was beginning to feel grudgingly infected with some of Lucy's enthusiasm as she turned up one after another, asking him about how they were taken, and giving him her own reaction.

She asked, 'Who's this with Jack?'

'Alison. She was cleaning out the darkroom cupboards, but I don't know what Jack was doing. Helping, or getting in the way I suppose.'

'He was giving you a super opportunity. See how Alison's trailing her cloth behind her, and Jack's tail's sticking straight up in the air? Two backsides perfectly framed and balanced.'

'That was the idea.'

'Oh, I know you didn't do it by accident, but if I can see these things at a first glance, how might they appeal to someone else?'

As they went through the rest of the pile, pictures turned up that he'd forgotten. There was one, to Lucy's delight, of Guy's niece, Naomi being cuddled to death by Jack, and another of his classics that Barry had taken on the pavement outside the studio. Jack was squaring up to one of the neighbourhood cats, and, it seemed, on the point of facing his adversary down. There were others, taken at the zoo with Alison and, of course, several horse pictures from recent times, as well as some he could scarcely recall. One that he'd printed and then thrown into the drawer was of a resentful basset hound puppy being vaccinated at the vet's surgery.

'When did you take that?'

'Quite recently, when I was doing some work for the vet.'

'It's perfect.' She looked at it for a moment longer and said, 'Do you know what all these have in common? They're all pictures of animals reacting in some way, either to people or to other animals.'

'Animal relationships.'

'Right. There's almost every situation here that you could

think of, and there's one more that you might have if Fenella's mare gets a move on. By my reckoning, she's overdue.'

'A mare and foal together. Yes, that would be marvellous.'

She turned to him triumphantly. 'So, Misery, it looks as if you've got your pictures for the competition. You just needed me to see something you'd missed.

It was late when he saw her to her door.

'Thanks ever such a lot,' he said. 'You were right. I'd missed the point completely about those pictures, and I'd never have seen it if you hadn't pointed it out.'

'It was no trouble,' she said, and then as an afterthought, she added, 'You know, you need to believe in yourself.' She leaned forward to receive a polite kiss in the usual way, and he held her rather longer than he had before. It felt so good, and she didn't move away, but simply gave him a squeeze before opening the door. 'Good night, Barry,' she said. As gestures went it was a small one, but he felt that they were just a little further forward.

# 27

# Final Approval

It was a few days later that Barry went into the bookshop and found Lucy eager to see him.

'I'm glad you're here,' she said, 'I was going to phone you if you didn't come in. I had a call from Fenella half an hour ago. She's had an awful time with the foaling. It happened three nights ago, and it was horrendous.'

'Oh, no.'

'Mandy's all right, but the foal was stillborn.'

'Oh hell,' he groaned, 'what bloody awful luck. Poor old Mandy as well.' It was particularly sickening because Mandy had become like an old friend. Visiting the farm as often as he had, he'd made a point of going to see her each time he called, and she'd been pleased to see him, too, especially as he was always good for a Polo mint.

Lucy held up her hand. 'But the vet located an orphaned foal – I suppose they have a kind of grapevine – and they introduced him to Mandy, and guess what? She's accepted him. Apparently, he's an Arab, so I imagine they'll look very odd together, but Mandy doesn't care. As far as she's concerned, he's hers. Fenella's excited too. I expected her to be in an awful state, and I imagine she must have been, after the foaling, but the orphan's given her a real lift. She's invited us over to eat with them this evening. She said she'd get something out of the freezer, but that's Fenella-speak for a superb meal. I suppose I should really have them over here soon. Anyway, we can arrange that later. Are you okay for this evening?'

'Yes, fine. What time?'

'The usual I imagine, but she said you wanted to photograph Mandy with her foal, so she suggested that we go early while there's still light.'

'Great, but I've got an appointment this afternoon and I can't see myself being back here before five.'

'Well, I can't close until five-thirty. Do you want to go straight there and I'll join you later?'

He thought about it quickly. 'No, let's go together. We'll have half an hour before we lose the light and that should give me ample time to get what I want.'

'Okay, you know best. We'll do that.'

Back at the office, he picked up the morning paper. He'd had no opportunity to look at it that morning, and, with half an hour to spare before he had to go out again, he browsed through the headlines. The main news was about the Stetchford by-election, which didn't interest him particularly. The election was reported at some length, so he ran his eye to the bottom of the front page and blinked with surprise.

*Man Charged With Kent Marsh Murder*, he read.

*A man is being held at Elmston police station, Kent, where he has been charged with the murder of Pauline Francis, whose body was found on Romney Marsh last September. He will appear at Elmston Magistrates' Court on Monday, the 4th of April.*

The piece went on to give his name and age, and the fact that he was unemployed. It seemed that his movements had been traced to an address in Dartford, where he was apprehended and taken for questioning. There were some background details and the story was continued on page two. Barry opened the paper and found the column on the second page, but it only gave some sketchy details about the man. Nevertheless, it gave him a lot of satisfaction to know that they'd got someone for the murder, and indications were that the man in custody was the missing photographer.

He closed the paper and put it down thoughtfully. The murder story was important, of course. Without realising it, he'd had that unfortunate girl at the back of his mind ever since the night on the marsh and, with all that had happened in the meantime, it was good to know that the loose ends were all-but tied up. A feeling of optimism had sprung, as if from nowhere, and he wondered if he really had reached a kind of watershed. One way and another he'd achieved a great deal in the past few weeks, he'd been given a second chance to enter the competition, and now he had an opportunity to take the animal shot he wanted, the one that with any luck would become the centre-piece of his entry. He also realised that he'd achieved the seemingly impossible, by not smoking a single cigarette since the night he was taken into hospital. Things had to be improving.

<hr />

They took Lucy's car as it was more reliable than his, and joined the traffic on the main road to Denford. At one stage they slowed down to a crawl because of a broken-down lorry, and they watched as cars came speeding past in the opposite direction. One of them, a white BMW was familiar to him by its number plate, although Lucy had already identified the driver.

'He doesn't look very happy,' she commented.

'I'm not surprised, the poor sod.'

She reached across and squeezed his hand. He wasn't sure why she did that, but he found it no less pleasing.

After some delay, they passed the lorry and picked up

speed again, but it was turned six o'clock by the time they arrived at the farm, and dusk wasn't far away. Barry knew he'd have to make the journey again, to take some daylight shots in colour but he wanted desperately to get something while the foal and its adoption were so recent. In reality, a lost day might amount to nothing; the foal would be no bigger, and Mandy would doubtless behave in much the same way, but his approach would be different. His excitement would have lost its edge, and that mattered, because it would affect the way he looked for shots, angles and all the lesser details that go to make a truly memorable picture.

Fenella came out as she heard the car in the yard, and to her credit, she lost no time in taking them to the paddock. She asked, 'Will you have enough light, Barry?'

'Yes, if we can get them so that the foal's not in shadow.' He had a ninety millimetre lens on the Leica so that he could get in fairly close without distorting the perspective. He could see Mandy at the far side of the paddock, and he waited as Fenella called her, the inevitable bowl of oats in her hand. Mandy lifted her head and came straight towards them, and it was then that he saw the foal for the first time, tiny, stilt-legged and vulnerable beside the mare's familiarly solid frame. They were the most perfect mismatch.

'I see you've brought that special camera,' said Fenella. 'I knew you would.'

'I didn't want to frighten either of them. They've been through enough already.'

'They've forgotten all that,' she said, 'but it was thoughtful of you.' She held out the bowl and Mandy shoved her nose into it, so Barry moved around to get a better view of the foal. Mandy turned her head, instantly protective, but Fenella cajoled her. 'Come on, Mandy, show us your baby.' She handed the bowl to Lucy, still talking to Mandy. 'You know Barry and Lucy. Come on, let's have a look at him.' She motioned to Lucy to bring the bowl towards her so that both mare and foal were illuminated by the fading sunlight, and Barry started shooting. As Lucy and Fenella backed away, he took frame after frame, with

Mandy occasionally showing some fleeting interest in what he was doing, but keeping her attention mainly on the foal, nuzzling at his shoulder or just keeping a maternal eye on him. He was vaguely conscious that Fenella and Lucy were talking to her, encouraging and reassuring her, but he could hear nothing they said, because, for a short time the world belonged to the mare, the foal and him. It was as if by some special consent that he was included for that spell. The light was going fast, but they seemed somehow happy to give him what he wanted and, in that early April sunset, he was able to capture their two heads together, barely lit by the remaining glow, the mare's, wide and honest, and the Arab foal's with its characteristic, delicate, curved face. He knew that if he could get the development right he would have the picture he wanted: twin tragedies that could never be reversed, but out of them, this small, touching consolation.

Then, without warning, like a manager bringing a celebrity photo call to a close, Mandy turned and walked away with the foal beside her. Barry was suddenly aware that the air was chilly, and he could smell the fresh, dewy grass of the evening.

'That's all you're going to get,' Fenella told him. 'I'll bring them in soon for the night, but they've had enough for now.'

Barry looked towards where the sun was setting behind a tall chestnut tree. 'The light's gone,' he said, 'but I think I've got all I need.'

They went back to the farmhouse, Fenella in front, and Lucy and Barry walking behind. Lucy put an arm round his waist. 'It was terribly dark,' she said. 'Will the pictures be all right?'

'Fine,' he assured her, 'I used a fast film, and I'll push the development a bit so they'll come out lovely and grainy. You'll see.'

'I should have known,' she said. 'Were you thinking of that when you were taking them?'

'No,' he admitted, 'I'd thought of it before. Just then, I wasn't really thinking of anything very much, only how marvellous it all was.' It was then that he thought he saw tears in her eyes, but he wasn't surprised. It was that kind of occasion.

He was absent-mindedly aware of entering the warm, brightly-lit house, seeing Dennis there and chatting with him. They had a friendly argument at some stage, about the Grand National, which was to take place on the following day. Barry favoured Red Rum, but Dennis was adamant that he couldn't win it a third time. The argument ran on into supper, until Fenella brought it to a halt. She wanted to tell them the story of the foaling and the subsequent fostering, but Barry heard little of it. He must have responded from time to time, but without any real concentration. He was conscious of Lucy looking towards him rather a lot, and he wondered at odd moments what she might be thinking but, most of the time, he sat, remembering the scene in the paddock, trying to recall every detail before the memory lost any of its magical fascination.

After supper, he was drinking cognac with Dennis while Lucy and Fenella went into the kitchen together. Dennis said something about women's chat, that they did it privately so that the men in their lives would never know what nonsense they talked. Barry agreed with him at the time, half-hearing what he said and catching odd bits of conversation from the kitchen. At one stage he thought he heard Fenella say something to Lucy about not leaving something too late, something about 'missing the boat,' and he wondered where he'd heard that expression recently. It came to him after a while. It was something that crook Hyman had said to him in his office. He didn't want to think about that, so he tried to concentrate on what Dennis was saying, only to find that the conversation in which he was taking only a passive part had moved on.

Later in the evening, they thanked Dennis and Fenella and went out to Lucy's car. They chatted easily on the way back, until they arrived at Lucy's place, and he got out to see her to her door. She unlocked it and stood in the half open doorway. 'Are you coming in?'

'If it's not too late.'

'I hope it's not,' she said, smiling as she switched on the staircase light. She turned to face him, still smiling, and it was then that he kissed her properly for the first time. He'd waited only a few weeks, but it had felt like months.

He opened his eyes and watched the first pale glimmer of light enter the room. Lucy stirred and moved against him, soft and warm, and he knew he hadn't imagined the previous night. It had been real, everything that had happened and all that had been said. He lay still for a while, content to feel her beside him and hear her gentle breathing, until he became increasingly conscious of a familiar, heavy mound over his left ankle. He moved one foot carefully so as not to disturb Lucy or the mound and, for a moment, he thought he'd succeeded, but the mound stretched and curled itself up again, purring so loudly that Lucy opened her eyes, smiling sleepily.

He said, 'I think he approves.'

She turned on her side to snuggle closer and murmured, 'I think he always did.'

# 28

## Epilogue

## BBC 1 *Arts in Focus*

### September 1981

Julie Stephens said, 'You never did win the competition outright, did you, Barry?'

'I'm afraid I didn't. That honour went deservedly to Russell Davies, the landscape photographer.'

'But your last-minute entry did win you First Prize in the Animal Category, and that marked the start of your career as a specialist animal photographer.'

'It did, Julie. I suppose you could say that some things are simply meant to happen.'

'That's perfectly true, and your services are now very much in demand in equestrian circles and among breeders, although you've always tended to play down your success.'

'Well, there are no prizes for boasting.'

'You're refreshingly modest, but before we end the programme, Barry, I must ask you who, or what, was your most important stimulus in setting out on your career in animal photography.'

Barry smiled self-consciously. 'If you're expecting the names of well-known photographers and artists, I have to disappoint you, because I was obliged to develop a style very much of my own, but that's only one kind of influence, isn't it? You see, I owe an awful lot to word-of-mouth recommendation by satisfied clients. Most importantly, though, I owe my initial success in animal work to my wonderful wife Lucy, who helped me realise where my true potential lay and, of course, in some way to the uncanny influence of our good friend Jack.'

'Jack, you told me earlier, was your cat,' said Julie, evidently still surprised and amused by the disclosure.

Barry smiled almost to himself, although still extremely conscious of being on camera. 'Oh,' he said, 'Jack was much more than that.'

## The End

www.ingramcontent.com/pod-product-compliance
Lightning Source LLC
Chambersburg PA
CBHW022012010726
47494CB00003B/1007